LIVE BY CHANCE
LOVE BY CHOICE
KILL BY PROFESSION

Passing the Torch

ROY MARK

Roy Mark
P.O. Box 294
Chiang Mai, 50000
Thailand

Roy@RoyMark.Org
www.facebook.com/Roy.Mark.Books

www.RoyMark.Org

Printed by CreateSpace
Available from Amazon.com and other retail outlets

ISBN 13: 978-1534947597
ISBN-10: 1534947590

Dedicated
To the Memory of
Melissa Clark

Melissa Clark attended the University of Kentucky before graduating from Longwood College at age eighteen. She was a member of Mensa International (www.mensa.org), the non-political society of intellectuals with IQs in the top two percent of the population.

Melissa was the daughter of Billy C. Clark, the highly acclaimed American author of eleven books and many poems and short stories. His writings were heavily influenced by his experience of poverty while growing up in Kentucky, such as his 1960 autobiography,

A LONG ROAD TO HOE. Melissa Clark was the ghostwriter for many of her father's works.

Melissa had a photographic memory, which was a gift she employed throughout her life including her work as a State of Virginia investigator. Working undercover, Melissa investigated corrupt judges and attorneys for the state.

Melissa Clark was an excellent communicator, both written and verbal. Her friends said that Melissa could talk a tiger out of his stripes.

On the morning of 9/11, with the shock of the terrorist attacks unfolding on the nation's TV screens, Melissa decided, as you'll read in this book, to marry Sterling Cody. Ironically, though Melissa had survived the 9/11 attacks, she died of pancreatic cancer on September 11, 2006—exactly five years later.

CONTENTS

Abbreviations & Acronyms

AHB	Assault Helicopter Battalion
AIT	Advanced Individual Training
ARVN	Army of the Republic of (South) Vietnam
AVG	American Volunteer Group
AWOL	Absent Without Leave
BCT	Basic Combat Training
C&C	Command and Control
CO	Commanding Officer
CSM	Command Sergeant Major
CWO	Chief Warrant Officer
DEROS	Date Eligible for Return from Overseas
EPD	Enterprise Police Department
FAC	Forward Air Controller
IP	Instructor Pilot
LOH	Light Observation Helicopter
LTC	Lieutenant Colonel
LZ	Landing Zone
mm	Milimeters (7.62mm = .3 inches)
MOC	Maintenance Operations Check
NVA	North Vietnamese Army
OMA	Three-letter code for Eppley Airfield, Omaha, NE

R&R	Rest and Recuperation
RAF	Royal Air Force
ROTC	Reserve Officers' Training Course
RPG	Rocket-Propelled Grenade
SP-4	Specialists Fourth Class
SP-5	Specialists Fifth Class
VC	Viet Cong
VFMA	Valley Forge Military Academy
WOC	Warrant Officer Candidate
XO	Executive Officer

Live By Chance, Love By Choice, Kill By Profession

About the Cover

The cover art for *LIVE BY CHANCE, LOVE BY CHOICE, KILL BY PROFESSION* is taken from a painting by renowned aviation artist Joe Kline. The painting depicts a Sikorski UH-60 Black Hawk in the foreground and a Vietnam era UH-1H "Huey" in the background. The Black Hawk, which is pulling pitch, contrasts with the ghostly Huey behind it; generations of helicopter aviation are portrayed in one image.

Mr. Kline's painting compliments the subject matter of this book, which features generations of aviators flying pre-World War II Boeing P-26 "Peashooters," Vietnam Hueys, and Black Hawks in South America and Iraq. The painting's title of "Passing the Torch" fit so well with the stories told in this book, that Roy Mark adapted it as the subtitle of this book."

Since the portion of this book that covers the Vietnam War focuses on Charlie Company of the 229th Assault Helicopter Battalion (AHB), Mr. Kline personalized his original artwork by painting the battalion's crest on the nose of the Huey and Charlie Company's blue circle on the pilot's door.

Limited edition prints of "Passing the Torch" and other paintings by Joe Kline are available for purchase at www.joeklineart.com.

Joe Kline is a Vietnam veteran and an Artist Member of the American Society of Aviation Artists. In Vietnam, Kline was a UH-1H crew chief with B/101 AHB Kingsmen from 1970 to 1971. He is a member of the Vietnam Helicopter Crew Members Association and a member of the 101st Airborne Division Association. Mr. Kline founded the Kingsmen Reunion Association in the late 1980s.

Joe Kline
6420 Hastings Place, Gilroy, CA 95020
408-842-6979
klinejd569@aol.com

www.joeklineart.com

Preface

I became acquainted with members of the U.S. Army's 229th Assault Helicopter Battalion in 2013 while researching a Vietnam War incident that took the life of my cousin, Mark Holtom. My initial contact was with Dan Tyler, who was the Air Mission Commander when two Huey helicopters collided mid-air, claiming the lives of four pilots and four crewmen including Mark.

While writing a short story about that incident, Tyler introduced me to other 229th veterans, who encouraged me to write more stories about their one-year tour in Vietnam. The short story evolved into my first book, *FIXIN' TO DIE RAG*.

After *FIXIN' TO DIE RAG* was published in 2014, a 229th veteran and friend of Dan Tyler known as Sterling Cody (a pseudonym) contacted me and explained that he was interested in collaborating on a book. He envisioned a book that detailed his long career with the U.S. Army, including flying Hueys in Vietnam.

I met with Sterling and discussed the specific incidents he wanted to cover most, as a book about his entire career would be a massive undertaking. To avoid writing a thousand-page novel, we whittled the scope down to the formative events of his childhood, his military training, and his experiences of war in Vietnam, South and Central America, and Iraq.

Though based on actual events, Cody insisted that aspects of the book must be fictionalized. Accordingly, he chose to use a pseudonym rather than his real name.

During the research process for this book, I interviewed many people connected with the events it describes, some of whom chose to not use their real names. In those cases, I have indicated the use of a pseudonym by adding an asterisk* after the first use of the name.

Roy Mark
April, 2017

Acknowledgements

During the research phase of this project, I received assistance from many sources. Without their input, this book would not have been possible.

Special thanks are due Major Roger C. Baker (U.S. Army, Retired) for permission to include an adaptation of an article he wrote titled "Yellow One" which appeared in the September/October 2015 edition of *The VHPA AVIATOR* magazine.

Many veterans of Charlie Company, 229th Assault Helicopter Battalion helped provide background information for events that occurred during their Vietnam tours. In addition to Major Baker, Gary Fowler, David Holte, Bob Jacobs, Jack McCormick, Doctor Craig Thomas, Dan Tyler, and Fred Zacher are among these army veterans. I wish to thank Gunnery Sergeant Charles D. Cox (USMC, Retired) for his help with Chapter Two. I am also grateful to Major General Scott Smith (U.S. Army, Retired) for his assistance and advice concerning aspects of this project. My thanks go to these veterans not only for their help with this book but also for their service to our country.

I thank Mister Orrie Swayze and Mister Mick Swayze for contributing biographical information about their brother, Captain Jerry Swayze. Although it required them to relive the painful memory of their brother's death, they were supportive of this project.

Mr. Ed Tatarnic contributed valuable information about the events of May 13, 1968, on Nui Ba Den (Black Virgin Mountain) in Vietnam. Mr. Tatarnic's cousin, John A. Anderson was killed defending the summit of Nui Ba Den. In later years, Mr. Tatarnic has done extensive research about that battle.

I'm grateful to the Curtiss-Wright Corporation historian and to Mister Doug Bradley of The Pea River Historical and Genealogical Society for their research assistance.

If I have forgotten to mention someone who assisted me with this project, I sincerely apologize.

1

FNG

Republic of Vietnam
3 May 1970

Sitting on a bar stool in Charlie Company's Officers' Club in Tay Ninh West, Warrant Officer (WO1) Sterling Cody and the other officers were relieving stress and tension, one beer at a time; Cody was several beers into the process.

The pilots and crews of Charlie Company were exhausted after three days of non-stop flying into Cambodia. Ten to fourteen hours of solid flying made for very long and tiring days.

Cody had been in-country for only two months, so he was still considered an FNG (Nam speak for *f---ing new guy*), and as such, his adrenaline had flowed double-time as green tracers streaked past the windshield of his Huey. His aircraft commander (Pilot in Command) had looked so calm, with a "just another day at the office" manner and tone to his voice, and he didn't seem to realize, or at least didn't acknowledge, that their lives could end suddenly with any one of the green tracers that whizzed by. Now that Cody was safely back at base and inside the O-Club, also known as the Officers' Club, Cody was replacing his diminishing adrenaline with beer—lots of beer.

South Vietnamese forces had crossed over the Cambodian border on 30 April 1970, and with U.S. forces following soon afterward, the Cambodian Incursion was in full swing. The political objective of the campaign was to demonstrate the success of President Nixon's Vietnamization program, to buy time so that U.S. forces could be safely withdrawn, and—according to a Nixon speech—to uphold U.S. ideals and credibility.

Political objectives meant little to the infantrymen— the grunts—and aircrews dodging bullets, mortars, and rocket-propelled grenades (RPGs). Their objective was to stay alive and to kill as many of the forty thousand enemy troops as possible that had amassed in the eastern border regions of Cambodia. Capturing or destroying munitions and supplies, although not as personally satisfying, was also part of their mission. They sent tons of rice stores back to South Vietnam. Rice that couldn't be sent back across the border was destroyed.

When Sterling Cody finally made it back to Tay Ninh West on 3 May, he, like his aircraft commander and crew, was physically exhausted. Nevertheless, he had one more duty to perform before he could call it a day. After shutting down, Cody's aircraft commander reminded him and his crew chief that the bird was due for an "MOC." An MOC was merely a "maintenance operations check." MOCs were performed periodically, and in this case, after 25 hours. MOCs were carried out by co-pilots and crew chiefs. They were not such a big deal, unless you had been flying in harrowing conditions for twelve to fourteen hours.

Cody instructed the crew chief, a young SP-5 named Greg Weber, to get everything ready for the MOC, saying that he would return shortly. Weber had been in-country a while and knew exactly where the FNG co-pilot was headed.

SP-5 Greg Weber

Being a pilot with the 229th Assault Aviation Battalion did come with the advantage of returning to base and cold beer, even if it was after dawn-to-dusk flying. Cody had come to the realization that flying combat missions was not only stressful but also physically exhausting. Cold beer always helped.

After his first cold beer at the O-Club, the tensions of the day began to subside. By his third or fourth beer, Sterling had lost track of time and didn't realize that it was past 2100 hours; he was past due on the flight line for the MOC.

Oh well, he thought, *I'll head for the flight line after I finish this beer.*

"OK sir, time for the MOC."

Cody only managed to catch a glimpse of his crew chief in his peripheral vision as he was lifted onto Greg's shoulders in the typical fireman's carry. Draped over the shoulders of his crew chief, his left wrist in Greg's firm grip, the other hand still holding his half-finished beer, Sterling protested, albeit a mild protest that came with a chuckle.

"How in the hell can I drink my beer with my head at the 6 o'clock?"

"I'll have you upright in a second, sir," was Greg's respectful but firm reply.

The other officers in the club glanced over, but they didn't think the site of a WO1 being carried out of the club over the shoulders of an enlisted man was at all unusual, surely not worthy of interrupting the business at hand—the consumption of copious amounts of alcohol.

Inside the O-Club at Tay Ninh West
Notice the bell in the background. Should anyone walk into the
club and forget to remove his hat, a mad dash to ring the bell
would ensue, which would require the Soldier wearing the hat to
buy a round of drinks for the entire bar.

At the flight line, Greg unceremoniously dumped the co-pilot into the right seat of their Huey.

On Greg's, "Untied and clear," Cody's attention was focused on the task at hand. He went through the starting procedure and brought the aircraft up to 6600 RPM. Then, after Cody had ensured that all gauges were in the proper range, Greg Weber walked up next to the co-pilot's seat.

"OK sir— shut her down."

With that, the MOC was completed. After securing their bird, co-pilot and crew chief headed back to the bar.

Inside the O-Club, Cody offered Greg a beer. It was a simple gesture; it conveyed, without spoken words, Cody's appreciation and that there were no hard feelings. Greg accepted the beer and headed off to his rack to stack a few Z's. Zero dark early came fast, and they had missions to fly the next day.

WO1 Sterling Cody arrived in Vietnam in mid-March 1970. He wanted to fly with and fight with the best, so he had volunteered for duty with the First Cavalry Division. The First Cav was, after all, known as "The First Team," and nothing short of The First Team would do for Cody. The First Cav had many units fighting in South Vietnam, so the only unknown to the FNG was where First Cav would see fit to send him. His orders were cut soon enough, and he learned that he was headed for the 229th Assault Helicopter Battalion.

When WO1 Sterling Cody reported to the commanding officer (CO) of the 229th in Tay Ninh West, he learned that the battalion was composed of three Huey Lift companies and one attack helicopter company. The Huey companies were Alpha, Bravo, and Charlie, and the attack helicopter company was Delta. The Hueys were primarily used for troop transport and were lightly armed with 7.62mm M60 machine guns mounted on each side. The Cobra attack helicopters of Delta Company were more heavily armed. They brought to the fight six M134 Miniguns that fired one thousand to four thousand rounds per minute of 7.62mm ammunition, 2.75-inch folding-fin aerial rockets, 40mm grenade launchers, and newer models that had the 20mm M61 Vulcan Gatling-style rotary cannon. The Cobra attack helicopter was a formidable offensive weapon. The attack helicopters were generally referred to as "gunships," and the lightly armed Hueys were called "slicks."

Over the course of a couple of quick orientation flights, Cody learned the lay of the land and Charlie Company's procedures. Radio call signs of the battalion's companies were committed to memory, along with radio frequencies. Charlie Company's call sign was "North Flag," which meant little to the nineteen-year-old FNG at the time, but he soon began to hear the older guys proudly refer to themselves as "North Flaggers." There was an esprit de corps within Charlie Company that Sterling Cody admired. Now, he too was a North Flagger, and he would soon learn why the title was a badge of honor.

"Hitting the ground running" may have applied had he been a grunt, but with Cody, it was more a case of "hitting the sky flying." The First Cav was pushing up into the Dog's Head Area of III Corps, and contact with the enemy became more intense as they got close to the border. Once they were inside Cambodia, the enemy seemed to be everywhere. A lot could be said about the Viet Cong (VC)—"Charlie" for short—and the more professional North Vietnamese Army (NVA) soldiers: they were brave, resourceful, numerous, and now, on the run.

The pilots and crews of Charlie Company would generally start the day flying combat assaults. They would rendezvous at a pre-designated location (usually a fire support base) and then hook up with the infantry troops and their Cobra gunship escorts.

It was all new and exciting for Cody, but he was glad to be flying as peter-pilot (co-pilot) with experienced aircraft commanders, who were good—really good. There was a lot to take in and a lot to learn.

After completing the helicopter assaults, the flights would break up and proceed with individual resupply missions. Everything seemed routine to the old hands, but to Cody and the other FNGs, it was indoctrination by fire.

Even the FNGs could tell that Cambodia was different from South Vietnam. The enemy inside Cambodia was not the irregular VC but regular NVA forces. They were well organized and well entrenched— a formidable foe.

The North Vietnamese had been moving troops and equipment south into South Vietnam for years using the so-called "Ho Chi Minh Trail." The trail's origins traced back centuries to when it was nothing more than primitive footpaths used to facilitate trade in the region. In 1959, the North Vietnamese began improving the trail to supply arms to the VC in South Vietnam. By 1964, the supply capacity of the trail had become over 30 tons per day, and the trail facilitated the movement of a steady stream of NVA regulars into the South.

At the time that WO1 Cody first set eyes on the trail, it was no longer—if it ever was—the muddy trail that he had been led to believe it was. At Valley Forge Military Academy in Wayne Pennsylvania, Junior Reserve Officers' Training Course (ROTC) Cadet Cody had studied military tactics and watched films that depicted the Ho Chi Minh Trail as anything but the modern, sophisticated system of roads he was now seeing from his Huey. The "trail" was now an impressive network of paved roads complete with supply depots and fuel pipelines. The roads even had telephone poles along the sides and signs along the way, indicating the locations of motor pools, ammo dumps, and hospitals.

Cody, like most nineteen-year-olds, felt invincible, but after witnessing the sophistication and determination of his enemy, he began to question his youthful immortality. Even so, for as long as Cody could remember, he had always trusted his gut. He now took solace in his gut feeling that despite the carnage around him, he was going to be okay.

The Cav was now placing fire support bases right across the trail, and the pilots of Charlie Company were starting their days before dawn to prepare for the day's missions. Each day that Cody flew into Cambodia, it seemed that there was yet another fire support base, each one a little deeper into Cambodia. The deeper the First Cav pushed into Cambodia, the more intense was the resistance they faced.

Missions usually called for a rendezvous at a predesignated location to hook up with First Cav grunts and Delta Company's Cobra gunships. The rendezvous was generally at a fire support base, but it was sometimes at sites in the field.

The areas they were to launch assaults on were often softened up with fifteen minutes of artillery prep fire. Air strikes were sometimes called in—depending on the enemy situation—and they were controlled by an Air Force forward air controller (FAC) flying overhead. The FACs flew O-1 Bird Dog or OV-10 Broncos. The Bird Dog was a small two-seat propeller aircraft, and the Broncos were turboprop light attack and observation aircrafts. They used 2.75-inch white phosphorus rockets to mark targets for the fighter aircraft.

And so it went on, mission after mission, day after day, as the North Flag Boys and the rest of First Cav systematically destroyed the previously untouchable enemy behind that imaginary line on the map known as the Cambodian border.

"What am I doing here?" was a thought that crossed the mind of every Soldier who found themselves in harm's way, and the sky warriors were no exception. Cody experienced those feelings, too, but had conflicting emotions about them. He actually liked the Army, the adventure, the flying, and the adrenaline rush that seemed to last all day.

Soon, WO1 Sterling Cody noticed something odd. It didn't happen often, but occasionally while flying in a combat zone, his mind would begin to drift. He would fly his Huey as if his feet on the rudders and his hands on the controls had a mind of their own. On these occasions, he would sometimes catch himself daydreaming of home. He often thought of his brother Jack, who was now back home after being wounded in Vietnam.

2

Devil Doc

Kam Ky, Republic of Vietnam
July 1969

Each time Sterling Cody saw a causality, he thought of his older brother. Jack Cody had joined the Navy in 1966 and had trained as a Hospital Corpsman. A few Hospital Corpsmen are further trained in Marine Corps tactics and assigned to Marine Corps units. These corpsmen are accepted by their Marine counterparts as brothers; to Marine Devil Dogs, their Corpsmen are "Devil Docs." In the Army, a wounded Soldier would call out "Medic," but wounded Marines always yelled, "Corpsman!"

Jack was now home from Vietnam after serving with a rifle company of the 3rd Marine Division. Yes, Jack was now home and safe, but it was a small miracle.

Corpsmen exposed themselves to enemy fire far more than the Marines they patched up. The casualty rate among Corpsmen was higher than that among their Marine comrades. Their bravery was on par with and often exceeded that of their Marine buddies, and their bravery has been proven over the years by the fact that they are the most decorated Sailors in the entire United States Navy. Corpsmen have been decorated with 22 Medals of Honor, 74 Navy Crosses, 31 Distinguished Service Medals, 946 Silver Stars, and 1,582 Bronze Stars.

Jack Cody had arrived in Vietnam as a Hospital Corpsman Petty Officer Second Class (HM-2) in June of 1969. After just a few days of in-country processing, he was assigned to Kilo Company, Third Battalion, Third Regiment of I Corps, Third Marine Division. In Marine speak, that was simply K/3/3.

After reporting for duty to the battalion commander, Jack was escorted to Kilo Company, where he met his platoon commander and the other Corpsmen and Marines who would be his brothers. Marines would sometimes shun an FNG, but they always accepted and wanted the best for their Corpsmen.

Upon arrival, Jack immediately noticed the intensity of the Marines of Kilo Company. Something was up: scuttlebutt (rumor) had it that a major offensive against the enemy was in the works.

The reason for the frantic preparations was revealed to Jack and the men of his platoon, when their platoon commander told them that they were moving out as part of an operation dubbed "Idaho Canyon." They were headed north to seek out the enemy west of Kam Ky in Quang Tri Province.

K/3/3 along with the rest of the 3rd Marines and the Army's 101st Airborne Division moved out as part of Operation Idaho Canyon on 21 July 1969. The Soldiers of the 101st Airborne and Marines of 3/3 were fighting the VC and NVA units in Quang Tri Province. Quang Tri was the northernmost province of the Republic of Vietnam (RVN or South Vietnam) and, of course, it was butted up against the demilitarized zone (DMZ) separating the two warring Vietnams.

The reaction of the enemy was swift; they didn't relinquish territory easily, and the fighting was sometimes intense.

Soon after arriving at 3/3's fire support base, Jack was sent forward to assist a platoon of Marines engaged in a desperate fight for survival. They were defending a hill near the DMZ. The enemy had zeroed in on the Marines' position with mortars and was firing for effect. The Marines pulled back a couple of clicks (kilometers) to Hill 162, where they set up a defensive perimeter.

Shortly after midnight—zero dark early to be inexact—all hell broke loose. Mortars began drubbing the Marines; screams of "Corpsman!" could barely be heard over the chaos. Jack Cody and his fellow Corpsmen were moving from casualty to casualty, trying, many times in vain, to save the life of a Marine. Then, enemy RPGs and small-arms fire began devastating the Marines inside their perimeter. The NVA was close—real close! AK-47 rounds were cracking over the Marines' heads, sometimes hitting their marks; mortar, RPG, and rocket rounds were hitting within their perimeter, creating havoc and tearing apart young healthy bodies. When hand-thrown grenades began landing inside their defensive perimeter, the Marines knew they might be in for some old-fashioned hand-to-hand combat.

No one on either side had the time or the inclination to pause and take in the eerie and strangely beautiful light show produced by the battle. Parachute flares swaying back and forth in the gentle breeze lit the area with alternating light and shadow. Incoming NVA tracer rounds were lighting the sky with horizontal green streaks. The Marines' red tracer rounds going in the opposite direction created a terrifying visual effect. Red and green tracer rounds were occasionally ricocheting and shooting skyward as if to highlight the deadly seriousness of the battle. It was all so surreal: the landscape lit up with flares; the noise of incoming mortars and rockets; the explosions; and the cracking noises of bullets overhead as they broke the sound barrier.

Amidst it all, Jack heard nothing; his vision narrowed until he saw only the Marine he was working on. The chaos around him became nonexistent. Jack ran, crouching, to a Marine rifleman who was moaning with a bullet wound to his chest. The injury was severe, but Jack thought that the boy—a Private First Class (PFC) who looked younger than his seventeen years—could be saved. Jack was on his knees, bending over the wounded boy. The boy became Jack's center of focus, and the battle faded from his consciousness.

Suddenly, an explosion rang loudly in Jack's ears, and a searing pain engulfed the crown of his head. A hand grenade had detonated some distance to his front, and a hot fragment had entered the top of Jack's skull. Blood began running down his forehead and into his eyes. Wiping the blood from his face did little to clear his vision or stop the stinging in his eyes. Jack was shaken— it hurt like hell—but he kept working on his patient.

After stabilizing the PFC as best he could, he gave the boy a reassuring pat on the cheek.

"You'll be all right, Marine. We'll have you outta here in a flash."

With that, HM-2 Jack Cody headed to the next "Corpsman!" call that he heard.

The call came from a nearby M48 Patton tank. Jack made his way to the tank and saw that the tank commander had been hit and was in terrible shape. Climbing high onto the tank to assess the commander's condition, Jack was more exposed to enemy fire than he had been at any other time during the fight. He ignored the risk, but not intentionally, as his mind blocked out everything around him except his mission—he had to save lives.

The tank commander was knocking on heaven's door with a massive wound to his upper chest; he could barely breathe. With his own blood still running down his forehead and into his eyes, Jack began a tracheotomy. As he began to cut the man's throat to create the emergency air passage, he felt a sudden sting on the right side of his neck.

What the hell? All this shit going on and I get stung by a bee?

Jack swiped at his neck with his bloody hand and continued what he hoped would be the lifesaving tracheotomy. But it was not to be. The captain died as Jack was working to save his life.

The battle continued and became hand-to-hand. When an NVA soldier climbed atop the M48 tank, Jack's platoon commander blasted him with his shotgun.

It was time to get the hell out of Dodge.

When the attacks tapered off a bit, K/3/3 moved back to the fire support base.

They hadn't been inside the perimeter of the fire support base for long before the enemy began a sustained attack. Jack and the other company Corpsmen had their hands full; they couldn't work fast enough.

When a CH-46 Sea Knight arrived to evacuate the wounded, Jack and HM-3 Aaron Burke*—a burly Irish lad from Boston—began loading the wounded onto the big bird. It was a tough physical job. Loading Marine after wounded Marine onto the Sea Knight sapped their energy, but the Corpsmen kept at it. When a second CH-46 arrived and they had loaded the last of the wounded, they finally had a moment—just a moment—to find their second wind.

C-46 Sea Knight on final during the 2002 Exercise Cobra Gold in Thailand
U.S. Marine Corps photo by Sgt. Stephen D'Alessio

Jack Cody stood before Burke, covered with the blood of wounded Marines, with his own blood running down the sides of his head and hair matted with gore. Jack's eyes looked glassy, staring but not seeing. Nobody was home!

Jack had been operating on training and instinct. Burke told Jack to get on the Sea Knight. It wasn't a request—it was an order issued by a caring friend. Jack didn't want to get on, but Burke was insistent and helped Jack onto the CH-46 for evacuation.

As soon as the big bird lifted off and the emotional stress was relieved, Jack's lights went out.

The CH-46 delivered Jack and the wounded Marines to the hospital ship USS *Repose* (AH-16). The *Repose* had been nicknamed "Angel of the Orient" and had been a lifesaver to America's wounded warriors since 1944.

When orderlies carried Jack to the emergency room onboard *Repose*, he was unconscious, and there was blood everywhere—his hair was matted with it, his face and neck were streaked with it, and his utility uniform was soaked in it.

An orderly, while quickly stripping Jack of his utility uniform in preparation for the doctor's examination, said, "This man looks like he just came from a slaughterhouse."

The orderlies didn't know and couldn't have guessed that most of the blood on their patient from the neck down had come from the dozen or more Marines that he had treated.

As part of the usual admission processes onboard the *Repose*, orderlies would record patients' names and serial numbers, sometimes right off bloodied dog tags.

"This man has no dog tags," one of the orderlies remarked.

"Look at that neck wound, must have lost them when he got hit," his companion said. "Look in his boots."

Many Army Soldiers and sometimes Marines would wear an extra dog tag strung into a bootlace for just such an eventuality.

"No such luck," the other orderly responded.

"Well, record him as another John Doe," his companion replied.

Jack was then taken to the operating room (OR), his prospects for survival undetermined.

In the OR, doctors removed a two-inch piece of Chinese Communist (ChiCom) grenade fragment from the top of Jack's skull. They cleaned bone fragments and other foreign matter from the wound and dressed it. His neck injury was not serious, but he'd live with a nasty scar as a reminder of Operation Idaho Canyon.

Jack Cody, now known as "John Doe," was taken to recovery.

Three days after Jack's injury, a Navy Chaplain and a senior Navy noncommissioned officer arrived at the home of Elizabeth and Buck Cody with the disturbing news that their elder son was missing in action. It was a terrible time for Buck and Elizabeth Cody. They didn't know if their son was dead, alive but alone somewhere in the jungles of Vietnam, or a prisoner of war in North Vietnam.

Onboard the Angel of the Orient, *John Doe* was unconscious for a solid week before he opened his eyes and looked around at the sterile environment of the hospital ship.

"Where am I?" were Jack's first words, uttered before he was even fully conscious.

A nurse told him that he was safe aboard a hospital ship and then asked the sixty-four-thousand-dollar question.

"What's your name, Marine?"

"Jack Cody...I'm a Corpsman."

The Navy finally put the pieces together and found their missing Corpsman. The news that Jack Cody was no longer missing in action was sent to Buck and Elizabeth Cody. It had been a terrible week, but their son was alive, and that was all that mattered.

After a rapid recovery, Jack was discharged and flown back to the world. He left the USS *Repose* with a souvenir in his pocket—a two-inch piece of ChiCom grenade shrapnel.

For his actions on that dark, terrifying night in Vietnam, Hospital Corpsman Petty Officer Second Class Jack Cody was awarded a Bronze Star with the Combat V to denote combat heroism. In recognition of his wounds, he was awarded a Purple Heart. Jack Cody's Devil Dog buddies honored him with the title "Devil Doc."

* * *

Sterling Cody's thoughts snapped back to reality. He realized that he had been subconsciously flying his Huey while his thoughts were occupied with his older brother.

Yes, Jack's home and safe.

Sterling pondered how strange it was that he could daydream while flying a helicopter. Skills that required supreme coordination seemed to—at times like these— need no input from his conscious mind. He didn't understand it and knew that it would be even harder for a civilian to understand, but amidst the carnage of war and the deaths of enemy soldiers and even his comrades, his thoughts would sometimes leave his body and transport him back to his youth. A youth filled with adventures aplenty shared with his brother, Jack.

3

The Right Brother

Emporium, Pennsylvania
1950

In 1950, young Sterling Cody began life much the same as most American boys. His was the quintessential American family: his stay-at-home mom doted on her new baby boy and the baby's older brother.

Young Sterling realized early on that his father was something special. Of Sterling's playmates' dads, his was the only father who was a pilot, and not just an ordinary pilot. Sterling would proudly announce to his friends that his dad was a test pilot. Sterling was proud of his dad, and he dreamed of someday soaring among the clouds like his father.

As Sterling grew, so too did his world. His older brother Jack began showing him the streams, hills, and trees on their two hundred acre dairy farm in Northern Pennsylvania. It wasn't an active dairy farm, but the old barn still stood, enticing the two adventuresome boys into exploring its every nook and cranny.

Sterling's dad had rented the old farm near Emporium, Pennsylvania, from the retired owner for $60 a month. In the 1950s, houses in the city were going at the same rate, so getting a nice house and a barn spanning two hundred acres with trees and streams and swimming ponds to delight growing boys was considered a bargain.

The farm was seven miles north of the city of Emporium. Emporium was a small town with a population of just 3,646 in 1950. Even though it was small in geographic size and population, Emporium was significant as the county seat of Cameron County. Several state highways passed through Emporium and Cameron County, but when the Interstate Highway system was later built, the county was bypassed, which perhaps explains the drop in Emporium's population to a tad above two thousand residents by 2010.

Young Sterling didn't realize it at the time, but Cameron County's most notable person was a man he would—albeit unknowingly—aspire to emulate. Joseph T. McNarney was a World War I flying ace who rose to four-star General and Deputy Chief of Staff of the U.S. Army during World War II (WW-II). Knowingly, the boy aspired to be like his dad.

Sterling's father, Edwin "Buck" Cody*, was born in Brooklyn, New York, in 1915 and reached adulthood at the height of the Great Depression. With about a quarter of adult males out of work, the chance of a lad of seventeen finding gainful employment was as likely as a New York minute lasting a full sixty seconds. Buck Cody had dropped out of school after finishing eighth grade.

Going to school was expensive, and there was no extra money in the family. With his schooling behind him—or so he thought—Buck Cody set his sights on adventure. He would sample the world and partake of the excitement offered by the world outside of New York City.

Sticking around Brooklyn and joining the swarms of unemployed men was not for Buck. He devised a master plan; the military was Buck's ticket to adventure. He would join the Navy and see the world. After a hitch in the Navy, he'd enlist in the Army, and after the Army, he'd join the Marine Corps. It made sense to the seventeen-year-old; he'd sample all three branches before deciding which one would be his career path.

When Buck's four-year Navy enlistment ended, he headed straight to the Army recruiter. After a battery of tests, the Navy veteran was offered Army flight school. Flying for the Army was everything he hoped it would be, and Buck excelled as a pilot. He was soon flying the Army's fighter, the Boeing P-26 Peashooter.

The Peashooter had made its first flight in 1932. The P-26 was state-of-the-art in the early 1930s: It had a 600-horsepower Pratt and Whitney Wasp engine that propelled the Peashooter at a cruising speed of 200 mph and a top speed of 234 mph. The Peashooter's wings were braced with wire, rather than with the rigid struts used on other airplanes, so it was lighter and had less drag. The P-26 was armed with two machine guns and carried a two hundred pound bomb load. The U.S. Army soon ordered 136 of the new all-metal fighters.

Boeing P-26 "Peashooter" of the 19th Pursuit Squadron in Panama

It was 1936, and the nation was still in shock over the human cost of World War I. The Great War—as it was called—had cost over 117,000 American lives. Returning veterans told of unimaginable horrors of charging into machine-gun fire and of mustard gas attacks. Over 204,000 wounded vets, some with missing arms and legs, and others with less visible scars, were reminders to the general population that The Great War had to be "The War to End All Wars."

The populace was not in the mood to support what was then called, "foreign entanglements." Even so, President Roosevelt knew that the Panama Canal was vital to the nation's defense.

Buck Cody was ordered to Panama to defend the canal and his country. When Buck arrived in the Canal Zone, he reported to the CO of the 24th Pursuit Squadron[1] at the Rio Hato Air Base[2] on Panama's Pacific coast. It was Buck's first duty station after his flight

---

[1] The 24th Pursuit Squadron was renamed 24th Fighter Squadron in 1942.

[2] Rio Hato was later renamed Albrook Air Force Station and later Albrook "Marcos A. Gelabert" International Airport.

training and his first time outside the United States. Everything was new and exciting.

Free time for the Soldiers at Rio Hato was little different than that at other Army bases around the world. The local bars and brothels were popular with many of the Soldiers, but they were not to Buck's liking. Buck was more of the outdoor type, so when he heard other flyers talk about their great hunting and fishing expeditions, Buck asked if he could join them. He acquired fishing gear for deep-sea fishing, and when a retiring first sergeant offered to sell his 12-gauge shotgun, Buck jumped at the opportunity and forked over the cash. Buck and his pals were soon bringing back wild game from the jungles and quantities of fish from the sea. Rio Hato's mess hall cooks were grateful and took all of the fish the pilots could bring them, as the Army's supply system did not provide them with fresh fish. The wild game—mostly wild boar and monkeys— was handed over to grateful Panamanians near the base.

Buck was having a ball in Panama; he loved the flying, the hunting and the fishing, and the experience of living in a foreign country. His tour passed quickly, and before he knew it, his enlistment in the Army was ending. It was time to return to the U.S.

After Buck's hitch in the Army ended in 1938, it was time for step three of his master plan; it was time to join the Marine Corps. World events, however, sent the now Navy/Army veteran into reevaluation mode. A few months or maybe even a year away from the regimentation, the spit-and-polish and the regulations of military life sounded good to Buck. Besides, he had a few greenbacks in his pocket and deserved a vacation.

Civilian Buck Cody still sought the fast life, and in that pursuit, he took to ice boating. On a cold winter day in 1938, Buck sat in the open cockpit of his homemade iceboat traveling lickety-split over the ice of Cupsaw Lake. The sixty-five acres of Cupsaw Lake in Ringwood, New Jersey, offered smooth ice and a straight-away to thrill any iceboat adrenaline junkie.

Buck had built his motorized iceboat from scratch. He had adapted a Model-T motor and attached a wooden aircraft propeller.

It was a terrible day for ice sailing, but the dead calm winds meant that Buck's Model-T-powered propeller boat would not share the ice with other boats. With 65 acres of ice all to himself, Buck opened the throttle. As his craft picked up speed and the icy wind began biting at his face, Buck had the sensation of flying in his P-26 Peashooter.

Let's see what this Model-T Peashooter can do, he thought, as he opened the throttle, balls to the wall.

Buck had no speedometer and nothing as sophisticated as an air speed indicator on his homemade boat, so he didn't know what speeds he was attaining. His aviation-experienced gut, however, told him he had it up easily over eighty miles per hour.

Buck made several passes and was engrossed in the unadulterated bone-chilling rush of speed and the wind on his face, and he didn't notice the older, nicely dressed man observing from afar. When Buck stopped for the day and began preparing his craft for his boat trailer, the older man approached and introduced himself.

"I'm Orville Wright," began the older man, "and I was impressed with your boat; did you build it yourself?"

Orville Wright in 1905

A little stunned at being in the presence of such a famous aviator—the world's first—Buck admitted that he had indeed built his boat and began explaining the specifications of his craft in scientific detail. Orville then told Buck about the iceboat he had built when he was in college in Minnesota, and the two men began comparing notes. Buck explained that some of the design features were inspired by his aviation experiences in the Army.

Charles A. Lindbergh's iceboat after the wreck
It is believed that Lindbergh's boat was parked near the shore one night when it was rammed by another iceboat. Notice the damaged wooden propeller.
Photo by permission of the Minnesota Historical Society

Orville Wright was impressed, and the conversation quickly shifted from the ice to the sky.

With aviation in the blood of both men, a bond was quickly formed—a bond that could only be understood by aviators such as themselves.

Orville asked about Buck's plans for the future, and Buck modestly explained that he hadn't yet formulated his post-Army plans. Orville Wright was quick to spot opportunities and to seize them. As Orville was talking with the young ex-Army aviator and iceboat builder, he was formulating a plan in his head. As Buck was speculating about his future prospects, Orville Wright whipped out what Buck thought was a very expensive fountain pen and a pad of paper.

As he was writing, he told Buck, "Take this to Curtiss-Wright over at Caldwell; they'll give you a job."

Buck knew that Curtiss-Wright Corporation had a facility at the Caldwell, New Jersey airfield; it was a stone's throw from his house near Cupsaw Lake.

Buck Cody left Cupsaw Lake on that cold winter day with a warm glow in his heart, optimistic that his future had been ordained by fate and the world famous Orville Wright.

Orville and Wilber Wright's company, The Wright Aeronautical Corporation, had merged with the Curtiss Aeroplane and Motor Company on 5 July 1929, forming the Curtiss-Wright Corporation. Orville was now a trusted consultant to the company, and a friend and confidant of Glenn Curtiss.

In 1938, Curtiss-Wright was—without question—the technological leader in U.S. aviation. They had pioneered the concepts of air-cooled engines as well as the radial engine. Curtiss-Wright engineers were pushing the output per engine and approaching the one thousand horsepower mark. In 1937, the Curtiss P-36 Hawk fighter plane was developed and tested. The Hawk was accepted by the United States Army in April 1938. It resulted in the largest peacetime aircraft order ever given by the Army Air Corps.

There was reason for Buck to be excited; the prospect of flying the latest and greatest—the P-36

Hawk—was within reach. The next day, Buck put on his best suit and drove to Caldwell. Once inside Curtiss-Wright's offices, he was directed to a secretary sitting just outside a large office. After a short wait, a well-dressed gentleman opened the door and invited Buck into his office. Buck presented his note from Orville Wright to the man and politely asked for a job. The man explained that the company wasn't hiring at that time.

Clearly disappointed, Buck explained, "Well, Orville Wright gave me that note and said that you were supposed to hire me."

Somewhat taken aback, the man stammered, "Well, if Mr. Wright said I was supposed to hire you, you're hired!"

Faster than he could comprehend what had happened, Buck went from unemployed and directionless to a Curtiss-Wright test pilot; he would be flying and testing the P-36 Hawk.

Curtiss P-36 Hawk

One of the first orders for the new P-36 was also one of the most unusual and most memorable. One P-36 Hawk was ordered personally by Soong May-ling, who was the First Lady of the Republic of China and the wife of Generalissimo and President Chiang Kai-shek, and as such, she became known as Madam Chiang. As China's First Lady, Madam Chiang took on duties far more significant than that of America's First Lady Eleanor Roosevelt. Among Madam Chiang's many responsibilities was her duty as Secretary General of the Chinese Aeronautical Affairs Commission.

Working directly for Madam Chiang in China was a former American Army pilot named Claire Lee Chennault. Chennault had retired from the Army in 1937 with the rank of captain, and had gone on to work as an aviation adviser and trainer in China. Chennault quickly became Chiang Kai-shek's chief air adviser. Since Chennault didn't speak Chinese and Chiang Kai-shek didn't speak English, Madam Chiang acted as their interpreter. Madam Chiang and Chennault formed an immediate and lasting bond.

When the P-36 Hawk was introduced, Madam Chiang knew that she had to have one. With her own money—pocket change for her—she ordered one of the first P-36 Hawks and presented it to Claire Chennault. Chennault would eventually lead The 1st American Volunteer Group (AVG) of the Chinese Air Force.

The AVG was supplied with an updated version of the P-36, which sported an improved supercharger and weapons systems. The Army designated the improved P-36 the P-40 Warhawk. With the new superchargers,

Warhawks could climb to greater altitudes and give the Japanese Zeros a run for their money.

Chennault's AVG painted a menacing shark's mouth on the nose of their P-40s and adopted the iconic name "Flying Tigers." A legend was now born.

Flight leader and fighter ace Robert "R.T."
Smith stands next to his P-40 fighter at Kunming, China. The
"Flying Tiger" insignia was created by the Walt Disney Company.

Curtiss-Wright was working at a frantic pace; everyone sensed that war between England and Nazi Germany was imminent. Buck stayed busy flying, writing reports and preparing for his next test flight.

On Friday morning, the first day of September, Buck made an early morning test flight. After landing his P-36, he walked to the hangar to talk with the engineers. They weren't interested in Buck's flight; they had a radio news broadcast playing and were talking among themselves—Germany had just invaded Poland.

England's Prime Minister Neville Chamberlain had signed an iconic agreement just the year before with Germany's Adolf Hitler for "Peace in Our Time." Chamberlain had said that if Hitler didn't abide by the treaty—and it was now obvious that he hadn't—he would declare war on Germany. Was the pacifist prime minister going to keep his word? Did this mean war?

Some argued yes but others, citing Chamberlain's history of appeasement, doubted that the appeaser-in-chief would actually make good his threat.

Buck woke to the news on Sunday 3 September 1939 that England and France had indeed declared war on Nazi Germany.

War!

It made newspaper headlines across the country and was all over the radio. The consensus seemed to be that the U.S. absolutely had to avoid getting entangled in Europe's war. The people at Curtiss-Wright, though, knew that they would be a part of the war even if the U.S. remained neutral.

Rumors began to spread around Curtiss-Wright of a contract the company was negotiating with the English government. The contract was not for airplanes (they had been supplying P-36s for some time), but rather, for people. Rumor morphed into reality when Curtiss-Wright put out the call for volunteers; they needed pilots and technicians to help assemble, test, and field the new fighters in England. Buck didn't hesitate; he was one of the first to sign the contract.

In October of 1939, Buck and other Curtiss-Wright volunteers boarded a ship loaded with P-36s and all manner of ancillary equipment. Buck was headed for England and the war.

Buck's job in England went well as the English geared up for war with Nazi Germany. Buck was flying again—not just regular sightseeing flights, but heart-stopping, adrenaline-pumping test flights.

Adolf Hitler's Luftwaffe was technically more advantaged than the Royal Air Force's (RAF) British and American-made fighters. The divergence in technologies began in 1929 when the Great Depression began to ravage the economies of the three countries and unemployment skyrocketed. Drastic action was required; jobs had to be created. The U.S. and Great Britain attacked the problem by slashing defense spending while simultaneously increasing spending on labor-intensive building projects. Adolf Hitler, on the other hand, drastically increased defense spending. He too created jobs, but Hitler's newly employed workforce created the most advanced military seen on the face of the earth.

While the Americans and English were sleeping, German aeronautical engineers were developing advanced superchargers, thereby increasing the maximum altitude attainable by their fighters. Altitude was a distinct advantage in a dogfight, and the Nazi superchargers were like German steel against English bronze. The English were outclassed.

The Curtiss-Wright engineers went to work alongside their English comrades, designing and improving new superchargers. The days of the Luftwaffe's Messerschmitt ME-109 out-climbing allied planes had to come to an end—and soon! Buck and RAF pilots took to the skies, testing the new superchargers and other modifications. They had a lot of catching up to do and little time—make that no time—to do it in.

Buck not only tested the P-36s, but also the Spitfires and Hurricanes built by the English. Buck loved every minute of it. Well, he didn't enjoy the report writing, but if that's what it took to stay in the sky, he'd learn to love that too.

The RAF replaced squadrons of British-built Hurricanes with U.S.-made Curtiss P-36 Hawks as fast as possible. In December of 1941, the RAF established a squadron in North Africa to go up against the Nazi's seemingly invincible General Erwin Rommel. The new unit—designated III Squadron by the British—was a fully equipped P-36 group that helped to establish air superiority over Rommel's Luftwaffe.

Buck continued his work in England until December 1941. After the Japanese attack on Pearl Harbor, the Curtis-Wright Corporation recalled him to their operations in New Jersey. His flying skills were needed at home.

Buck Cody settled into his job and began thinking of marriage and a family. When he met Elizabeth Hart*, he knew that she would become his wife. From Maywood, New Jersey, Elizabeth was nineteen years old and a real beauty. Elizabeth Hart became Mrs. Edward Cody* soon after they met.

The new couple settled in Ringwood, New Jersey, near Cupsaw Lake. By 1950, the family was complete. John, or Jack as he was called, was born on 3 June 1945. Jack's little brother, future playmate, and partner in all things adventurous was born on 11 October 1950.

4

Flap Your Wings

Cameron County, Pennsylvania
October 1957

The sun was beginning to dip behind the Allegheny Mountains, and there was a chill in the early October air as twelve-year-old Jack Cody strapped the homemade canvas wings to his seven-year-old brother's arms. Sterling knew that this was going to be their best adventure yet. He stood proudly atop the chicken coop roof and listened intently to his older—and presumably wiser—brother's final instructions for the impending flight.

This was it. Jack and Sterling had been talking, planning, designing, replanning, and redesigning all summer. Now, in the brisk October air, atop their chicken coop launch pad, Sterling Cody confidently prepared for flight. He affixed his "aviator goggles"—last summer's swimming goggles—to his face and was now ready to soar.

With total confidence only a boy of seven can muster in an impossible task, Aviator Sterling Cody began his first flight, and soar he did—straight to the ground.

...and soar he did—straight to the ground
Illustration by Guadalupe Rivas

Jack, being older and wiser—at least wiser than a seven-year-old—picked his little brother up from the dirt and niggled his technique.

"You didn't flap your wings fast enough; you gotta flap harder!"

Sterling's second trip to the top of the chicken coop wasn't quite as enthusiastic as his first, but he now knew the secret—flap faster, flap harder. Now, armed with the secret of flight, Sterling knew that this time, he would surely fly.

With a little encouragement from his "ground crew," Sterling began flapping to beat the wind and launched himself from the apex of the chicken coop, not into the wild blue yonder as he fully expected, but straight into the ground, again!

Jack rushed to the crash site to help his moaning sibling. He untangled legs and arms from canvas, wood, and string, and helped Sterling to his feet.

Dirty and disheveled and with wings still strapped to his arms, Sterling was a sight to see. But a few scrapes and bruises were minor compared to the disappointment that Sterling felt after his failure to fly. Determination, however, and a desire to soar into the heavens like his father were part of the boy's nature from his earliest consciousness. He *would* fly, someday!

With the late October sun in their face, the brothers walked home, anticipating each new day and the new adventures to come.

5

Drinkin' Wine Spo-Dee-O-Dee

Cameron County, Pennsylvania
Christmas 1957

Like most boys, Sterling Cody liked the Christmas season. Now that he was seven years old, he was too big for Santa Claus, but that didn't mean he didn't look forward to the gifts. He also liked the cold weather that seemed to herald the Christmas festivities. Most of all, Sterling loved the freedom that came with his school holidays—freedom to explore the woods and streams of his father's farm, freedom to play games with his friends, freedom to pursue adventures as yet unimagined.

On the afternoon of Christmas Eve 1957, Sterling met with two neighbor boys, Jim Manning* and Darrel Bennett*. Jim and Darrel were not only neighbors but also classmates and two of Sterling's best friends. Adults know that second-grade friendships rarely last more than a few years, but second graders—with their unwarranted wisdom—have the knack of convincing themselves that their friendship will last forever.

Sterling, Jim, and Darrel enjoyed that special kind of bond.

It was a cold day that was getting colder. A light snow had begun that morning and continued into the afternoon. The boys decided that it was an ideal day for ice-skating, and Sterling knew the perfect spot.

One of the streams that fed into the Susquehanna River originated on Keating Summit, just ten miles north of the Cody Farm. As it meandered south, it intersected with a trout stream on the farm. It was one of the Cody boys' favorite spots; along with their friends, they would fish there on lazy summer afternoons and skinny dip on days that were more adventurous. On this freezing Christmas Eve, however, Sterling and his friends had ice-skating on their mind.

The boys knew that the best spot for fishing in the summer was also the best place for ice-skating when the river froze over. They headed for the widest section, where the two streams came together in a "Y." The ice was thick and strong, except for one spot at the center of the "Y," where the mixing of the waters from the two streams created a turbulence that restricted the formation of ice. The boys were instinctively aware of the danger of skating near the center of the "Y."

The three fifth-graders were having so much fun that, at first, they didn't notice the older boys approaching. The older boys were Sterling's twelve-year-old brother Jack, Darrel Burnett's brother Dean*, and their buddy Don Keller*. They were laughing and cutting up, which wasn't that unusual, but their laughter and antics were strangely amplified.

The younger boys approached the creek bank to see about the commotion.

"Whatcha doing?" from the younger boys was answered by Dean with a cryptic, "Drinkin' wine spo-dee-o-dee."

It meant nothing to the younger boys, but it caused the older boys to convulse in uncontrollable laughter.

Sterling and his buddies smiled and even laughed a bit, even though they didn't get what was obviously an inside joke. Jack tried several times to explain the meaning of the phrase, but he couldn't get past, "Drinking wine spo..." before the trio of older boys burst into another fit of laughter. Finally, after four or five attempts, Jack was able to explain that *Drinkin' Wine Spo-Dee-O-Dee* was a Jerry Lee Lewis rock-n-roll song popular on the radio. The younger boys were not yet into rock-n-roll, so they had never heard the song. But by now, it didn't matter since the significance was apparent.

Sterling knew that his dad had a ten-gallon barrel of homemade elderberry wine that he kept in the barn. He knew what that wine smelled like, and he recognized the smell permeating the air. When the older boys began nipping from little flasks—acquired from who knows where—there was no doubt. What the hell...it was Christmas and everybody was having fun.

The six boys took to the ice. It was more fun with six, and the elderberry wine lightened the mood of even the younger ones, even though they hadn't drunk any of the forbidden fruit.

Amidst the chaos of six boys skating this way and that, suddenly, Dean Bennett deliberately skated towards the hole in the ice and the turbulent waters within. The other boys watched in awe as Dean approached the hole at breakneck speed. Some cheered, while others stood flabbergasted as Dean leaped into the freezing water.

It took a moment for the boys to process what had just happened and for panic to set in. The fast moving current began carrying Dean downstream from the hole in the ice. Dean—obviously panicking now—was fighting to keep from going under the four-inch thick ice. They all knew that if Dean went under the ice, the fast-moving current would carry him downstream to his death.

Without hesitation, Don Keller leaped into the water, grabbed his friend by the jacket collar, and kept him from going under. The other boys formed a human chain and pulled the two drunken scoundrels from the icy water.

The "Y" where the two streams merge
This photo was taken before the streams froze over.
From the Sterling Cody Collection

Back on solid ground, Dean and Don began to shiver in their wet clothes. Even though the party was obviously over, most of the copious quantities of elderberry wine—so rapidly consumed—had yet to enter the older boys' bloodstream. They would soon realize that there was a price to pay.

Dean and Don were freezing and needed to get out of their wet clothes and into something warm pronto. Jack and Sterling's house was the closest, so the boys decided to go there. Besides, in their condition, they didn't want to face parents and Jack knew that his parents were out Christmas shopping. Close and safe seemed like the best option.

The boys entered the Cody house, and as expected, Mr. and Mrs. Cody were still Christmas shopping. They had time to cover their tracks and come up with their stories.

Dean and Don shed their wet clothes and took hot showers. After his shower, however, Dean seemed to be drunker. The alcohol was still kicking in, and his stomach was beginning to kick it out. Dean started vomiting into the commode. Jack helped Dean to his bedroom and put him in his bed, but not before getting a pan from the kitchen so that Dean wouldn't make a mess on the bedroom floor.

Don Keller dried himself off and Jack—the least drunk of the three—handed Don some dry clothes from his closet. Don first tried putting on Jack's jeans the conventional way, standing up, but standing only resulted in his falling on his ass. After chuckling over his clumsiness, he picked himself off the floor, and with Jack's help, sat on the side of the bed. Even while seated, putting on the jeans was difficult, since he could see four pant legs instead of two. After several attempts, he finally threaded his legs into the proper pant legs. The alcohol was still kicking in.

Don decided that he had best get on home. Darkness comes early during the winter months, and on this Christmas Eve, it was already dark. The boys never walked on the road between their houses because it was much faster to cut through the woods following the railroad tracks. What boy could resist walking on railroad tracks?

With Buck and Elizabeth Cody still out on their last-minute Christmas shopping, the evening progressed normally for the two boys home alone on Christmas Eve.

They turned on the lights on the Cody's Christmas tree, and they fixed themselves sandwiches as the Evening Flyer (a passenger train) roared past the Cody Farm, sounding its whistle on its way to Emporium. Everything was as it should have been, until the phone rang at about eight in the evening.

Mr. Keller* was on the line, and he was worried about his son Don. It was late on Christmas Eve, and it was not like Don to be out this late. He should have been at home with his family, celebrating Christmas with his brothers and sisters.

The Cody boys' hearts sank in their chest as they remembered—almost in unison—that Don had left for home just before the Evening Flyer had announced its passing. They knew that Don was way yonder drunk and would have been walking home—make that stumbling home—along the Evening Flyer's tracks.

Now Don was missing? The Cody boys feared the worst. They rushed out the front door to begin searching the railroad tracks for their friend and ran headlong into their parents returning from their Christmas shopping. What else could go wrong?

"Dean's upstairs in bed, and he's awfully sick," blurted Sterling, hoping against hope to avoid getting into trouble.

Jack took the lead in explaining their haste, "Don's missing, he went home on the tracks, and now he's missing...We gotta go find him."

With that, the boys ran toward the railroad tracks. They walked the entire mile and a half of the track, one on each side; they occasionally crossed over and checked the other's side to make sure they hadn't missed anything.

Jack and Sterling were relieved, yet concerned, when they approached the Keller's house. They were relieved that they hadn't found Don in a heap of blood and guts, but concerned for their friend and the trouble they all were in.

How were they going to come clean with Mr. Keller? Were they going to have an all-out search with police, search dogs, and helicopters?

Sterling and Jack approached the Keller's house slowly and reluctantly. As they were about to walk up the porch steps, they spotted an unfamiliar lump huddled under the porch. It was Don with a piece of canvas wrapped around him, trying to sober up. Don, who was still showing the effects of the elderberry wine, didn't want to go inside.

"You got to Don; you can't sleep out here all night," said Jack. "I know, go in through the basement; then you can go up the kitchen stairs and just blend in."

It was a good thing Don had twelve brothers and sisters, because as it turned out, he was hardly noticed as he made his way to his upstairs bedroom.

Don changed into his own clothes and explained that he had been doing chores in the barn and stoking the house furnace with coal. Mr. Burnett never suspected a thing.

It turned out to be a good Christmas for the boys after all. Well, not so much for Dean and Don, as they spent Christmas day nursing their first hangovers.

6

Parker's Tomb

McKean County, Pennsylvania
November 1959

Adventuresome boys are seldom dissuaded from outdoor activities by a little foul weather. Sterling Cody and his older brother Jack were headstrong; they had a mission, and—like their mailman—neither snow nor rain nor heat nor gloom of night would keep these boys from their next adventure.

It was the fall season in Northern Pennsylvania when the boys set out on their mission. It was cold; it was snowing large wet snowflakes; and the ground was wet and soggy. Despite this, the boys decided to set out on an epic camping trip, which would later become a legend and make the newspapers and TV stations around the region. This was not a spur-of-the-moment camping trip. The Cody brothers had been planning this expedition for months, and finally, everything was coming together.

The brothers left their house with the usual admonition from their mother, "You boys be careful now."

"We will Ma."

"Promise me now...and Jack, you look after your brother."

"We promise Ma, bye."

As with most boys, their "we promise" was a contract with their mother that was void beyond her line of sight.

The boys headed first for the old barn, where Jack picked up the tools that they would need.

"Let's see now Sterling...a hammer, a crowbar, maybe this big screwdriver, definitely need the flashlight...that should do it."

And with that, the boys picked up their sleeping bags and their food supplies, and set off down the railroad tracks to meet up with their friends and co-conspirators, Dean and Darrel Burnett.

After a short trek down the railroad tracks, the Cody boys met their friends at the Burnett place, and the foursome set out for their campsite close to Gardeau Baptist Church. Just beyond the church was Parker's Tomb. Their chosen campsite near the church was not incidental—it was strategic.

The Cody boys and their friends believed that Colonel Noah Parker of Parker's Tomb had led raids of slow-moving trains as they struggled up the incline to Keating Summit in the late nineteenth and early twentieth century. The boys were intending to visit the departed Colonel Noah Parker, but not to pay their respects.

The boys had heard of Noah Parker's connection to Captain Blackbeard. But what they may not have known was that Parker's Blackbeard was not the famous Edward Teach—aka Blackbeard the famous pirate—of the early eighteenth century. Although they may not have known all the details of Noah Parker's dealings with Captain Blackbeard of the early nineteenth century, they knew enough to set them off on their tomb adventure.

The warm waters around the Bahamas are famous for spawning tropical storms and hurricanes, which are in turn infamous for sending Spanish galleons into the depths. In 1680, a particularly ferocious storm sent a Spanish galleon along with its crew and a king's fortune in silver to the bottom. The wreck, although plainly visible in shallow water, was firmly in the grip of Davy Jones' Locker. The treasure would only be freed by a unique type of man capable of salvaging such treasures. A century and thirty-one years later, the British Admiralty commissioned just such a man.

The Admiralty had the perfect candidate: Captain Blackbeard, of the early nineteenth century, was perhaps the greatest marine salvager, ever. Blackbeard accepted the commission and the challenge. It didn't present that much of a challenge to the resourceful Blackbeard; within a month, the prized cargo was en route to Baltimore. Blackbeard's commission required him to turn over the salvaged riches to the Admiralty at an English port. Since England was then at war with France, shipping the prized cargo to England risked having it fall into the hands of Napoleon Bonaparte's Navy or returned to the deep by French warships.

In Baltimore, news of Blackbeard's salvaged riches soon spread, first through the taverns around the docks and then to the American authorities.

At the time, the British were mired in the Napoleonic wars and were forcefully impressing American sailors into the Royal Navy. It was a common practice back then, but the Americans protested and considered it tantamount to an act of war. England considered the American protest to be whining on the part of an upstart nation and the pretext for a war designed as an American attempt to annex Canada. War between the Americans and the Crown seemed imminent.

Blackbeard was keen to get his treasure into English territory as quickly and as safely as possible. He decided that his best bet was travelling over land to Canada, which was some four hundred miles away. He assembled his crew, loaded silver bars into the false bottoms of ox-drawn wagons, and loaded the wagons with all manner of supplies to sustain the party overland to Canada.

Blackbeard's race to Canada went well at first, but soon conditions became more difficult, and the going became dangerously slow. On the 18th day of June, Blackbeard lost the race; the United States declared war on England. Blackbeard found himself with the King's treasure in enemy territory with only a few options, all of them bad. Burying his treasure and returning after the war seemed to be the least risky option. He would return to reclaim the silver bars after what he thought would be a quick English victory.

The king's ransom in silver was believed to be buried

somewhere near Keating Summit, not far from where two adventuresome boys named Jack and Sterling Cody would reside a century and forty-eight years later.

Blackbeard continued on to Canada and eventually to England to wait out the War of 1812. When the war ended in 1815, Blackbeard returned to America and contracted Noah Parker to guard the treasure site. The coy Mr. Parker guarded the site well. Interlopers never stumbled upon the silver, and although treasure hunters searched, their efforts were in vain. Blackbeard never again saw the fortune, and King George's silver was never again seen by human eyes, except—legend would have it—by Colonel Noah Parker, who would, throughout his lifetime, show bouts of sudden unexplained wealth.

Throughout the years leading up to the mid-twentieth century, every schoolboy within a hundred miles of Keating Summit knew of the legend of Blackbeard, Noah Parker, and King George's silver bars. Speculations that Noah and his crew had collected riches from slow-moving trains ascending Keating Summit added to the allure.

Endless hours of dreaming of untold wealth were, for most boys just that, a dream. This was not so for Sterling and Jack Cody, as they were boys of action. Their campsite near Parker's Tomb was indeed strategic. They would break in and retrieve whatever riches were entombed within. Riches that some said—and the boys with their youthful optimism knew positively—Noah Parker took to his grave.

The boys were excited as they bid their mother

farewell and promised they'd be careful. They carried their sleeping bags, canteens of water and military-style mess kits. Their diet for the next two days would consist of hamburgers, hot dogs roasted over an open fire, chips, and cookies—lots of cookies. They remembered essentials like matches to start their campfire and a flashlight. The flashlight was not for telling scary stories around the campfire; it was for their real-life spooky adventure.

Trudging through the thick forest with all their gear and supplies to their campsite was more difficult than they had expected due to the wet ground and slippery mud. There was still an hour of Saturday afternoon daylight, so they managed to make it to their campsite and set up before dark. They collected firewood from around their campsite, and after great effort, managed to get a fire started from the dead but damp wood. It was after dark by the time the boys broke out the hot dogs and roasted them over the open fire.

It was a dark night; cloud cover obscured the moonlight before it could penetrate the thick canopy of hemlock and evergreen trees. The boys were relieved to see that the nearby Baptist Church had no activity scheduled; the little church was dark and deserted.

Setting the mood, Jack observed that Parker's Tomb would be, "Daaark as a witches' heart!"

They all laughed. The younger boys gulped but they would not be deterred by a little spooky talk.

With the mood set, the boys set out on their mission. They walked past the darkened church for about one hundred yards and then stopped. Looking down at them from a slight incline was the famous Parker's Tomb.

The tomb was built into the base of a mountain and was about thirteen feet tall and circular in shape; it resembled the military Quonset huts that both Cody boys would become familiar with in a few short years. An obelisk extended upward another thirteen feet from the crest of the tomb.

As they made their way up the slope, Jack shined the flashlight above the doors to the inscription:

PARKER
—1895—

Parker's Tomb
Before the break in, solid wood double doors protected the
entrance. After the break in, the entryway was sealed with cinder
blocks and cement.
From the Sterling Cody Collection

It was clear that Jack and Dean were in charge of the operation, as both older boys approached the door to assess their challenge. Pushing against it with all his might, Jack realized that the hardwood door was solid and firm. With that initial assessment, they broke out the crowbar, hammer, and screwdriver.

The door actually consisted of two doors hinged on either side, connected with a locking mechanism in the center. Jack and Dean took turns at trying to bust the lock with the screwdriver and hammer. After several failed attempts at breaking the lock, Jack mumbled to the younger boys, "Hand me the crowbar."

Jack and Dean worked the crowbar into a small gap where the wood door met the cement wall. Prying as hard as they could, they managed to increase the gap to about half an inch. With that, they could tell where the hinges were, so they began prying first at one and then at the other hinge. They soon had the gap open to about an inch.

"Let's just bust it open," offered Jack.

Dean, in agreement, said, "Yeah, come on, put your shoulder into it."

The two older boys played football on their junior high school teams, so they began ramming the door with their bodies just like they did with the tackling dummies at practice. They first tried from one foot away, but as the door's failing hinges proved stronger than first thought, they began hitting it with two and then three-foot running starts. After four or five hits, the door fell flat into the tomb with a thunderous S-P-L-A-T!

Afraid that the noise would have been heard five miles away, they all held their breath.

Nothing! Not even a dog barked. They were safe.

It was pitch dark inside the tomb. Sterling found their one flashlight and began to shine it around the interior. Hearts were beating overtime, not only from the exertion required to get in, but also from the realization of actually being inside the forbidden Parker's Tomb.

It was dark and scary inside. The tomb extended deep into the side of the mountain and was a lot bigger than they had thought. They had seen the tomb from the outside hundreds of times, and they were just realizing that the exterior was like the tip of an iceberg. The boys kept close to each other as they began slowly exploring inside the tomb. They found empty crypt after empty crypt. Partly following the beam of their one flashlight and partly feeling their way, they continued searching for Noah Parker's Crypt.

"We should've brought more flashlights," offered Darrell, which prompted a "No shit Sherlock" from his older brother.

"Wow," said Sterling, "there're a lot of crypts in here."

Searching the tomb for Noah Parker's coffin took a considerable amount of time; it was about thirty minutes—or what *seemed* like thirty minutes to the boys—before Sterling finally locked the beam of light on a casket that was sitting on a stone table. The casket was old and looked just like the wooden ones the boys had seen in hundreds of cowboy movies. It had a single metal handle—brass, Jack reckoned—extending across the foot and another across the head of the casket. Attached to the foot of the coffin was a dusty old metal plaque that was hard to read at first. Sterling brushed away dirt and cobwebs and began to read aloud:

Here lays Noah Parker

My Days are Gone,
My Days are Done,
Now I'll Let the Worms,
Have Their Fun

Laughter echoed off the cement walls of the inner tomb.

"Ole Colonel Parker had a warped sense of humor," Jack said.

"Yeah, but the worms got the last laugh," Sterling quipped.

The tomb filled with more laughter.

The mood within the tomb was now light as the boys set about the task at hand—finding Parker's treasure.

"It's got to be inside the coffin," someone said.

"Sure it is...let's get it open!" Jack commanded.

They began trying to open the lid, but it was sealed tight.

They worked on the lid until someone said, "Let's pull it down, it'll bust open."

With Sterling holding the flashlight in his armpit, awkwardly shining the flashlight on the foot of the coffin, all four boys began tugging the handle at the foot of the coffin. As they were pulling, the handle and the entire piece of wood to which it was attached suddenly and, without an inkling of warning, broke off, sending four boys ass end over teakettle against the west wall. The flashlight slowly rolled toward the entrance, sending its beam rotating eerily across the opposite wall. Sterling crawled over on all fours and grabbed the light.

"Let's get the treasure and get outta here," Jack said.

They walked gingerly to the foot of the coffin. The four boys stood silently for a moment; their brief moment of reverence and awe soon passed. So much for reverence! The boys had come for treasure, and they weren't to be denied it by some old dead geezer.

The casket was now open at the foot; the darkness inside was hiding its resident and—the boys were confident—untold riches. Sterling directed the flashlight's beam into the open-ended coffin.

Aaaaaaah!

The sight of two boney feet sent the boys scurrying over each other in a race for the tomb's narrow exit.

As the four boys squeezed against each other to be first out, Sterling pulled out of the human traffic jam and said, "Whoa! I came for treasure, and I'm not gonna let no dead guy stop me."

Jack concurred as forcefully as he could, "Yeah, screw the dead guy."

Jack was actually a little embarrassed that his younger brother was the first to recover from the frightening sight.

Regaining his composure, Jack commanded, "Come on, let's see what the old fart stashed in his box."

They walked gingerly to the now open-ended casket, and someone shone the light into the enclosure. The old guy had been sent to the hereafter wearing socks but no shoes. The socks had rotted away over time revealing boney feet wrapped in strands of cloth. The body was small and all shriveled up. They looked deep into the coffin near the corpse's shoulders; something caught their eye. Sterling reached in, but his arm was too short to reach whatever it was lying next to the body. Jack then pushed his brother aside and reached in. He felt something solid; it felt like a brick. He could barely grasp the object with the tips of his fingers, so he pushed the boney feet to the side and stuck his head into the coffin. He slid his whole body shoulder deep into the box, and was able to get a slightly firmer grip. He pulled the object maybe half an inch before his fingers slipped off. He pushed his body a little deeper into the casket. With his head now at Colonel Parker's boney knees, Jack was able to grasp the object firmly. He pulled himself out of the coffin holding what looked like a brick.

All four boys stood in silent awe as the flashlight shone on a silver bar.

The silence lasted for a few seconds as the boys looked at each other and back at the silver bar. A thousand thoughts rushed through four young minds.

The silence was broken with the jabbering of "Wow!"

"I can't believe it!

"I knew it!"

"We're rich!"

Someone said, "Let's get outta here," and the boys headed for the door and ran all the way back to their campsite.

Back at camp, they sat around their campfire, cooked hamburgers, roasted hot dogs, and talked about their adventure. They passed the silver around and speculated on how much it weighed and how much it was worth. Estimates ranged from five to ten pounds and from a thousand to a million dollars. They couldn't agree on the value, but finally decided that it weighed about seven pounds.

In the early morning hours of Sunday, with sleep finally overcoming their excitement, the boys began to contemplate on what they had done. They couldn't agree on whether grave robbing was a hanging offense or would just get them five to ten years in the pen. In the waning light of their campfire, the boys made a solemn promise. They promised each other that they would keep this night a secret for twenty years, and twenty years, as any schoolboy knows, is longer than all the "begats" of the Old Testament.

The boys awoke late on Sunday morning, packed their gear, and headed home. About half-way home, Dean and Darrel Burnett broke off to follow the railroad tracks to their house; Jack and Sterling continued on to their home a short distance away.

The Cody boys knew better than to enter their house with their wet, muddy boots. They had been on many camping trips, and they knew the drill. They removed their boots and hung them on the clothesline to dry before going inside to clean up. They entered through the kitchen door and headed to their bedroom, but then Jack stopped suddenly. The Sunday edition of *The Cameron County Press* was sitting on the table. Jack did a double take and tried not to overreact when he saw the headline:

GRAVE ROBBERS RAVAGE PARKER'S TOMB

After taking showers, the boys tried to act as normal as possible. They went outside and began their chores, which included feeding the chickens and collecting eggs. They were on the second floor of the barn when, to their horror, they saw a state trooper pull up in his cruiser. The boy's mom was in the yard as the trooper approached and began conversing with her.

The boys were out of sight, but close enough to hear everything. The officer asked about the muddy boots hanging on the line. He said that considering the break in at the nearby tomb, the wet boots were—he didn't say "suspicious"—a little curious. Mrs. Cody didn't hesitate—and rightfully so—when she said, "Oh, my boys go camping all the time...whenever they come home with wet boots, they always hang them on the line."

"How old are your boys?"

"They're fourteen and nine."

The trooper knew that it was common for kids to be camping around the area and so was apparently satisfied with Elizabeth Cody's perfectly plausible explanation. He thanked her for her cooperation, climbed into his cruiser and left to continue his investigation into the highest profile crime to hit the area in years.

Late Sunday afternoon, the boys passed by Parker's Tomb. The temptation to have a look was too great, and they had never heard about how criminals always return to the scene of the crime. They walked past the tomb as casually as possible, but they couldn't help but pause and watch as workers enclosed the entrance with cinder blocks and mortar. Workers would later cement over the cinder blocks.

The brothers walked on and renewed their pledge to remain silent about the incident for twenty years.

"I think we dodged a bullet this time Sterling," Jack reassured young Sterling, and they both breathed a sigh of relief.

Little did they know that one day they would be dodging real bullets, and not always successfully.

7

DNA

Wayne, Pennsylvania
1964

Sterling Cody, the thrill-seeking little boy who made his first "flight" from the roof of the family chicken coop, grew up to be a broad-shouldered teenager.

In his thirteenth year, he followed his elder brother Jack to Valley Forge Military Academy (VFMA) at Wayne, Pennsylvania. Sterling entered his plebe year—9th grade—in September of 1964 with the rank of private.

Being away from home for the first time didn't bother Sterling a bit; it was just another adventure for him. Brother Jack was a senior and gave his younger brother tips, but Sterling generally nodded and ignored the advice; he'd do things his way.

VFMA had a proud history of athletic excellence. Sterling was on the wrestling team, and he also excelled as a guard, center, and linebacker on the varsity football team. The boy took to military life and did well at the academy. After finishing his plebe year, he entered 10th grade with the rank of corporal. By his junior year,

Sterling Cody was promoted to sergeant and was made platoon sergeant of Golf Company. Leadership came naturally to the young cadet, and in his senior year, Sterling was promoted to second lieutenant and made the regimental athletic officer.

As the athletic officer, Lieutenant Cody ran the entire intramural sports program, which was a big responsibility; it involved organizing flag football, basketball, table tennis, and softball tournaments. But Cody rose to the challenge. He was assisted by a kid named Schultz, who was a sergeant. With the TV series *HOGAN'S HEROES* in its prime, Sergeant Schultz was often teased for "knowing nothing."

The studies, sports, military drills, parades, and other extracurricular activities kept Sterling Cody busy, and there was little time to dream of adventures to come. Somewhere, however, deep within his gray matter, he felt the urge to fly. He always knew that someday he would fly like his father. He was as sure about it as he was about growing to be a man; it was in his DNA.

Sterling Cody graduated from VFMA in June of 1968 at the age of seventeen. His father, Buck Cody, was proud of his younger son and was thrilled that he had received a full football scholarship to West Chester State College in West Chester, Pennsylvania.

Buck Cody expected his son to play football for four years, attend law school, and then pursue a career in law. Sterling Cody, however, had a different vision for his future. Sterling couldn't envision himself in a pinstripe suit arguing cases in a courtroom; his future was in the clouds.

At the age of only seventeen, Sterling was too young to join the Army without parental consent, and he knew that his father would never sign away what he considered his son's promising future. So the Army and his dream of flying would have to wait, but not for long.

Sterling went to classes and played football, but he was marking time. On 11 October, his eighteenth birthday, Sterling Cody visited his Army recruiter. The recruiter was prepared to offer the perspective recruit some options, but Sterling was only interested in flying. The recruiter explained about the Army's Warrant Officer Candidate (WOC) program and offered him the chance to fly helicopters. Cody was hooked. It was decided that Sterling would take the required physicals and tests, and if everything went well, he'd join the Army after finishing his first semester at WCSU.

Over the next few weeks, Sterling took the flight physical, which was more demanding than the Army's standard physical. When the recruiter called with the results, he congratulated the young man on passing and arranged for Cody to take a psychological exam. Unknown to Cody at the time, the exam was designed to weed out the timid; the Army needed helicopter pilots for the war in Vietnam. They needed risk takers.

The psychological test consisted of 565 written questions followed by an interview with a psychologist.

Sterling Cody, the boy who had once strapped homemade wings to his arms and twice attempted to fly from the roof of a chicken coop, was interviewed to see if he was a risk taker. Sterling Cody, the boy who had broken into a tomb and rummaged through an old coffin, brushing bony feet aside in a search for treasure, needed to pass some stupid psychological test to see if he was a risk taker.

The Army had just tested and interviewed the quintessential type-A risk taker.

Sterling Cody's Army recruiter informed him that he had passed the psychological test. The recruiter said that the WOC program called for him to go to boot camp at Fort Polk, Louisiana. He would go through boot camp as a private (E-1), after which he would be sent to rotary wing (helicopter) flight school at Fort Wolters in Texas. At Fort Wolters, Cody would become a WOC with E-5 (sergeant) pay, and he would be taught how to be an officer and a gentleman.

No shit, Sherlock? crossed Sterling's mind, but he offered a more respectful "Really?" to the recruiter.

Then, if he were successful to that point, WOC Sterling Cody would begin learning how to fly helicopters.

On 31 January 1969, Sterling Cody—barely eighteen years old at the time—raised his right hand and swore "to support and defend the Constitution of the United States against all enemies, foreign and domestic..."

On 2 February, Private Sterling Cody left for Fort Polk, Louisiana. The adventure had just begun.

***

Omaha, Nebraska
1969

Ozzie Daniels*, just two days past his twentieth birthday, and his nineteen-year-old buddy Phil Seefeld sat at the departure gate at Omaha's Eppley Airfield (OMA)[3] waiting for their flight to be called. It was the second day of February 1969. It was also the beginning of a new and life-altering adventure for the two Army recruits.

Ozzie Daniels was a farm boy from a few miles outside of a tiny farming community called Polk, which was twelve miles from Central City, the nearest decent-sized town in Central Nebraska. Ozzie, the first son of Wayne* and Mary* Daniels, made his grand entrance into the world on 31 January 1949.

Wayne Daniels had flown B-24s in the Pacific during WW-II. After the war, he had given up flying and settled into family life and farming. He grew corn and raised hogs. Wayne and Mary were blessed with two sons and a daughter.

By age twelve or so, young Ozzie had set his sights on becoming a cadet at the Air Force Academy. The allure of a military career appealed to Ozzie, but he didn't begin thinking of becoming a pilot until one fateful day when he was sixteen. That day would change his life forever.

It was a Sunday afternoon, and the Daniels' took

---

[3] Unique three-letter codes are used by The International Air Transport Association's (IATA) to identify airports throughout the world. OMA is the identifying code for Eppley Airfield.

Ozzie to Central City Airport, a couple miles west of the city. Wayne had accepted an offer that the U.S. Government's Soil Conservation Service (SCS) had made to local farmers to view their farms by air. The SCS plan was to let farmers see their farms from the air so that they could more easily see the effects of soil erosion. Mr. Daniels had been scheduled to view his farm in a Cessna 172, a small, four-seat, single-engine plane.

After arriving at the airport, Wayne Daniels helped his wife and sixteen-year-old son into the back of the 172. The pilot took his seat on the left, and Mr. Daniels took the co-pilot's seat.

It was Ozzie's first flight and the highest he'd been off terra firma since his last two-point jump shot at his high school gymnasium. The Daniels' were thrilled to see the countryside, particularly the family farm, from the air.

After assessing their farm for soil erosion, the pilot banked the small plane and headed back toward Central City. Wayne mentioned to the pilot that he had been a WW-II bomber pilot, and the pilot immediately offered to let Wayne take the controls. As Wayne placed his hands on the controls and began banking the plane this way and that, his passion for flying was ignited again. Unknown to him at the time, his sixteen-year-old son also felt the heat of this passion for the first time, and it would not be extinguished anytime soon.

As they approached the airport, Wayne asked the pilot if he could land the Cessna. The pilot—a licensed flight instructor—was clearly impressed with the old bomber pilot's skills, so he gave his consent. He filled

Wayne in on the Cessna's proper approach speed for landing and then watched with amazement as the WW-II bomber pilot greased his first landing in eighteen years.

Later that same Sunday, Wayne dug through his war memorabilia and found his old Civil Aeronautics Board [4] pilot's license. Looking closely, he saw that there was no expiration date. This meant that after passing a Federal Aviation Administration medical, he was good to go. And go he did—to the airport, as often as he could.

On his first flight as pilot-in-command since WW-II, Wayne brought along his son Ozzie. Wayne even allowed Ozzie to take over the controls for a while, and when he did, father and son connected as never before. It was a moment that defined the boy's destiny. Flying was in the father's blood and the son's DNA.

Ozzie began flying lessons soon afterward, and he made his first solo flight just before starting his senior year of high school. By then, he had mentally mapped his career path in aviation: he would attend the U.S. Air Force Academy and make a career as a pilot in the Air Force.

With just twenty hours of total flight time in his logbook, Ozzie scheduled his first solo cross-country flight as a student pilot. He would fly solo to Colorado Springs, where he had an appointment to visit the Air Force Academy.

A student-pilot's first solo cross-country flight is a big deal and a test of sorts. The aircraft has to be thoroughly checked, fuel consumption calculated, weights and

---

[4] The Civil Aeronautics Board was renamed Federal Aviation Agency in 1958 and Federal Aviation Administration in 1967.

balances checked, weather checked and re-checked, waypoints plotted; headings calculated and adjusted for wind direction, and routing plotted on an aviation map.

Under normal circumstances, what the student did when he reached this destination would be anti-climactic, but Ozzie's flight would end with a visit to the Air Force Academy. It would be the biggest day in the young boy's life.

Ozzie Daniels skipped school on Friday, 28 October 1966, but not for fun and games; a cross-country flight and a visit to the Air Force Academy was serious business.

Wayne Daniels let his son do all the flight planning, but he checked every aspect of the young aviator's plans and calculations. Wayne Daniels ensured that his son's flight was planned as meticulously as he had planned B-24 bombing missions. Ozzie would begin his flight from the Grand Island Airport (GRI)[5]. Grand Island, Nebraska's third largest city, was about thirty-five miles from the Daniels Farm. Wayne had arranged to rent a Piper Cherokee-180 at GRI, which he figured would be better for his son's cross-country flight since it was larger and faster than the Cherokee-140 trainer that Ozzie had been flying out of Central City.

The thirty-minute car ride to the airport gave Mr. Daniels time to review Ozzie's flight plans for the umpteenth time. Finally, after his preflight inspection of his aircraft, it was time to leave. Wayne Daniels watched

---

[5] Unique three-letter codes are used by The International Air Transport Association's (IATA) to identify airports throughout the world. GRI is the identifying code for Grand Island Airport.

as his son yelled "Clear!" and started the Cherokee's 180-horsepower Lycoming engine.

Wayne Daniels was proud and a little apprehensive. He waved as his son began to taxi to the runway. Ozzie looked back and caught a glint of moisture in his dad's eyes.

Ozzie's 360-mile flight to Colorado Springs was uneventful but nevertheless a thrill for the novice aviator.

After landing at Peterson Field, he was met by a U.S. Air Force Major. The major—on the cadre of the Academy—shepherded his young charge off on a whirlwind tour of the Air Force Academy. Ozzie was impressed with The Academy, the people he met, and his VIP treatment; he was now more determined than ever to become a cadet after graduating high school.

Ozzie Daniels' senior year in high school seemed to be a thrill a minute. U.S. Senator Carl Curtis nominated him to the Air Force Academy. His career was on track.

Offutt Air Force Base in Omaha was Ozzie Daniels' next stop en route to becoming an Air Force Cadet. In perfect physical health, Daniels was optimistic—perhaps overly so—when he arrived at the base hospital to take the Class 1 medical. The Class 1 was a requirement for all pilots and, of course, a requirement for entrance into the academy.

Everything went well until a dentist began poking around in Daniels' mouth.

"Oh, my!" was the last thing he expected or wanted to hear from a doctor.

As the dentist continued to probe with his fingers

and instruments in the boy's mouth, Daniels' heart sank.

What is it? What's wrong? A thousand thoughts ran through Daniels' mind in the ten seconds or so that it took the doctor to extract himself from Ozzie's mouth.

As soon as he could, Ozzie spat out, "What is it?"

"Son, I count twenty-two teeth; standard issue is thirty-two."

The doctor went on to explain that it was a rare congenital condition in which fewer than the normal thirty-two teeth develop. He said, too, that some of the uppers were not perfectly aligned with the lowers.

Ozzie knew that he had fewer than the usual number of teeth, but it had never been a problem for him. He asked the dentist if his condition would disqualify him from entrance into the academy. The doctor was non-committal.

I hate wishy-washy; just say it, Ozzie thought, but he was respectful, and thanked the doctor.

It didn't look good.

Two weeks later, the Air Force gave Ozzie the bad news: He had failed the Class 1 Physical and his nomination to the Academy had been rejected.

Ozzie Daniels was devastated. He would not attend the Air Force Academy, would not become an Air Force officer, and would not become an Air Force pilot. He was crushed.

Later in his senior year, Ozzie received a Regent's Scholarship to the University of Nebraska. To Ozzie, it was like a consolation prize.

Knowing that their son was still hurting from the Academy's rejection, his parents tried to emphasize the value of a good education. Ozzie was not pacified. He wanted to fly, and he wanted to be a military pilot.

Being rejected by the Air Force only strengthened Ozzie's determination to get his pilot's license. He continued his lessons and got his pilot's license in March before graduating high school in June of 1967.

During the summer of '67, Ozzie was making plans to attend the University of Nebraska in Lincoln and building flight hours toward his commercial pilot's license. The university was about ninety miles from his home, so he would be living at a dorm on campus. He was pleased to learn that the University of Nebraska had a flight club, which would make it convenient for him to continue to build hours.

Then, a ray of hope appeared when Ozzie overhead a couple of his friends talking about joining the Army on a Warrant Officer Flight Training Program. They said that they would be flying helicopters.

Helicopters aren't jets, Ozzie rationalized to himself. *The medical for helicopters can't be as demanding as that for jets...Can it?*

Ozzie decided that he'd go for it. When he told his parents of his plans, they threw a fit. They tried all kinds of logic to convince their son to go to college instead. They even brought up the escalating war in Vietnam, not knowing that it was part of the allure for their son. But logic seldom works on eighteen-year-old boys, and Ozzie's innate desire for adventure trumped all logic.

At the Army recruiting office, Ozzie began filling out the paperwork to become an Army WOC. The questions were routine and mundane; Ozzie filled in the blanks with little thought. Then a question stood out as if in bold print:

Have you ever been rejected for military service?

Wow, does my nomination to the Air Force Academy count?

Ozzie hesitated.

Better ask the recruiter.

Ozzie caught the recruiter's attention and explained the situation.

"Well, if you failed the Academy's medical, then you'll fail the Army's flight medical too," the recruiter explained. "They all use the same medical standards for pilot training."

Ozzie Daniels was crestfallen, but then the recruiter offered a ray of hope. He said that with the Vietnam War escalating, the Army was having trouble recruiting enough suitable candidates to fly helicopters and that some of the medical standards might be relaxed soon. The recruiter said that he'd keep Ozzie's file handy, and if the rules changed, he'd get in touch.

So for now, it was back to Plan B, which was his Regent's Scholarship to the University of Nebraska.

Ozzie Daniels entered the University of Nebraska. He would major in civil engineering and sign up for Army ROTC. He found ROTC much more interesting than his regular classes and soon signed up for the precision drill team.

The precision drill team, he learned, was part of an extracurricular military fraternity known as the National

Society of Pershing Rifles. It was organized when then Lieutenant John J. Pershing (1860–1948) was a Professor of Military Science and Tactics at the University back in the early 1890s. Pershing organized the special drill team and named it the Varsity Rifles. In 1895, however, the group renamed itself the Pershing Rifles after its mentor and patron John "Black Jack" Pershing. Pershing later became General of the Armies and commanded the Allied Expeditionary Forces during World War I.

Ozzie joined the Pershing Rifles' military police squad and participated in ceremonies and in the color guard at home football games.

Ozzie kept his grades up, but his heart was more into the military aspect of his life on campus. In his spare time, he continued with his flying lessons. He was a very busy freshman indeed.

Ozzie lived on campus in a two-man dorm room. When he first met Phil Seefeld, his new roommate, the two boys made an immediate connection. They were both Nebraska farm boys. Phil wasn't in ROTC, but he always showed an interest in Ozzie's military activities. They both loved the outdoors, and as their friendship grew, their interests merged.

One day soon after they met, Ozzie took Phil for a ride in a University of Nebraska Flying Club plane. Ozzie showed Phil the campus and the city of Lincoln in a Cherokee-140 (PA-28-140).

Riding in a small plane for the first time evokes different emotions in different people. For some, it is a frightening, white-knuckled nightmare. In people like Ozzie, the thrill is beyond exhilarating. The feeling of floating among the clouds and looking down on the world below is life-altering. Just as it was with Ozzie a year earlier, so too it was with Phil, and he too began taking flying lessons. Both boys, it seems, were adventuresome. Had the term been coined back in the 1960s, they might have been called *adrenaline junkies*.

ROTC, Pershing Rifles, the precision drill team, and MP Squad weren't enough for Ozzie; he soon joined the Lincoln Sport Parachute Club. Phil joined too, and the two friends made several parachute jumps.

By the end of his first semester of college, Ozzie was promoted to Pershing Rifles Cadet Sergeant, was the squad leader of the MP squad, and a squad leader of the regulation drill squad. He had adapted well to, and was enjoying everything military, but not so his studies, although his grades were acceptable.

After a summer of working on the family farm, Ozzie returned to school, but again, his heart was not in the books. His studies bored him; Pershing Rifles, ROTC, flying and jumping out of perfectly good airplanes were the only things that gave him any satisfaction.

After just a few weeks into his sophomore year, a call from the blue reinvigorated his zest for life. It was his Army recruiter on the line. The Army was unable to fulfill their quota for Warrant Officer Flight Training candidates, so they had issued a new class of Flight Medical. The new Class 1A Medical was more relaxed with regard to some of the less critical requirements, and the recruiter had remembered Ozzie...and his teeth.

"No guarantees son, but if you're still interested, we can arrange for you to take the medical." The recruiter continued, "We can send you to Omaha to take the medical and the Flight Aptitude Selection Test."

The recruiter had trouble talking over Ozzie, who was saying, "Okay...Yes...I'm still interested...When do I leave?"

The recruiter told Ozzie to come in to sign some papers, and that he could go to Omaha on 13 November 1968 to take the test.

Phil Seefeld had heard one side of his roommate's phone conversation. When Ozzie filled him in on the news, Phil said, "Gimme that phone...What's that recruiter's number?"

In Omaha, Ozzie passed the Class 1A medical and was sent down the hall to take the Flight Aptitude Selection Test (F.A.S.T.). He was confident when he sat down to take the F.A.S.T. He had logged over one hundred hours as a private pilot and had done well on the written test for his private pilot's license.

After the allotted time, the Army sergeant who administered the F.A.S.T. came back into the room and collected Ozzie's test. He said that he'd return in a few minutes with the results. Ozzie was confident; he knew that he'd done well on the test.

The sergeant returned and surprised Ozzie with the results.

"Ozzie, I've been administering this test for two years," the sergeant said, "and you've just chalked up the highest score I've ever seen."

With a "well done" and light pat on the back, the sergeant said, "You'll make a fine pilot."

Phil Seefeld passed his physical and F.A.S.T., too, and

the two friends were accepted for Warrant Officer Flight Training. A date was set for them to return to Omaha for their induction into the Army as Privates (E-1); they'd have to earn the rank of Warrant Officer.

Privates Ozzie Daniels and Phil Seefeld joined other recruits on 2 February 1969 in Omaha, where they boarded a jet for the first leg of their trip to Fort Polk, Louisiana. They would fly to Dallas Love Field and then transfer to a turboprop for a shorter flight to Louisiana.

Eleven hundred miles to the east, in Philadelphia, Army Private Sterling Cody waited curbside at the Army's processing center for a ride to the Philadelphia National Airport.

Buck Cody, the Army P-26 Peashooter pilot who went on to become a test pilot with the Curtiss-Wright Corporation, had since retired, and had taken a job at the Philly airport working for Boeing Vertol, in charge of the instrument lab at the test flight facility. Buck and his crew were working on improved instrumentation for the CH-46 Sea Knight and CH-47 Chinook helicopters. Little did he know that in just five months, a Sea Knight would evacuate his first-born son—Navy HM-2 Jack Cody— from a battlefield in Vietnam.

Buck broke away from his work to pick up his second son at the Army's processing center. Together, father and son drove back to Philadelphia National, this time to the passenger terminals on the opposite side of the runways from Boeing Vertol's hangars.

Private Cody, a Soldier for less than twenty-four hours and in civilian clothes, boarded a jet bound for Houston. There, he'd connect with a Trans-Texas

Airways (TTA) turboprop—colloquially known as "Tree Top Airways"—for a short flight to Fort Polk, Louisiana.

Sterling Cody, Ozzie Daniels, and Phil Seefeld's destinies were set to merge among the pine trees of Fort Polk and extend to the rice paddies and jungles of Southeast Asia.

8

All You Can Be

Fort Polk, Louisiana
February 1969

Camp Polk was created in 1941 in Central Louisiana as the United States began preparing for entry into the world war that was raging in Europe. In deference to their Southern host, the Army named their new base after Leonidas Polk, a Confederate General of the American Civil War.

The Army's new camp was huge, occupying over 309 square miles (801 square kilometers) of Louisiana Piney Woods. The Army quickly built thousands of wooden barracks to house Soldiers training for the possibility of entering the European war. Soon afterward, Camp Polk became the center of a statewide exercise that became known as the "Louisiana Maneuvers," in which over half a million Soldiers from nineteen army divisions took part. The Louisiana Maneuvers were conducted over an area spanning 3,400 square miles (8,800 square kilometers) during August and September of 1941.

During WW-II, Camp Polk served as a training facility, as well as a military prison. The first German prisoners of war began arriving in Louisiana in July 1943. Most were from Field Marshal Erwin Rommel's Afrika Korps. The Germans were housed in a large fenced-in compound in the area now encompassing Honor Field, Fort Polk's parade ground.

From the end of WW-II until the early 1960s, the post was closed and reopened numerous times. During much of this period, it was open only during the summers to support reserve component training. However, Soldiers were stationed there for the duration of the Korean War.

In 1955, Camp Polk was renamed Fort Polk and became the center of another large-scale military training exercise—Operation Sagebrush. This operation lasted for fifteen days and was undertaken to evaluate the Army's effectiveness in the nuclear age. During Sagebrush, over 85,000 Soldiers operated over much of Louisiana.

In 1962, Fort Polk was converted into a center for Advanced Individual Training (AIT) and Basic Combat Training (BCT). BCT was colloquially known as boot camp.

In early February of 1969, young men from around the U.S. began arriving at Fort Polk's reception center, anxious to begin their basic training. Many of the arrivals looked around and felt that they were caught in a time warp. The landscape reminded them of scenes from Hollywood's WW-II movies, with wooden barracks of that era dotting the landscape. They were soon brought back to reality, however, as they began days of processing into the modern Army.

Sergeants directed the new privates through the course of filling out countless forms. They were marched to medical facilities where they underwent examinations. Dentists probed their mouths, medics with jet injector guns vaccinated trainees mass-production style, and barbers sheared them like sheep.

Sterling Cody and most of the new privates were alone and friendless for the first time in their memory. Ozzie Daniels and Phil Seefeld, however, had joined the Army together, and they were determined to stick together.

After ten days of processing, over a thousand trainees were herded into a semblance of a formation by a dozen sergeants. When ordered to attention, the trainees snapped to what they envisioned the Army's position of attention to be. Some stood overly rigid; some with their chest extended grotesquely and their chin angled up at forty-five degrees. When the sergeants were satisfied that they had their charges in some semblance of a military formation and at attention, they stood back and observed their creation. Over a thousand trainees stood before them, sixty-four across and sixteen deep. At the back of the formation stood Privates Ozzie Daniels and Phil Seefeld, confident that they would train together during boot camp.

One of the sergeants addressed the group and told them that they would be split into four training companies. The other sergeants then began walking down the line, counting trainees. When they reached sixteen across and sixteen deep, a sergeant commanded that group, "Forward...march!" One company down, three to go. From the back of the formation, Daniels and Seefeld watched as a sergeant began counting the next sixteen. The count got closer to Daniels. "Fourteen...Fifteen..."

Oh, Shit! Daniels realized that he would be number sixteen and that his friend would be number seventeen.

Damn, we'll be split into different companies.

There was nothing Daniels could do except maintain his military composure—eyes straight ahead.

Phil Seefeld also saw what was happening, but he wasn't about to keep any sort of military composure. He watched the sergeants carefully, and when the moment was right, he stepped back, went around Daniels' back and grabbed trainee number fifteen—the trainee to Daniels' right—by his collar and yanked him back out of formation. Number fifteen fell head over heels and landed in the dirt behind the formation. When the commotion caught the sergeants' attention, all they saw was a trainee flat on his ass with a dazed look on his face, and an empty slot where Seefeld had been.

What the hell? Daniels was in the last row and could not see the commotion that had happened behind him.

Half a dozen sergeants converged on trainee number fifteen with a cacophony of commands: "Get off your ass! Get back in formation! You got two left feet boy? This ain't no summer camp!"

Fifteen was in a daze and clearly intimidated. Afraid to speak, he jumped to his feet and entered the formation at the only open slot. Private Fifteen was now Private Seventeen.

Ozzie Daniels was confused at first, but with the sergeants' attention planted firmly on Private Fifteen, he glanced to his right and saw Phil—a shit-eating grin on his face—standing proudly in Fifteen's stead. Phil and Ozzie would not be separated that easily.

The newly formed company—Alpha Company, 5th Battalion, 2nd Training Brigade—was marched off to buses. With the processing completed, their training began when drill sergeants commanded the new trainees off the buses and ordered them into formation. Then—without first instructing the trainees on how to comply—the Drill Sergeant began barking commands, "Right Face...Left Face...About Face!"

Chaos ensued. Some of the trainees apparently didn't know left from right. The command "About Face" resulted in confused stares from several bewildered men. Amidst the turmoil, several trainees executed the commands with military precision. The Drill Sergeants' experienced eye picked out several trainees from the confusion and pulled them from the herd. The method to the madness was to identify trainees who had some sort of military background or training.

One of the trainees had particularly impressed the Drill Sergeant with his military bearing. Private Sterling Cody, who rose to the rank of second lieutenant during his four years at VFMA, had performed every command precisely. His poise seemed to command respect. His newly issued uniform, unlike the trainees in the rest of the herd, was impeccable on his 5-foot 10-inch muscular frame.

Sterling Cody was given a black brassard with

Sergeant First Class (E-7) Chevrons to wear on his left sleeve. The three stripes with two rockers designated Cody as the company "Field First." Ozzie Daniels and the other trainees who had demonstrated military bearing and knowledge of the commands were given brassards with corporal chevrons and were appointed squad leaders.

The trainees were told that they were now in Alpha Company, 5th Battalion, 2nd Basic Combat Training Brigade, and that their basic training would last for eight weeks, beginning "NOW!"

Alpha Company was composed of four platoons, two of which contained mostly draftees and enlistees. After BCT, many of them would remain at Fort Polk for an additional twelve weeks of infantry training at AIT, while the others would move on to technical training at other locations. The other two platoons of Alpha Company consisted entirely of Soldiers enlisted under the Warrant Officer Flight Training Program. If they completed BCT successfully, they would be shipped directly to Fort Wolters in Texas to begin their training as Warrant Officers and helicopter pilots.

Basic training went well for Ozzie Daniels and Phil Seefeld. They were in good physical shape and took their Drill Sergeant's mental games in their stride.

Ozzie and Phil, as with all trainees of Alpha Company became familiar with Alpha Company's Field First, but they had not yet met the man, Sterling Cody, with whom they would share their Vietnam War experiences.

In the third week, Alpha Company headed for the shooting range. They had learned the Manual of Arms with their M14 rifles and would now fire them on the range.

The trainees knew all about their M14s by now, and they could recite the specifications by heart: "The M14 is a 7.62mm, magazine-fed, gas-operated, air-cooled, semi-automatic shoulder weapon." It was now time to test their knowledge of their M14 rifles on the range.

Sterling Cody, Ozzie Daniels, and a few other trainees knew that the Army was replacing the M14 with the more modern, lighter M16, which was already in use in Vietnam. Cody, being the Field First, was first to get the word that they would be the last training company to fire the M14. He passed the word to the rest of the company. To Cody, it seemed a little silly to be training with an obsolete weapon.

On the range, the trainees learned that the M14 had a hell of a kick. Most trainees did well on the range; Ozzie Daniels shot high score and received a trophy for his effort.

After eight weeks of boot camp, the trainees on the WOC Program could say goodbye to Fort Polk. Unknown to them, a few would wash out at Wolters and be back within weeks to continue their infantry training.

After a graduation ceremony, Privates Sterling Cody, Ozzie Daniels, and Phil Seefeld and the other aspiring aviators received their orders to report to Fort Wolters near Mineral Wells, Texas.

9

Officer Material

Fort Wolters, Texas
April 1969

The signs on the front of the commercial buses read, "Charter–Fort Wolters, Tex." With their duffel bags stowed in the cargo bay, excited Soldiers filed onto the buses and took a seat for the seven-hour ride from the piney woods of Louisiana to the ranch lands of North Texas. Excited to be free of drill sergeants and boot camp and filled with anticipation, the Soldiers were in a jovial mood. Some were reminded of recent high-school class trips.

"You think all the Drill Sergeant Mickey Mouse bullshit's behind us now?" Phil Seefeld asked his buddy.

"Sure," observed Ozzie Daniels, "we'll be Warrant Officer Candidates. They'll teach us to be officers and gentlemen. I'm sure they'll treat us like gentlemen." More than a few jokes were exchanged on that ride, with the Soldiers addressing each other whimsically as "Sir."

After a rest stop for lunch along the way, the buses arrived at the entrance to Fort Wolters in the late afternoon. Above the entrance, an arched sign announced:

U S ARMY
PRIMARY HELICOPTER CENTER
FORT WOLTERS TEXAS

On each side of the sign, sitting on pedestals, were two small helicopters. Soldiers leaned left and right to get a better glimpse of the helicopters. Few could identify the make and model; they were as foreign to most of the Soldiers as the Apollo Lunar Excursion Module that would put Americans on the moon later that year.

A few minutes later, the buses pulled into the parking lot. As soon as the driver opened the door, an Army warrant officer entered the bus and began screaming instructions at the new arrivals.

Oh shit, so much for being treated like gentlemen. Ozzie was taken aback.

"I thought you said..." Phil didn't finish his sentence before Ozzie's "Shhhh!" made it clear that the situation needed to be taken seriously.

With the Soldiers in formation, the warrant officer, who identified himself as a Tactical Officer (Tac Officer), emphasized that they were not warrant officers; they were warrant officer *candidates*! They could be dropped from the program at any time for any number of reasons—academic or disciplinary.

"Future officers and gentlemen don't cuss. Future officers and gentlemen don't get into trouble with the local civil authorities," the Tac Officer admonished, "and if they do get into trouble, even so much as a traffic ticket, then they aren't considered to be officer material."

"And if you make it through the four weeks of preflight," the Tac Officer continued, "any of you uncoordinated dipshits that can't master the skills required to fly our helicopters will be dropped and reassigned by the Army to finish your enlistment."

Most of the WOCs took the Tac Officer's last threat to mean that they would be shipped back to Polk for infantry training and Vietnam. Meanwhile, Sterling Cody, the former VFMA lieutenant and boot camp Field First, took it all in his stride.

The new WOCs settled into their quarters and prepared for their first four weeks of preflight training. The insignia of their new rank—the letters "WOC"—was issued to be worn on their collars.

Tac Officers conducted close-order drills, harassed the WOCs, held inspections, harassed the WOCs, and when they were bored, harassed the WOCs.

Preflight was like a mini Officer's Candidate Course combined with aviation ground school. They studied leadership and were assigned and evaluated on leadership positions within their platoon. Aviation subjects were taught by warrant officers, commissioned officers, and civilian instructor pilots. The WOCs spent a lot of time learning about and mastering the E6B flight computer, which was a circular type slide rule that was used in flight planning. Their instructors gave the WOCs endless sample problems to solve using the E6B, such as calculating fuel burn, wind correction, time en route, ground speed, and estimated time of arrival. Courses were taught in navigation, meteorology and the unique flight characteristics of rotary-wing aerodynamics. They learned about the components of the helicopter and about the pilot's instruments and controls. During preflight, it was sometimes hard for the WOCs to not drift their attention off their instructors and Tac Officers, and upward to the many helicopters being flown by WOCs already in flight training.

Finally, after four weeks, they began to fly, but classroom instructions remained an important part of each day.

The WOCs had become aware that commissioned officers were at Wolters training in separate classes. It was evident to the WOCs that the Commissioned Officers were treated as officers and gentlemen. The Officers had more freedom than the WOCs; the WOCs were marched to classrooms and bussed to the flight line while Officers drove their personal cars. One car—a brand new 1969 red Cadillac convertible—stood out. It stood out not only because it was out of the price range of the average lieutenant or captain in the Officers' classes, but also because of the colonel's insignia—a silver eagle—attached to the front bumper. A full-bird colonel training to be a helicopter pilot was a bit unusual.

In his first week after preflight, Ozzie Daniels' parents and younger brother came to Fort Wolters for a visit. They drove down from Nebraska in two cars, the family car and Ozzie's 1966 Plymouth Satellite. The

Plymouth stayed when Ozzie's family drove back to Nebraska. Ozzie was proud of his candy apple red Plymouth, but it dimmed in comparison to the red Caddy convertible seen around the base. Ozzie's Plymouth stayed parked most of the week, to be used on the occasional weekend pass.

The WOCs had been given a stern warning: "You can be dropped from the program, and if you wash out, you will serve the remainder of your enlistment at the Army's discretion." With the war in Vietnam raging, the not-so-subtle reference to the Army's "discretion" was not lost on the WOCs. The Army needed all the infantrymen it could get—the sooner, the better. To be dropped from flight training almost guaranteed a quick trip back to Polk for Infantry Training and a quicker trip to Vietnam to join the grunts. The seriousness of their situation became apparent when—at an alarming regularity—men were dropped and shipped out. Men who were having trouble with the academics were suddenly gone. Others were dropped because they couldn't master flight training. Rumor had it that one man was dropped for having lied on his application; he hadn't disclosed a problem with civilian authorities. It became apparent to the WOCs that getting into trouble with the law could be the end of their aviation career and the beginning of their career as an Army grunt.

One part of flight training that could result in a WOC being dropped was the requirement to solo by the end of twenty hours of flight with an instructor pilot. Most WOCs celebrated their first solo between the minimum ten hours and fifteen hours. A few pushed the twenty-hour cutoff. Sterling Cody was first in the class to solo. From day one, the helicopter had felt like an extension of his body, and he soloed at ten hours. He was ready earlier, but rules are rules, and he wasn't allowed to solo until he had completed the required ten hours.

By mid-July of 1969, things had settled into a routine. On some days, the WOCs flew in the mornings with classroom instruction in the afternoons, and on other days, the order was reversed. The Tac Officers still harassed the troops, but most WOCs now took it in their stride and wrote it off as just more silly games.

The WOCs were now getting weekend passes. Time away from the base was welcomed, even if it was just for a few hours in Mineral Wells on Friday or Saturday night. WOCs with cars, however, could explore Texas beyond Mineral Wells.

Ozzie Daniels and Phil Seefeld, with Ozzie's candy apple red Plymouth, didn't limit themselves to Mineral Wells. On weekend passes, they traveled south to Galveston Island and east to Dallas. In their travels around North Texas, they met a couple of girls from Texas Women's University in Denton. The girls invited Phil and Ozzie to a weekend gathering and barbecue at their family cabin on Lake Texoma. They would meet the girls at their home in Alvord on Friday at 6:30 p.m. before driving to Lake Texoma. It promised to be an exciting weekend for the boys.

After Friday afternoon's flights, Ozzie and Phil hit the barracks at about 5 p.m., anxious to change into their khaki uniforms and hit the road. Their Tac Officer, however, had other plans. He began a series of harassing maneuvers that continued to delay the expected weekend pass. The drive to Alvord would take about an hour, and the Tac Officer's little games were eating into their drive time by the minute. Finally, at 6 p.m., the Tac Officer handed out the coveted passes. The guys only had half an hour to make the hour's drive to Alvord.

Daniels and Seefeld hit the road, intending to make up as much as they could of the thirty minutes lost to the Tac Officer's silly games. Ozzie—usually very respectful of speed limits—pushed well past the 65 mile per hour speed limit on stretches of open road. After all, this wasn't a Sunday drive, and girls were at stake. Ozzie slowed down close to the speed limit as they passed through the town of Weatherford. The conflicting thoughts of the consequences of getting into trouble with civilian law and jeopardizing their rendezvous with the girls were ever present in his mind. A simple speeding ticket would be cause enough for termination from flight school, and that probably meant being shipped back to Polk for infantry training and a trip to Vietnam as a grunt. Girls today versus the rice fields of Vietnam tomorrow; it was a hard choice for a twenty year old.

In Weatherford, Ozzie turned north onto FM-51, a state farm-to-market road. He'd traveled that route before, and he knew that it was a straight shot to Springtown. The twenty-mile stretch cut straight through open ranch lands. There were no towns and virtually no traffic on the two-lane asphalt road, and the posted speed limit was sixty-five miles per hour all the way to Springtown. The road was exceptionally wide for a farm-to-market road, with wide shoulders on each side. Rolling hills would be an obstacle to passing slow-moving vehicles, but there was very little traffic to slow the red Plymouth.

Phil was impatient, "Come on Ozzie, if we're late, they may leave without us."

"I'll push it a little, but I sure can't afford a speeding ticket." Ozzie eased the Plymouth up to seventy-two miles per hour.

Damn, thought Ozzie, *This is risky!*

"Help me keep an eye out for cops."

Both boys watched for police cars hiding behind trees and billboards, but there were scant hiding places for lurking officers of the law. There were, however, those rolling hills. A couple of miles from Springtown, they topped another of the never-ending hills, and there, approaching from the north, was a black-and-white state trooper's car.

"Shit!" Both WOCs uttered the expletive simultaneously.

"I hope he's not trolling with radar." Ozzie's "hope" was more of a prayer.

Ozzie took his foot off the accelerator, knowing that if the cop had him on radar, that it would be too late. He looked down at his speedometer, which was coming off seventy-five miles per hour. By then, the black-and-white had passed the Plymouth. Ozzie looked in his rearview mirror, hoping against hope that he wouldn't see brake lights on the cruiser.

When he saw the brake lights light up, Ozzie made a

snap decision and floored it.

Phil's excited "Go! Go! Go!" heralded his approval of his friend's decision.

As the Plymouth picked up speed, Ozzie rationalized his decision to himself. There was a lot to lose by getting a speeding ticket, and running from the cops would result in the same trip to the rice paddies as a simple traffic ticket.

"Why not chance it?" Ozzie asked his friend.

Phil took it as a rhetorical question and responded with "Go...go...stomp it you dumb shit!"

Ozzie knew that his Plymouth wouldn't outrun the cruiser for long, but Springtown was about a mile ahead around a sweeping bend, and he knew that if he could get into town before the cop, he could take a turn on one of the several intersections and possibly shake the cop.

Phil looked back, reporting to Ozzie that the cop was pulling a "U" turn and that they were putting distance between themselves and the cruiser. As they approached Springtown, the Plymouth's speedometer needle was touching one hundred, and the cop was gaining on them—Fast!

Ozzie figured that his Plymouth was more maneuverable than the cruiser and knew the intersection where he wanted to turn in his attempt to shake the cop. He hit the brakes and made the turn.

"Oh, Shit! Wrong road!"

Ozzie had turned a city block too early and had entered a driveway into a farm implement dealership. The driveway—which was more like a road—wound around to the back of the dealership's main building into an empty parking lot. End of the road!

Without hesitating, Ozzie floored it again and barreled-ass off the parking lot and into a field of weeds taller than the hood of the Plymouth.

"Shit, I can't see a damn thing!" Ozzie was looking through the windshield at weeds slamming into the grill; waves of seed, leaves, and pollen were rolling up the hood to the windshield like waves breaking on a beach. They were flying blind and had no idea where they were or where they were headed.

Suddenly, a rusty old farm implement whizzed by about eight inches from Ozzie's side-view mirror.

"What the hell was that?"

"What was what?" Phil hadn't seen a thing. "Go! Go! Go!"

Suddenly, and with a thud, they were out of the field and onto an old gravel road. The Plymouth had obliterated an old fence of some sort, as it broke free of the field.

The only choice now was to wait patiently for the state trooper to catch up or to follow the gravel road to who knows where.

Phil's "Go! Go! Kick it in the ass" left little doubt about where he stood on that matter.

They followed the gravel road for several miles before they came to another farm-to-market road and could get their bearings.

Ozzie checked his rear-view mirror regularly, but the state trooper's image didn't reappear.

"I think we've lost him," Ozzie said.

"He must've chickened out when we went into the field," observed Phil.

"I don't blame him," said Ozzie, "we almost hit that old farm thing, whatever it was."

"What farm thing?" Phil hadn't seen a thing and didn't even remember Ozzie's panic from when the rusting hunk of metal had almost killed them both.

It was one hell of a day for the boys. Their overnight rendezvous with the beautiful girls paled in comparison to the high-speed car chase. It was a weekend the boys would relive throughout their long friendship.

Back at Fort Wolters, the training continued, and the WOCs could finally see the goal line. They felt like accomplished pilots, and the Tac Officers' games now seemed more comical than threatening.

WOC Sterling Cody finished the required cross-country flights and check rides well before he logged the course's required one hundred hours. To build his hours, the instructor pilots were assigning him extra flight hours ferrying ships from maintenance to the flight line. Then, with three hours short of the hundred required for graduation, Sterling was assigned an additional cross-country flight.

"You'll be flying with a senior officer," Cody was told, as he and the instructor pilot walked to the flight line. "He needs this required cross-country flight and you'll be his co-pilot."

"Go ahead and do the preflight, and he'll be along shortly."

A senior officer? Sterling wondered who the senior

officer could be. *The base commander? Oh well...no big deal.*

Flying with a senior officer might have rattled any of the other WOCs, but Sterling had dealt with senior officers in high school at VFMA, so this assignment didn't faze him. Finishing up with his preflight, Cody looked up to see a shiny red Cadillac convertible drive up to the flight line. The silver eagle on the black license plate attached to the front of the red Caddy caught Cody's eye.

So this is the high-ranking officer I'll be flying with.

WOC Sterling Cody greeted the colonel with a snappy salute and received a nonchalant salute in return as the colonel entered the cockpit. Cody noticed the nametag on the colonel's uniform: PATTON.

Rumor around base had it that this was the son of the legendary General George Patton of WW-II fame. Cody knew that Army scuttlebutt was wrong more often than not, and besides, he knew a Colonel Patton at VFMA who was not related to General Patton. This was probably just another coincidence.

In the cockpit, it was all business. Colonel Patton was pilot-in-command and WOC Cody was his co-pilot. Cody did the navigating, checking his map against predetermined landmarks. Cody stayed busy operating the radio; calculating ground speed against air speed, wind direction and speed; and suggesting heading adjustments to the Colonel. They passed over the northern tip of Possum Kingdom Lake as they headed northwest to Graham, Texas. From Graham, they changed direction and flew southwest over open countryside to Breckenridge. The last leg of their cross-country—Breckenridge back to Mineral Wells—was the longest. There was little time to enjoy the scenery—there wasn't much to see anyway—as Cody calculated heading adjustments, operated the radio and plotted their position against their intended course.

Cody, having finished his required cross-country flights days before, was comfortable with his position as the colonel's co-pilot. The hour-and-a-half flight presented no technical problems for Cody, and as they landed at Mineral Wells, he sensed that Colonel Patton was pleased with himself.

If the Colonel's happy, I'm happy.

When they landed at the Mineral Wells Heliport, Cody began the cool-down procedure.

"Well sir, why don't you go ahead and fill out the log book," Cody offered, "and I'll do the post-flight inspection."

The Colonel barely acknowledged his WOC co-pilot, but he did glance toward Cody as if to say, "Of course you will."

Cody was still doing his post-flight when Colonel Patton—without saying diddly-squat—walked away.

After securing his ship, Cody walked into the briefing room where he knew there'd be donuts and coffee and where he knew that he could unwind for a few minutes. The instructor pilot came up to Cody and asked how the flight went.

"No problem sir, by the way, was that Colonel Patton, General George Patton's son?"

"Sure was, that was Colonel George Smith

Patton IV."

Well, I'll be go-to-hell...I'm not impressed, Cody thought, but maintained his outer military bearing and respect for the rank.

George Smith Patton IV
Undated photo in Vietnam
Patton's father was George Smith Patton III.
George Patton IV later legally changed his name to George Smith Patton (dropping the "IV").

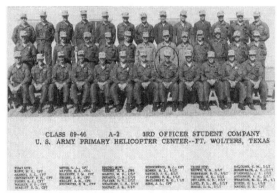

CLASS 69-46   A-2   3RD OFFICER STUDENT COMPANY
U. S. ARMY PRIMARY HELICOPTER CENTER--FT. WOLTERS, TEXAS

Patton was in Class 69-44 during most of his training but graduated Class 69-46.

In late August 1969, WOCs Sterling Cody, Ozzie Daniels, and Phil Seefeld graduated from the 7th

Warrant Officer Candidate Company (7th WOC Co.) and received their orders. Daniels and Seefeld were transferred to Fort Rucker, near Enterprise, Alabama, and Cody to Hunter Army Airbase, Savannah, Georgia.

Two days before the WOCs were relieved and free to make the trip to their new training base, Sterling Cody was called to the CO's office.

The CO—a major—returned Cody's salute and told him to sit down. The major then came straight to the point. "Mr. Cody, we've received a report that your brother has been reported as missing in Vietnam." The major went on to say that they didn't have any details.

Wow...How the hell can he just be missing? Sterling's thoughts ran a mile a minute. *Jack's a Corpsman for crying out loud, the Marines don't just misplace their corpsman!*

There was nothing Cody could do except wait for more news. He decided to report to Hunter Air Base; maybe there would be more news in a couple of days.

Ozzie Daniels and Phil Seefeld packed their duffel bags and a few personal items in the candy apple red Plymouth and drove out of Fort Wolters for the last time. As they drove past the two training helicopters mounted atop the pedestals on each side of the road, they both became a little nostalgic. They had set eyes on those strange machines twenty weeks before, and at that time, they had not known a thing about them. A lot had transpired since then. They could now name the component parts; they understood the aerodynamics; they had flown those machines; they'd soloed in those birds. And while Sterling Cody, Ozzie Daniels, and Phil Seefeld were learning to fly helicopters, Neil Armstrong had piloted the Apollo Lunar Excursion Module to a soft landing on the moon.

WOCs Daniels and Seefeld drove to their homes in Nebraska for a two-week leave before reporting to Fort Rucker. On the state highway, Phil said, "Okay Ozzie hit it...Go! Go! Go!"

The two friends looked at each other and laughed. Ozzie vowed to keep the Plymouth's speedometer needle below the speed limit until warrant officer bars were pinned to his collar.

10

Mother Rucker

Fort Rucker, Alabama
September 1969

WOC Sterling Cody drove directly from Fort Wolters to his new training post at Hunter Army Airfield, Savannah, Georgia, where he joined Warrant Officer Candidate Training Class 69-47.

For WOCs Ozzie Daniels and Phil Seefeld, their two-week leave with their families flew by quickly, and before they realized it, the two friends had to hit the road again for another long drive to their new training base at Fort Rucker, near Enterprise, Alabama.

The 63,100 acres that comprise Fort Rucker in southeastern Alabama has its roots in WW-II. After the Japanese had attacked Pearl Harbor, the War Department converted government land known as the Pea River Land Use Project, into a new Army training camp. The new camp was named Camp Rucker in honor of Confederate Colonel Edmund W. Rucker. The first trainees began arriving in May of 1942. In 1955, the Army Aviation Center was established at Rucker, and later that year, Camp Rucker became Fort Rucker.

The drive to Fort Rucker was exciting for the two Nebraska natives; they had never been to Alabama and didn't know quite what to expect. As they drove deeper into The Heart of Dixie, the combination of mid-August heat and Gulf Coast humidity became enervating.

As the Plymouth approached Enterprise, the two-lane U.S. Highway 84 widened into four and became North Main Street. At College Street, the boys caught a red light and came to a stop. There, in the middle of the intersection, the boys witnessed the strangest sight they had seen on their entire trip.

* * *

Enterprise was a small—some would say sleepy— Southern town with a population of about 15,000[6] people in the southeast corner of Alabama. The town was founded in the latter part of the 19th century, and by the early 20th century, Enterprise was a thriving town that was primarily supported by the cotton crops grown by farmers in Coffey and Dale Counties. Cotton was king, and the king flourished in ignorant bliss, unaware of the oncoming hordes of invaders from the South.

The boll weevil[7] is a quarter-inch-long insect that eats the buds and young bolls of cotton plants. It is sometimes known as a "snout beetle" because of its long beak or snout, which it uses for feeding. Native to Mexico and Central America, the boll weevil invaded

---

[6] The population of Enterprise, Alabama, was 15,591 in 1970.

[7] The scientific name of the boll weevil is *Anthonomus grandis*

Texas in 1892. Once inside the United States, the horde of beetles ate their way east at the rate of seventy to one hundred miles each year. When the ravenous insects reached Louisiana, cotton farmers in Mississippi and Alabama took solace in the common belief that the Mississippi River was a natural barrier that the boll weevil could not traverse. When the boll weevil reached the rich alluvial areas of the Mississippi Delta, however, it was as if they had reached the weevil promised land. In 1907, they crossed the Mighty Mississippi without skipping a meal.

When word spread that the boll weevil had crossed the river into Mississippi, farmers in Alabama became concerned but continued planting the only crop they knew—cotton.

In 1915, the boll weevil invasion reached Coffee County, devastating the area's only cash crop. Farmers who had borrowed money to plant their crops couldn't repay their loans. Merchants who had loaned money to farmers for food and supplies were not repaid. As the population of weevils increased, the money supply in the local economy dwindled.

Something had to be done about the havoc-wrecking pests, but what should be done was the question of the hour.

Enterprise businessman H.M. Sessions came to the rescue of the town. Sessions was a local banker and a cotton merchant. He realized that failing cotton crops and failing cotton farmers would result in his businesses failing in very short order. He therefore started a campaign based on the work of Dr. George Washington

Carver, who was the Director of the Agricultural Department at Tuskegee Normal and Industrial School in Tuskegee. Sessions first traveled to Virginia and North Carolina, where he purchased a load of seed peanuts that he shipped back to Enterprise. Back in Enterprise, he offered the seed peanuts—North Carolina Runners— to one of the many farmers who had a loan outstanding with his bank. Sessions proposed that the farmer plant his entire 125 acres with peanuts, and he guaranteed the farmer one dollar per bushel for the resulting crop. Free seed crop and a generous guarantee on the future crop was too good an offer for the failing cotton farmer to resist.

In the spring of 1916, Coffee County farmers—with one exception—planted cotton as they had done for generations. The boll weevils had a field day in the cotton fields but ignored the 125 acres of peanuts planted by the lone farmer. When the farmer harvested his bumper crop of peanuts, Sessions—as promised— bought the farmer's crop of eight thousand bushels at the price of $8,000[8]—an inordinate sum in 1916. The farmer was able to pay off his loan and bank a tidy profit.

Other farmers in the area took notice, and when Sessions announced that he had eight thousand bushels of seed peanuts for sale, the demand outstripped supply.

Within two years, King Cotton was dethroned, and residents were trumpeting the diversity of their new

---

[8] Adjusted for inflation, $8,000 in 1916 would be worth $176,910 in 2016.

peanut crops. Cotton oil mills were converted to produce peanut oil; farmers fed the peanut plant to livestock; and sharecroppers fed their families with the unsold crop. The demand for peanuts grew as Doctor Carver continued to find new uses for the humble legume. Within two years, Coffee County was the leading producer of peanuts in the United States.

The residents of Enterprise had survived an agricultural and economic disaster, and the economy was now more vibrant than it was before the arrival of the Mexican boll weevil. Enterprise residents now looked upon the boll weevil as a godsend.

An Enterprise merchant, Roscoe Owen "Bon" Fleming, began promoting the idea of erecting a monument in honor of the insect that had transformed the one-crop economy. Some thought of it as a crackpot idea, but Bon Fleming would not be deterred. On his own hook, in early 1919, Fleming placed an order in Italy for the construction of a statue that would be part of the monument.

The statue was that of a lady in a flowing white gown standing with her arms extended above her head and holding a vessel containing a fountain. The city built a solid protective abutment in the middle of the intersection of Main Street and College Street and placed the statue on a cast iron base inside the abutment. The basin created by the abutment was filled with water in which small fish were released. Enterprise's creation stood thirteen-and-a-half feet above street level.

At the base of the monument, a bronze plaque read:

In profound appreciation
Of the boll weevil
And what it has done
As the herald of prosperity
This monument was erected
By the citizens of
Enterprise, Coffee County, Alabama

The city planned a dedication ceremony to be held on 11 December 1919. Festive bunting was strung along the streets leading to the monument. A young lady was selected as Miss Peanut, and a young man as King Cotton. Dr. George Washington Carver was invited to make the dedicatory speech.

The townspeople became very concerned in the days leading up to the big day, as heavy rains threatened to dampen the festivities. However, on the morning of 11 December—as if on cue—the clouds parted, and the sun shone on the little monument. The assembled crowd was disappointed to learn that Doctor Carver was unable to make it to Enterprise because a bridge on the Atlantic Coast Line Railroad had been washed out due to the heavy rains.

After the speeches, the fountain at the apex of the monument was turned on to cheers from the crowd. When a gust of wind sprayed water on the crowd, adults cheered and children danced in the mist. The spray from the fountain, however, became an ongoing problem, and the fountain soon fell into disuse.

The Boll Weevil Monument in Enterprise, Alabama soon after its dedication in 1919
From the collection of the Alabama Department of Archives and History, Montgomery, Alabama

Twenty-nine years later, in 1948, a local artisan decided that a monument to a boll weevil should actually feature a boll weevil. Since the fountainhead at the top of the monument had been in disuse for years, he decided to cast a boll weevil and attach at the apex. His masterpiece was about the size of a man's fist and appeared quite small at the top of the monument. Although the artisan was quite talented, he wasn't much of an entomologist, and he fashioned the boll weevil with four legs instead of the proper six. The little boll weevil sat happily upon its perch atop the monument for five years. Then, one morning in the winter of 1953, someone noticed that the boll weevil was missing. The "bugnapping" was investigated, but there were no leads—only rumors. One such rumor had it that the

AWOL bug had been seen in the hands of a Soldier in Korea, who was using it as a paperweight.

Enterprise was quick to replace the little boll weevil, this time with one that was four times larger. The new, anatomically correct six-legged weevil was added to the monument in a ceremony on 1 May 1954, and to this day, Enterprise celebrates "Boll Weevil Day" on the first day of May.

* * *

It was this strange sight of the boll weevil monument that mesmerized Ozzie Daniels and Phil Seefeld as they sat at the corner of Main and College Streets, waiting for the traffic light to change. When the light turned green, Ozzie said, "We gotta take a look at that," and pulled the Plymouth into a nearby parking space.

They walked into the street to examine the strange monument. Both boys being farmers knew what a boll weevil was, but they had never actually seen one. Now, they stood—jaws slightly ajar—looking at a boll weevil perched upon the top of a monument. In this part of the South, they would not have been surprised to see a monument dedicated to Robert E. Lee or Stonewall Jackson, but a boll weevil?

After admiring the monument and exchanging a few jokes at the expense of the memorialized insect, the two WOCs drove into Fort Rucker and reported for duty to the CO of 3rd Warrant Officer Candidate Company (3rd WOC Co.).

Daniels and Seefeld settled into the training routine

and were pleased when it became evident that the Tac Officers weren't as hard-ass as they had been at Wolters. There were inspections, but they were less demanding. The Tac Officers didn't seem to notice as swearing slowly found its way back into the WOCs' vocabulary. There were no more threats of being dropped from the program for a simple traffic violation, not that Daniels intended to get a traffic ticket within the state of Alabama.

Even with their flying, classroom instruction, and field exercises, the WOCs had much more free time than before. During their free time, the Boll Weevil Monument in Enterprise was often a topic of conversation. One WOC told the story of how a WOC in 1959 had stolen the boll weevil from atop the monument. According to the story, the AWOL bug was later apprehended some two hours away in Panama City Beach, Florida. Then there were other tales of how the boll weevil had been taken from its perch. The stories inevitably began with "This ain't no shit," and they were usually told by someone who knew someone who knew the heroic perpetrator.

Daniels took the rumors with a grain of salt. They probably weren't true, and even if they were, they were probably just pranks, like high school kids putting laundry detergent in a fountain. When Daniels first learned about the history of the monument, he took offense; he thought that the memorial should have been of Doctor George Washington Carver. He vowed to himself that he would correct what he perceived to be an injustice and appropriate the bug and install it in the

3rd WOC Company area on post.

Daniels wasn't one to set off on a plan half-cocked. To kidnap Enterprise's famous weevil successfully would take careful thought and complex planning. The gears were now set in motion, and Daniels approached the project as one would a military operation.

Meanwhile, training for combat as a Huey pilot in Vietnam continued. They spent many weeks learning to fly solely based on their instruments. Flying into inclement weather in Vietnam was a given; instrument flying was a skill that could save their lives. The WOCs learned techniques for carrying heavy loads and low-level flying. They learned about formation flying and troop insertions and extractions. They honed their autorotation skills by practicing night and low-level power-off landings.

The WOCs were not only being trained as helicopter pilots, but also as officers, gentlemen, and most importantly, leaders of men. As pilots, they had to be prepared to lead their crew and passengers if they were forced down in enemy territory. Their training included escape, evasion, and survival tactics.

At Fort Polk, the Army made the infantry exercises as realistic as possible with the use of artillery simulator grenades. During exercises, the instructors would throw artillery simulators—sometimes called stun grenades, concussion grenades, or simply flash bangs—close to the trainees as live rounds were being fired above their heads. The trainees, their faces painted black, brown, and green with camouflage grease paint, crawling through dirt and mud, live fire above their heads and flash bangs on all sides, got the feel of the real thing.

During the course of his training, the boll weevil mission was not far from Ozzie Daniels' mind. He had begun some very serious planning for "appropriating" the boll weevil from its perch atop the monument. He thought of the flash bangs back at Fort Polk and how they could be used in his plan.

Daniels knew—as they say in crime novels—that he had to "case the joint." He and Phil would make a point of driving down Main Street each weekend while on their weekend pass. They'd cruise the main drag three or four times each day checking and rechecking each detail.

How was the boll weevil attached? It looked like there was a long bolt extending from the weevil and through the mount, which was held in place with a nut. Daniels couldn't tell what size the bolt was, but he figured that an adjustable wrench[9] would do the trick.

Would he need a ladder? It did not seem so, as Daniels saw that he could easily jump the fence, climb up the monument, and stand on the light fixture to have easy access to the bolt.

Enterprise was the quintessential little Southern town, to which the phrase "roll up the sidewalks at nine o'clock" could easily apply. Daniels figured that the heist would have to be a night operation. It was not that darkness would offer concealment—the entire intersection and monument were well lit—but rather, it

---

[9] The adjustable wrench is known by various names around the world. In the U.S., it is known as a crescent wrench, but in other countries, as a spanner wrench, English key, Swedish key, or French key.

was to minimize the possibility that a local yokel would spot him and raise the alarm.

Daniels knew that a small town of 15,000 or so couldn't have a huge police department. He located the Enterprise Police Department (EPD) about five blocks away off South Main Street, and as he had expected, it appeared to be a small force. But the EPD—small as it was—could be a major problem. Many nights of surveillance soon revealed their routine. Each night, EPD sent out two roving police cruisers with two officers in each car, and they stationed a K-9 unit on Main Street, about one hundred yards from the monument. The canine, a large, all-white German Shepherd, along with the K-9 handler, seemed to sit and watch the monument all night. The two roving cruisers and the K-9 unit would have to be distracted somehow. Daniels ran different scenarios through his head.

This is gonna take some serious planning, Daniels thought. He decided that he'd take as much time as was necessary to cover all bases and get every detail right.

The days and weeks passed.

Finally, Daniels ran his plan by his confidant, Phil Seefeld. He said that they'd need three diversions in various parts of town. If they could set off three flash bangs in different parts of town, it'd distract the two roving patrols and pull the K-9 unit away from the monument. Daniels knew that the flash bang grenades were not dangerous; they'd been set off near him many times during training. He knew, too, that they were deafening and would rattle windows in the area. On a quiet night, a flash bang would draw the cops to the sound like a boll weevil to a cotton boll. He'd then simply climb the monument, remove the pest, and make his escape.

Phase one of Operation Boll Weevil was to get their hands on three artillery simulators. Daniels knew that the artillery simulators—the flash bangs—were stored in the armory near the training range. Since the practice range and its armory were well within the confines of Fort Rucker, he figured that there'd be minimal, if any, guards around the facility. Besides, he'd stood guard before, but never with live ammunition. *What's more*, he thought, *even if there is a guard, and even if he does have live ammo, he wouldn't have orders to shoot...would he?*

Daniels had seen the flash bangs stored on shelves inside a bin attached to the range armory. The bin's door was hinged at the top so that the door was raised up like the door of a hot dog stand. When the bin was locked up at night, Daniels noticed that the hasp and padlock were in the middle of the wide door. There appeared to be some wiggle room at the bottom right and left corners of the door.

Daniels thought, *I should be able to pry that door out just a little, reach in, and snatch three grenades. Surely, the Army wouldn't miss just three.*

Daniels watched carefully from the back of the deuce-and-a-half (two-and-a-half-ton Army truck) each time he and his fellow WOCs were transported to and from the training range. He made mental notes of the route and landmarks, knowing that his plan called for him to follow that route surreptitiously in the dark of the night.

When Daniels felt that phase one of Operation Boll Weevil was planned as well as the Army had taught him, he and Phil Seefeld pulled the trigger.

After evening chow, Ozzie and Phil dressed in their green Army fatigues and waited for darkness to descend on Fort Rucker. They were anxious but presented a casual facade to their fellow WOCs around the barracks. At about nine o'clock, they drove Ozzie's candy apple red Plymouth away from the brightly lit area around their barracks into the darkness near the practice range. For once, Ozzie wished his Plymouth's color was something other than candy apple red; camouflage green would have been nice. They parked about a mile away from the practice range and the armory where they knew the flash bang grenades were stored.

Working as a two-man unit, they then "cammed up" by painting their faces with black, brown, and green camouflage grease paint. When both men were satisfied that their faces wouldn't stand out in the dark like a full moon, Ozzie's "Let's go" indicated the start of the mission. They softly closed the doors to the Plymouth and began the trek on foot to the armory. As the two friends walked the dark path to the armory, their eyes slowly adjusted to the low-light conditions. By the time they reached the armory, they were wishing that they'd picked an overcast or moonless night. When they spotted the armory, they paused, crouched, and approached cautiously. Ozzie and Phil then took a position in some bushes so that they could watch for sentries. After what seemed like thirty minutes, but was actually about ten, they were convinced that the armory was not guarded.

They approached the armory cautiously. The bin containing the flash bangs was, as expected, locked with a sturdy padlock. The lock was at the bottom center of the wide door. As Daniels had expected, with the hinge at the top, he could pull the wooden door away from the bin at the bottom edges of the door. He pulled on the right side of the door, and it pulled away by about eight inches, which was just enough room for him to reach into the bin and feel around. He pulled his arm out and displayed to his partner an artillery simulator—a flash bang.

"What'd I tell you," said Ozzie as the two smiled at their cunning.

Ozzie reached into the bin and pulled out a second flashbang. They'd need one more flash bang for their mission. So Ozzie reached into the bin to get the third one. He reached in confidently to pull out the third, but felt nothing but empty space.

"Damn, I can't feel any more," Ozzie said.

"Let's try the other side," said Phil, as they walked to the left side of the door.

Ozzie reached in and felt around. He felt empty shelves and wooden pegs, but no flash bangs.

"Oh well, we got two; that'll have to do," said Ozzie, "I'll have to think of something else for the third diversion."

The two WOCs began making their way back to the Plymouth. Their spirits were high; their mission had gone well, except for that last flash bang. They were softly chatting as they walked; suddenly, they saw a sentry somewhere off in the dark. They both dropped into some bushes and froze. This was no drill; this was not a training exercise. Ozzie and Phil—face down in the bushes—watched and listened. They could hear talking.

Must be more than one, Ozzie thought.

They could hear rustling in the bushes and more talking.

Must be searching for us.

The sounds seemed to get closer before finally fading. The guys stayed put for about thirty minutes and were about to make their move back to the Plymouth when a deuce-and-a-half full of Soldiers arrived at the range. One Soldier—probably an officer—jumped out of the cab and began directing the Soldiers as they dispersed. Flashlights started lighting up from all points. It was an eerie and frightening sight; twenty or more beams of light were shining in all directions.

Ozzie and Phil held their breath as one searcher walked right by them, directing his light into the bushes. Ozzie's heart was beating so loudly that he thought it would be audible to the searcher. The beam of the flashlight must have passed right over Ozzie, but the searcher walked away as calmly as he had approached. Eventually, the searchers returned to the truck and piled on. Ozzie and Phil watched as the deuce-and-a-half pulled away, leaving behind the single sentry who must have raised the alarm.

The sentry resumed his routine patrol. The guys waited until he began walking in the opposite direction, and then made their move. Slowly, cautiously at first, but picking up speed as they increased the gap between them and the sentry, the boys made their way back to the Plymouth.

"That was close," Ozzie said as he started the Plymouth and pulled away.

"Uh huh," Phil said, "But we got the flash bangs."

"We got two, Phil. There're three patrol cars; we'll need three diversions. I'm not going back for more; I'll think of something else for the third diversion."

Ozzie drove north; he didn't want to take the direct route back to the barracks. After thirty minutes of driving north, he turned east for another twenty minutes before finally returning to the post by way of the towns of Ozark and Daleville. On the way back, Ozzie decided on his third diversion.

"Gasoline," Ozzie announced. "We'll get a plastic jug; use a gasoline-soaked rag for a fuse; and set it ablaze in the middle of the street. That should do the trick."

The guys got back to post late that night and made it to their rooms without anyone noticing their dirty fatigues or the camouflage grease paint still showing behind their ears.

Over the next couple of weeks, Ozzie honed his plan to "liberate" the boll weevil from its perch atop the monument. He selected strategic locations for the diversions on the northern, eastern, and southern edges of Enterprise. He recruited two other buddies, who would, along with Phil, set off their diversions at the appointed time.

Ozzie and Phil located and checked out an alley to the west that would be ideal for observing the monument and the K-9 officer. He decided that he needed a driver for his getaway.

Better to have a driver waiting with the motor running for a quick exit.

He considered using his beloved Plymouth for the job, but it wasn't the hottest thing on the road. Besides, its candy apple red color might as well be glow-in-the-dark red. Ozzie thought of a buddy with a very hot 1969 AMX Javelin. The Javelin sported an orange paint job, which would be just as conspicuous as Ozzie's red Plymouth, but the Javelin concealed a 390-cubic inch V8 with a four-barrel carburetor and racing transmission. The Javelin was a street legal drag racer that would beat any small town squad car; hell, it would outrun any police car in the nation. When the Javelin owner agreed to help, all the pieces came into place. It was now a matter of picking the day and time.

On an Indian summer night in late November 1969, Ozzie initiated the final phase of Operation Boll Weevil. He briefed everyone on their role. The first flash bang would go off at exactly 21:00 hours (9:00 p.m.). The second flash bang would be set off forty-five seconds later, and the gasoline jug would be set alight forty-five seconds after that. When the K-9 officer lit up his lights and sped away from his position near the monument, Ozzie would sprint across the intersection, climb the monument, and snatch the boll weevil.

In a scene straight out of a B-Movie, Ozzie went over everyone's part, had everyone set their watches, and asked for questions. In the parking lot, he checked that each car was carrying the proper device: flash bangs in two cars and the jug of gasoline in the other. Ozzie placed his adjustable wrench in the front seat of the Javelin; they were ready to go.

Ozzie's "Any questions?" elicited a few negative nods, and his "Let's go" set Operation Boll Weevil in motion.

The three diversion drivers drove to their assigned positions on the north, east and south sides of Enterprise. Ozzie and his Javelin driver drove to the alley near the monument and parked facing out. As they sat, the tension mounted. They watched and waited for nine o'clock and the expected diversions.

The K-9 officer was in his position. He, too, was sitting and watching, but was probably bored to tears.

At precisely nine o'clock, Ozzie and his driver heard a distant BOOM to the south. About 30 seconds later, a siren pierced the night. The siren began at the police station and began to fade toward the south.

The second artillery simulator was similarly detonated in the distance, and another police siren headed north.

So far, so good...

Then...BOOSH! A flickering orange light lit the eastern sky.

"This is it," Ozzie said to himself more than to his driver.

Ozzie glued his eyes on the K-9 cop car, "If he doesn't take the bait..."

About 30 seconds later, the white dog began a steady bark, the cruiser's flashing lights lit the intersection, and the cruiser sped off, his siren and lights fading as he raced east.

Ozzie grabbed the wrench, leapt from the Javelin, and raced across the interception to the monument. He scaled the little wall with its steel fence in a single bound.

Ozzie Daniels stood on the light fixtures while detaching the boll weevil.

He climbed the cement pedestal and stood with one foot on each light fixture. Ozzie adjusted his wrench to fit the nut. He had a good bite on the nut as he pulled, but the nut was old and the threads were rusty; it took all of Ozzie's might to break it free. The statue's upstretched arms restricted the wrench to a partial rotation before he had to pull the wrench off and get a new bite. The rusty bolt slowed him down, and there were another two inches of the bolt to go before the bug could be liberated.

Then the situation changed from bad to worse. A

light came on in a window above a shop near the intersection, and Ozzie could see movement inside.

Must be an apartment above that shop. Oh, shit...I've been made!

About a minute later, Ozzie heard sirens again, but this time, the sirens seemed to be approaching from all directions. Just then, the Javelin with its loud pipes roared out of the alley and skidded to a stop beside the monument. The passenger door flew open, and the driver screamed, "Daniels, if you're coming, you'd better get in now because I'm leaving!"

With an inch of rusty bolt remaining before the bug could be freed, Daniels knew that he was defeated. Reciting a series of expletives to himself, he climbed down the monument, leapt the fence, and landed in the front seat of the Javelin. The Javelin accelerated, burning rubber before Ozzie could get his door closed. They headed north on Main Street through the small downtown area and made a sharp left turn onto Watts Street—a side street that would take them to Highway 134 and out of town. When the Javelin straightened out on Watts Street, Daniels looked back to see the three police cars fishtailing as they rounded the corner. Just as Ozzie turned around to tell his driver, the Javelin crossed over a railroad track, sending the orange dragster and Ozzie airborne. Ozzie hit the roof hard before being squashed back into his seat when they bottomed out on the asphalt. It was only then that Ozzie thought of fastening his seat belt.

West Watts Street was a two-lane road that ran straight through a sparsely populated part of Enterprise.

It was perfect for the street legal dragster, so the driver gunned the orange Javelin, leaving the black-and-white police cars far behind. In a couple of miles, they made a right for a block and then turned left onto State Highway 134, which would take them out of town and hopefully to safety.

Highway 134 was a two-lane asphalt road that was straight enough for the Javelin to show its mettle. When the telephone poles passing by began to look like a picket fence, Ozzie leaned over to see that the speedometer needle was buried. He looked back again, even though he knew there was no way those local cops could be within a mile. Finally, when they began running in and out of patches of late night fog, they slowed down a bit. They did a little zig-zagging through some country roads and made their way back to Mother Rucker.

To Phil Seefeld and the others, it was an adventure; for Ozzie Daniels, it was a major disappointment. He had failed.

Ozzie thought of the "Seven Ps," the military gold standard for mission planning: *Proper Planning and Preparation Prevents Piss Poor Performance.*

Why hadn't I measured the nut and brought a ratchet wrench? Why hadn't I thought to bring a can of penetrating oil?

It was a lesson learned that would serve him well in the not-too-distant future. Vietnam was calling.

An estimated ten thousand people crowded the area around the Boll Weevil Monument for the Golden

Anniversary Celebration on 11 December 1969. The monument had been repainted and a double-ring fountain installed. The lady in the flowing white gown held the insect of honor proudly above her head. The spectators had no idea how close their lucky bug had come to being a no-show for the festivities.

WOCs Daniels and Seefeld graduated from class 69-45 on 25 January 1970, and they were appointed Warrant Officers (W-1). The next day, they were awarded their wings and given their marching orders: Report to the CO of 90th Replacement Battalion at Long Binh, Republic of Vietnam.

11

Yellow One

Republic of Vietnam
1969–1970

Author's Note: This chapter is an adaptation of an article written by Roger C. Baker and published in the September/October 2015 edition of *The VHPA AVIATOR MAGAZINE*. I am grateful to Major Baker for his permission to adapt his story, as it fits seamlessly and gives the reader greater insight into the events depicted in this book.

Major Baker's original *Yellow One* is available on the internet at:
www.roymark.org/yellow-one.html

—Roy Mark

Before arriving at Tay Ninh West in August of 1969, Captain Roger C. Baker had never heard of the term "Yellow One." The term had no particular significance, and he could not have imagined the unique and demanding responsibilities that were attached to it, but he was about to learn.

Yellow One was the Army's term for "Combat Assault Flight Leader." Yellow One was responsible for leading several echelons of three Hueys each. Yellow

One's bird was designated Yellow One and was accompanied by Yellow Two and Yellow Three. The second echelon was designated White One, Two and Three. Occasionally, a third echelon—Blue—was added to a combat assault mission.

Yellow One was the Combat Assault Flight Leader; Yellow One was also his bird.

Yellow One was—in the vernacular of the time— "The man." He controlled all aspects of the combat assault. He controlled all of the Hueys in his flight and the escort gunships, and if needed, he called in artillery. It was a big job, and not all Huey pilots were up to the task. The pilots of Charlie Company were the best, and Charlie Company's Yellow Ones were the best of the best.

Stepping off the chartered flight from the States alongside warrant officers and second lieutenants, Captain Baker was an atypical FNG. From Syracuse, New York, the twenty-six-year-old captain exuded an external air of confidence for the benefit of the junior officers. However, he shared their apprehension, their wonderment, and yes, their deep-seated primal fear. This was, after all, a war zone, and rotary wing pilots were being killed every day.

Captain Roger C. Baker

When Baker finished flight school in July of 1968, most of his graduating class headed for Vietnam. Lieutenant Baker was one of the few to be given a stateside assignment; he was headed to Fort Carson in Colorado.

Flying out of Fort Carson involved a lot of mountain flying, and Baker was learning from experienced combat veterans. The pilots he flew with were mostly young warrant officers who had just returned from Vietnam. They were good—damn good—and they taught him things about flying in a combat zone that were not in the lesson plans at Fort Wolters.

Baker's roommate at Carson turned out to be an excellent mentor. Chief Warrant Officer (CWO) Bill Davis had just returned from a Nam tour as a gunship pilot with the First Cav. Davis was able to give Baker a perspective of the operations that would be vital to the future Yellow One.

After he had logged three hundred hours of flight time, Baker was elevated to Aircraft Commander. He was then sent to the UH-1 Instructor Pilot (IP) course at Fort Rucker, Alabama. After finishing the IP course, Lieutenant Baker was promoted to captain and given orders that read "Vietnam!"

As a seasoned aviator fresh from IP School, Baker felt prepared for the challenges ahead, but he was about to be confronted with the most difficult challenge of his military career.

Captain Roger Baker was assigned to Company C, 229th Assault Helicopter Battalion, First Cavalry Division (Air Mobil). Charlie Company was a down-and-dirty Huey Lift Company. Lift companies carried troops, supplies, and when necessary, the wounded and killed in action. Lift company Hueys were lightly armed with two M60 machine guns that fired 7.62mm rounds at the rate of five hundred to six hundred rounds per minute. The lightly armed Huey became known as a "Slick," and Baker's new Slick Company had the distinct radio call sign "North Flag." Baker would soon learn that the officers and enlisted men of Charlie Company referred to themselves as "North Flaggers," and that North Flaggers had a proud tradition of living up to high standards.

Having just flown with combat vets at Fort Carson, Baker knew that his captain's bars would mean little in the cockpit. The warrant officers at Carson had prepared him for the Nam reality—time in-country was a rank of its own.

Captain Baker was assigned as a section leader in the first flight platoon. When he flew his first real mission, it was as a co-pilot flying with IP Jim "Lunchmeat"

Lungwitz. Jim was tagged with the nickname "Lunchmeat" for obvious reasons, and "Lunchmeat" became his personal radio call sign. Lunchmeat was an experienced combat pilot on his second Nam tour.

His first combat mission taxed all of Baker's IP skills. Lunchmeat had been assigned as Yellow Two that day, with Baker as his co-pilot. From morning liftoff until after sunset, they flew over ten hours of combat assaults. During that first day, Yellow Two was a very busy aircraft, and Lunchmeat had little time to tutor his FNG co-pilot on the finer skills of combat formation flying. Lunchmeat spent most of his time passing artillery clearances to Yellow One, while Baker spent most of his time just trying to keep Yellow Two behind Yellow One.

It was a memorable day for Baker. His Yellow Two came under enemy fire several times during the day, but Baker was so overwhelmed with the complexity of the operation that he didn't have time to be terrified—ignorance was bliss! When his first flying day ended that night and Baker rolled the throttle off, he was convinced that North Flaggers were all nuts and that he was in way over his head.

It had been a long day, and Baker was glad it was finally over. Then, Yellow Two's radio crackled to life. Lunchmeat and Baker were given a new mission. They were part of a mission to fly to a landing zone (LZ) and retrieve the bodies of a downed crew. A Light Observation Helicopter (LOH) had been forced down in War Zone C. The Loach—Army slang for LOH—had hit hard, killing the crew of two. Baker sat at the controls, as the bodies of a fellow helicopter pilot and his observer were unceremoniously loaded onto a nearby Huey. The gravity of his situation now etched itself in his mind, and it would remain there throughout the coming year, and indeed, for the rest of his life.

As time went by, it became apparent to Baker that more often than not, he was being assigned as co-pilot on White One, the back-up flight lead aircraft. The White One Huey was always assigned to a Flight Leader, and Flight Leaders held the title "Yellow One." Pilots who had earned the Yellow One title led the mission from the Yellow One Huey or backed up the Flight Leader in White One.

As co-pilot in White One, Baker was flying with the unit's Flight Leaders, North Flag's Yellow Ones. He was learning from the best.

Each of the Yellow Ones took great pains to keep Baker informed about what the flight leader was doing and why. It wasn't long before he was told that he was to begin training as a Yellow One. Being chosen as a North Flag Yellow One wasn't an arbitrary process; it wasn't like winning the lottery. The selection process was based on Baker's flying skills, his understanding of tactics, and his demeanor under fire; indeed, his every action since arriving at C/229th was considered. Most importantly, input from the unit's aircraft commanders was considered in the selection process. Being chosen was a unique distinction, and Captain Roger Baker felt honored, humbled, and a little overwhelmed.

Charlie Company's three Yellow Ones were Captain Hewitt "Buck" Lovelace, First Lieutenant Larry Matchett, and First Lieutenant Don Robert "Thumpy" Thompson.

Baker was a little apprehensive about stepping into the position of Yellow One, so he sought out Thumpy Thompson and discussed his feelings. Thumpy was easy to talk with, and Baker valued his advice.

"Don't worry about it" was Thumpy's advice. "I felt the same way Roger, and besides, they wouldn't turn you lose until you're so well trained that you can't screw up."

It was sound advice, but Roger Baker would comment many times in the years to come, that it was the only time Thumpy had ever lied to him.

Captain Baker then spent the next few months as co-pilot in the Yellow One Huey. He flew with Charlie Company's three Yellow One pilots, trying to soak up as much information as they could throw at him. Each of the three Yellow Ones had a distinct style of running the lift, but they were all very effective at accomplishing the mission.

Captain Hewitt "Buck" Lovelace was an impressive young man, who was handsome and well groomed. To Baker, Lovelace always seemed a little lax with his flight planning. However, he soon found that to be a misconception, since most of Buck's planning was done in his head. Buck had a somewhat photographic memory and an outstanding knowledge of the Area of Operation. After a few missions, Baker figured that Lovelace could fly most missions without a map. Buck smoked Camel cigarettes—the short, unfiltered kind. When things got hairy, with tracers streaking every which way, Baker would often glance over and see Lovelace casually taking a drag from his Camel. He was the coolest Yellow One under fire.

First Lieutenant Larry Matchett was another Yellow One to mentor Captain Baker. Lieutenant Matchett was a tall, lanky cowboy from Montana and was really a warrant officer at heart, who was more interested in flying and had little tolerance for Army protocol. However, he was all business in the cockpit. Baker felt that he learned more easily with Matchett, who was methodical in running his missions and never varied far from his system that worked so well. Larry smoked Marlboros and an occasional Garcia de Vega cigar. He didn't hesitate to show his concern under fire, and Roger Baker could relate a little more to Larry than the cool-under-fire Buck Lovelace.

Then there was First Lieutenant Don Robert "Thumpy" Thompson—truly an unforgettable character. When Thompson first arrived in Charlie Company in April of 1969, he immediately stood out from the crowd. From Arkadelphia, Arkansas, Thumpy was about 5 feet 6 inches tall and had a gymnast's build. Thompson was a little on the hyperactive side, and when he spoke, his Southern accent and hillbilly dialect immediately caught the attention of Charlie Company pilots. Thompson's flight leader took note of the hyper little FNG, who reminded him of the Disney cartoon character Thumper. Thumper was the little rabbit that appeared in the film Bambi and was so named for the way he thumped his hind paw. For this reason, Thompson was tagged with the nickname "Thumper," and after a few days, "Thumper" had morphed into "Thumpy."

Thumpy Thompson's mission briefings would knock

your socks off. Pilots in his flight would hear something along the lines of, "Flight this here's Yeller One, we all gonna sashay up the blue a mite with a six plus two." No one ever needed to ask who the flight leader was.

Thumpy was trained as a Yellow One by both Buck and Larry, and he seemed to exemplify the best qualities of each. His planning was thorough, and he was always able to adapt to tactical changes. When things got bad, Thumpy got better.

Roger Baker, an upstate New York Yankee, and Thumpy, with his Southern bumpkin veneer, got along surprisingly well. Roger quickly realized that this Yellow One was a highly intelligent, brave, and skilled pilot who cared deeply for the men of his flight. They related in many ways, down to their choice of smokes; they were Winston men.

One of Baker's most memorable flights with Thumpy Thompson was something short of an aviation triumph. It began routinely with Thumpy making a visit to Tactical Operations Center to check for any last-minute changes to the mission, and Baker doing his preflight inspection on Thumpy's Huey, 68-16123. Thumpy's Huey had its last three digits "123" painted on the nose. Above the 123 was painted "Thumpy 1," which indicated Thompson's status as a Flight Leader.

UH-1H 68-16123
"Thumpy One"
Photo courtesy of Jack McCormick

When Thompson and Baker met at Thumpy 1, they put on their body armor—dubbed "Chicken Plates"—and settled into their seats in the cockpit. In the midst of their mission—a combat assault—Thumpy began shifting around in his seat and cussing a blue streak. That was unusual enough, but he then took off his chicken plate and stripped to the waist. It took a few seconds for Baker to figure out what was going on, but among the cuss words were references to the heritage of red ants. Thumpy was busy killing red ants that were stinging his chest and stomach. It seemed that Thumpy had spilled coffee on his chicken plate the day before; the sugar had attracted the ants, and they had made a temporary nest between the nylon outer layer and the aluminum oxide ceramic plates of Thumpy's chicken plate.

The three Yellow Ones were each unique: Captain Hewitt "Buck" Lovelace with his photographic memory, First Lieutenant Larry Matchett with his Warrant Officer approach to the war, and First Lieutenant Don Robert "Thumpy" Thompson with his Southern good-ol'-boy mannerisms—each unique and each highly effective. They could not have been more different, yet all three led by example. They were Roger Baker's mentors, and he followed them unhesitatingly into some nasty battles.

Years later, at Charlie Company reunions held at cities around the United States, Roger never failed to mention that he would still follow those three guys anywhere.

Captain Roger Baker continued his Yellow One training throughout the months of August, September, and October of 1969. As co-pilot of the Yellow One bird—the lead Huey of the flight—Baker became painfully aware of the fact that while the lead sled dog always gets the best view, he doesn't always like what he sees. The Yellow Ones and flight leaders of Charlie Company, however, did like what they were seeing in Roger Baker. They recommended, and the CO approved, his elevation to Yellow One. Baker considered it quite an achievement to have been selected by such great pilots as CWO Tom "Ogre" Agnew, CWO Wayne Miller, CWO Mark Panageotes, CWO Reggie Baldwin and the other warrant and commissioned officers of Charlie Company. It was a source of pride, and he would cherish this achievement throughout his thirty-year military career and into retirement.

After three months of training, Captain Baker's time had come; he was cut loose to see if he could cut the mustard as a Yellow One.

Crew chiefs and door gunners were assigned a Huey, and they stuck with that ship, sometimes for the entire duration of their tour. Pilots, on the other hand, were assigned a new ship each day; they flew many different Hueys manned by different crews. Yellow Ones, however, rated their own ship and the crew that manned it.

As a new Yellow One, Baker was assigned Huey 68-15648. When he first laid eyes on his new bird, he was less than impressed. Two bleeding, bright red cherries adorned the nose below the words "Cherry Buster." *That's gotta go*, was Baker's first thought even before he met his new crew. *Easy Rider*, he thought, *would be a great name*.

Baker's new crew chief was Specialists Fourth Class (SP-4) Dave Holte, a laid-back, skinny, twenty-year-old blond from Kansas who made a career out of keeping pilots out of trouble. When Baker first broached the subject of changing Cherry Buster's name, Holt would have none of it. He respectfully explained to his new boss that his ship had been named "Cherry Buster" because many pilots, passengers, and crew—including himself—had had their cherries busted in 648. The meaning was clear to Baker; there was a tendency for hot lead to hit 648 when new guys were onboard.

"Besides," Holte said sealing the deal, "changing her name would be bad luck."

Captain Baker (L) and Dave Holte (R)
with Huey 68-15648 "Cherry Buster"
Note the .51 Cal bullet hole between them.

Holte was a seasoned crew chief, and "bad luck" was a persuasive argument. As an aircraft commander, Baker had quickly learned to heed the advice of his crew, so 648 remained "Cherry Buster." As a concession, Holte allowed Baker—an accomplished artist—to remove the two cherries nose-art and paint a muscular cartoon character with "Cherry Buster" written across his chest.

Baker realized very quickly that Cherry Buster was a great aircraft and that it was manned by an excellent crew.

On Baker's first mission as a Yellow One, his assigned co-pilot was WO1 Neil "Beeper" Blume. Blume was from the small Minnesota farming community of Herman. Neil had picked up the nickname "Beeper" early on in his tour. His aircraft commander had directed Blume to beep up the engine rpm, and Neal had accidentally beeped it down instead. He went on to be one of the best pilots in Charlie Company, but he never shook the name.

WO1 Neil "Beeper" Blume

Baker managed—with the help of his crew—to struggle through his first mission without any major blunders. Aircraft commanders can be brutally critical of their Yellow Ones, but on Baker's first mission, each of the aircraft commanders of the flight did everything they could to make things easier for the new Yellow One. Back on the ground, many of them extended their congratulations and compliments. The congratulations and compliments, however, came with a price. Drinks at the O-Club that night were on the new Yellow One. For his part, Captain Roger Baker was glad that his initiation into the ranks of Charlie Company Yellow Ones was over.

The months passed. As Roger Baker led combat missions as a Yellow One, he got a feel for how his aircraft commanders and pilots handled themselves under fire. On the ground, the other pilots and he exchanged views on their situation in Vietnam. About mid-way through his one-year tour, like many of his comrades, Baker began to realize that tactically, nothing was really being accomplished. That realization led to his being more conservative as a flight leader. He became less willing to expose his flight to unnecessary risk.

As the 229th Assault Helicopter Battalion expanded its operations closer to Cambodia, ground-to-air fire became more frequent and intense. The NVA began to deploy what the pilots referred to as an anti-aircraft battalion. It consisted of three .51 caliber machine guns and three infantry support companies. The enemy's new battalion proved to be very effective.

By late 1969, Roger Baker had been in-country for five months. He was no longer an FNG and was now leading combat missions as a Yellow One. A special comradery had developed between Roger and his fellow pilots. They were excellent pilots, and they knew it; they were Charlie Company pilots—North Flaggers. They had faced the enemy every day of Baker's five months in-country. There were hairy missions and close calls, but neither a ship nor a man had been lost to enemy fire. Charlie Company was charmed, or so it seemed. As 1969 faded into 1970, however, their luck changed.

On 30 December 1969, Captain Baker was leading a flight into an LZ when a sniper shot and killed Captain

Gerald Clifford Swayze, the co-pilot of one of his ships.

(Note: The story of Captain Swayze's death is covered in detail in Chapter 12, beginning on page 147)

It was the first loss of a pilot as a result of ground-to-air fire since Charlie Company's dark days of 1968 in the A Shau Valley. Swayze's loss had a sobering effect on the men of Charlie Company. Baker was personally affected by it, and for the first time, experienced the pain and sorrow of not bringing everyone home alive. The North Flaggers now realized that until now, luck had been on their side. What they didn't know was that their streak of bad luck was just beginning.

Charlie Company honored Captain Gerald Clifford Swayze with a missing man formation flyby over the Tay Ninh base camp the next day. It was an emotional experience for every North Flagger. It affected Roger Baker especially hard, and the experience didn't get any easier when more missing man formations were flown in the months to come.

After the loss of Captain Swayze, Roger Baker decided that his formation's best defense might be a more aggressive offense, so he began insisting on maximum gunship coverage on every mission. He instituted the "JUDGE." The Judge was one of the company's Nighthawk aircraft reconfigured for extra firepower. On The Judge's starboard side, the door gunner carried out the Judge's sentence with twin M60 machine guns dispensing 7.62mm lead at a combined rate of 1,000 to 1,200 rounds per minute. On the port side, the crew chief saturated the enemy with the same 7.62mm rounds, but at a maximum rate of four-thousand rounds per minute from his M134 Gatling-type minigun. When The Judge passed a death sentence upon the enemy, the sentence was carried out unequivocally and swiftly; there was no appeal. The Judge carried no troops, flew in the tail-end Charlie position, and provided close-in fire support from a high hover in the pickup and landing zones. The Judge was also used as a recovery aircraft for the recovery of downed aircraft crews. It came in handy on a few occasions.

The Judge was named after the T.V. comedy skit *Here Comes the Judge*, which was first performed by Pigmeat Markham and later by Sammy Davis Junior on Rowan & Martin's Laugh-In. The phrase "here come the judge" quickly entered the American lexicon.

When Captain Baker arrived in Charlie Company in August of 1969, he made an immediate connection with the executive officer (XO), Captain Bill Lorimer. Lorimer was a career officer from St. Cloud, Minnesota. The two captains became friends; each respected and admired the job the other was doing. In February of 1970, Bill Lorimer was appointed as Charlie Company's CO. Lorimer's career in the Army was on track. Roger Baker was thrilled for his friend, and as expected, he soon realized that Bill Lorimer was an excellent CO. Lorimer was liked by his officers and men, but more importantly, he was well respected.

Captain William Lorimer IV
Commanding Officer, C/229th

On the 10th day of March, Lorimer joined a flight led by Lieutenant Don "Thumpy" Thompson. Lorimer would fly as co-pilot in the fourth of six Hueys. Their mission was to extract Army of the Republic of Vietnam (ARVN) troops from a pick-up zone and transport them to a new location. After picking up the ARVN troops and ascending through five hundred feet, an enemy soldier opened up with his Kalashnikov AK-47, spraying 7.62mm rounds at just one of the six Hueys. Of all of the rounds fired, not one hit the Huey. One round, though, entered the open door of Lorimer's Huey, passed by the door gunner, passed between the armor plating on the back of Lorimer's seat and the sliding armor plating on his

143

right side, and then entered his body just above the seam of his armor-plated chicken plate. It was a real fluke if ever there was one.

It had only been forty-two days since the missing man formation honoring the memory of Captain Jerry Swayze had flown over Charlie Company's base at Tay Ninh. Now, Roger Baker was saddened as Hueys flew overhead honoring his friend Bill Lorimer. A 21-gun salute was performed at a memorial service, and then life, not to mention the war, had to continue.

Surprise would be an understatement to describe Baker's reaction when he learned that he had been chosen as Charlie Company's new CO. The position called for a major to fill the slot, and Baker was not only a captain, but a junior captain at that. He considered it an opportunity to honor his friend by continuing with the policies that Captain Lorimer had initiated.

Captain Baker settled into his job as CO, knowing that he had big boots to fill. The officers in his command, especially the Yellow Ones, were supportive, as was the battalion commander, Lieutenant Colonel Robert Patton. Patton gave Baker the freedom and authority to do things his way. Baker wasn't as thrilled with the colonel's staff and considered them a royal pain in the ass.

FNG Captain Roger C. Baker had arrived in-country one year earlier a little naïve, a little idealistic, and overly optimistic as to what the Army could achieve in a troubled land. He was happy—make that ecstatic—to be leaving, but at the same time, saddened to be leaving behind *his* company and the officers and enlisted men he had come to admire and respect. As a Yellow One, he had been determined to bring every man home at the end of each day; logic told him that in a shooting war, that was an unrealistic goal. But not achieving his goal still hurt...a lot!

When Roger Baker boarded his "freedom bird" for stateside duty at Fort Stewart, Georgia, he went through a range of emotions: relief that he had made it and was still alive; joy that he would be with his family soon; gratitude to the pilots and enlisted crewmembers of C/229th who flew the missions; admiration for the officers and men who never flew, but made flight possible—the cooks, the clerks, the supply specialists, the mechanics, and all the others who did important jobs; sorrow for his friends and men under his command who would remain forever young—boys really—and didn't live to catch their freedom bird home; and sympathy for the families of the fallen, for their friends and loved ones who would continue their lives with broken hearts, perhaps not knowing, not understanding, and questioning why it had to be. Baker thought of the men he was leaving behind. David Holte, his first crew chief, was back in the world and safe, but Larry Heale, his second crew chief, was still in harm's way and keeping another pilot out of trouble. Names and faces flashed through his mind's eye: Painter, Jeremiah, Townsend, Guest, Cristelli, Griffith, Zennie, White, Haskins and many more. He could see them all, and they would remain etched in his memory, each wearing Army green.

As the chartered jet passed over the coast of South Vietnam, homeward bound, Baker thought that he was leaving Vietnam behind. As with all Vietnam veterans, however, he would come to realize over the years and decades to come, that Vietnam would always be a part of him.

12

Golden BB

Republic of Vietnam
1969

Captain Jerry Swayze had been in Vietnam for five months. Most of those five months had been spent as the battalion's supply officer (S-4). Being the supply officer wasn't exciting, but it was a good experience for a career-focused officer. Besides, the slick companies were always short of pilots, and he was able to fly occasionally.

Then, in November of 1969, the full-time supply officer and part-time pilot was transferred to a flight platoon in Charlie Company. After the transfer, Captain Jerry Swayze became a full-time pilot and a Charlie Company North Flagger.

The leadership of Charlie Company was about to be shuffled by the CO's DEROS (Date Eligible for Return from Overseas). Major Dick Antross[10] would be replaced by his XO, Captain Bill Lorimer[11]. Jerry Swayze, being the next senior captain was expected to become Lorimer's

10 Richard C. Antross, Colonel, U.S. Army (Retired)

11 William Lorimer IV (16 July 1942 – 10 March 1970)

new XO. Experience as XO—second in command—would be Swayze's first step toward greater command responsibility. His future in the Army looked bright.

Gerald Clifford Swayze was a small-town boy from Wilmot, South Dakota. Situated in the northeast corner of the state, the community of Wilmot had a population of just 467 when Jerry graduated from Wilmot High School in 1959. Wilmot was a vibrant community, and unlike many small towns in America, the population was holding its own. In fact, from the turn of the century until 1960, the population had increased by some 115 residents.

As it is with most small-town boys, young Jerry Swayze grew up with close ties to his community and closer ties to his family. Jerry was the oldest of four children born to Cliff and Rose Ella Swayze.

The United States was enjoying a fragile peace when Gerald Clifford Swayze entered the world on 5 May 1941. War had broken out in Europe in 1939 and would engulf the United States seven months after Jerry's arrival. The Swayze's second son, Orrie, was born two years later, and he was followed by their daughter Sharellyn in 1945 and third son Mickey in 1947.

WW-II was over before young Jerry was old enough to appreciate the meaning of war. As a pre-teen, however, he was captivated by the stories of his Uncle Murel's service during the war. It was a time when comic books depicted heroic Americans defeating hordes of buck-toothed bespectacled Japs. Jerry was old enough and wise enough to realize that real enemies were not caricatures and that war stories didn't always have comic book endings. His Uncle Murel had fought the Japanese in the Philippines, and in 1945, he was killed in the effort to wrest the island of Luzon from the Japanese. War was real to Jerry.

Jerry grew up with a sense of mission and adventure. He loved the outdoors and became an accomplished bow hunter. He even entered archery contests and did well. After graduating from Wilmot High School in 1959, Jerry Swayze studied drafting at Gale Institute in Minneapolis for a while before entering the U.S. Army on a three-year enlistment. He liked the Army, but he did not necessarily like being at the bottom of the totem pole. He felt that he was more of a leader than a follower. Jerry saw his future as an officer.

When Swayze's Army enlistment ended in 1962, he returned to Wilmot and enrolled at South Dakota State University (SDSU) in Brookings. Jerry had shown talent as an artist, so he majored in art. With his career path in mind, he enrolled in Army ROTC. Jerry excelled in ROTC. His military bearing garnered over three years of enlisted service set him apart from the teenagers in his freshman class. When, in his junior year, Jerry's ROTC class began studying Army aviation, he set his sights on an aviation career. In June of 1966, Jerry graduated from SDSU with a Bachelor of Arts and Sciences degree. Along with his sheepskin, Jerry received a commission in the U.S. Army. Second Lieutenant Gerald Swayze's first assignment was to attend Jump School. Jumping out of airplanes wasn't Jerry's first choice. What he really wanted was to fly airplanes, but it would do...for now.

After Jump School, Jerry was ordered to Korea.

Swayze spent his time in Korea near the DMZ, which separated the Republic of Korea (South Korea) and the Democratic People's Republic of Korea (North Korea). The warring parties of the Korean War had signed an armistice ending the fighting in 1953, but an armistice is not a peace treaty. The United States and North Korea were still at war, and Jerry was eyeball-to-eyeball with the Communist enemy across the DMZ. There were skirmishes from time to time, and the situation remained tense, but Jerry completed his tour without incident.

Lieutenant Gerald C. Swayze in Korea

Before leaving Korea, Jerry applied for flight training to become a helicopter pilot. Once he was back in the U.S., he passed his flight physical and received orders to report to the Army's Primary Aviator Flight School at Fort Wolters, Texas.

During his four months at Fort Wolters, Swayze mastered basic flight maneuvers of the helicopter. He then learned to apply those maneuvers to small and unimproved landing areas. He was introduced to formation flying, air navigation, and night flying. From Fort Wolters, Swayze was sent to Fort Rucker in Alabama where he transitioned to the much larger, more complex UH-1 (Huey). Finally, Swayze was flying the helicopter of Vietnam fame. In the Huey, students were taught the tactics used in Vietnam.

It came as no surprise to Jerry Swayze or to any of his Fort Rucker classmates when they were ordered to Vietnam.

When Jerry arrived in Vietnam in late July 1969, the U.S. was coming off its deadliest year of the war: 16,899 Americans had been killed in 1968. The New Year brought with it a new U.S. President and new hope. President Richard Nixon introduced the strategy of "Vietnamization," according to which U.S. troops would be withdrawn and replaced by RVN forces. It made little difference to the Huey pilots; they were needed to support U.S. troops and the RVN troops that were slowly replacing them.

Captain Jerry Swayze, like Captain Roger Baker before him, was not the typical FNG; both men had several years of Army experience under their web belts and Captain's Bars on their collars. Like Baker before him, Captain Swayze soon learned that time in-country outranked silver bars.

As the battalion supply officer, Jerry was kept busy at headquarters, but he volunteered for missions and flew as often as he could.

As a North Flagger, Jerry flew almost every day as co-pilot (peter-pilot in Army slang) with seasoned pilots (Aircraft Commanders, ACs). Most of the ACs were young warrant officers and lieutenants who were Jerry's juniors, except in the cockpit. New peter-pilots were generally assigned flights with the most experienced ACs. The ACs were charged with getting new pilots up to speed as soon as possible. Each AC's approach to training new pilots was different. Some were tough taskmasters, while others were more easygoing but methodical. It didn't matter to Jerry. He was happy to be learning from the best. As he logged more hours flying combat missions, he became familiar with North Flag's procedures and Area of Operations. He absorbed everything North Flag's ACs threw at him. He was learning practical combat flying, which were skills not taught at Fort Wolters and Fort Rucker.

As 1969 faded into 1970, Jerry Swayze's future looked bright. He was new in Charlie Company, but he was the senior Captain behind XO Bill Lorimer. With CO Major Antross rotating back to the world soon, the domino effect would move Lorimer into the CO's position and elevate Swayze to Executive Officer. Yes, his future looked bright, but in combat, no man's future is assured beyond the next mission.

The men of Charlie Company were working long hours seven days a week. Jerry flew with different ACs each day, and his confidence grew with each combat mission. Around the base, he felt that he was beginning to fit in and that he was being accepted as a fellow pilot. In his hootch, Jerry became friends with Captain Fred Zacher. Fred's bunk was next to Jerry's, and they spent some of their limited free time just shooting the breeze. Fred particularly enjoyed Jerry's sense of humor. They exchanged stories of friends back home, and their experiences in the Army. Jerry had just returned from R&R (Rest and Recuperation) in Australia, and Fred enjoyed Jerry's recounting of the great times there.

The United States was not the only country fighting to prevent a Communist takeover of the Republic of Vietnam. The member states of the Southeast Asia Treaty Organization (SEATO), all of which were anti-Communist, contributed troops to the effort. The SEATO countries of South Korea, Australia, the Philippines, New Zealand, and Thailand had forces scattered throughout South Vietnam.

The Republic of the Philippines sent a civic action group consisting of an engineer construction battalion, medical and rural community development teams, a reinforced infantry battalion, a reinforced engineer battalion, a support company, civic action personnel, a Navy contingent, and an Air Force contingent. The 1st Philippines Civic Action Group (PHILCAG) arrived in South Vietnam in 1966 and set up their base just behind the 229th Assault Helicopter Battalion area inside the Tay Ninh Base. A group of Filipino doctors and nurses lived off base; they worked at the province hospital and lived in a villa in Tay Ninh City. PHILCAG's mission was to provide civic action assistance to the Republic of Vietnam by the construction, rehabilitation, and development of public works, utilities, and structures. PHILCAG's strength eventually topped two thousand military and civilian personnel, but in 1968, the Philippine government had begun withdrawing personnel. When Jerry Swayze arrived at the Tay Ninh base in July 1969, PHILCAG was down to 1,500 personnel. The PHILCAG personnel were friendly and hospitable, and most spoke excellent English. PHILCAG staff and 229th Soldiers would often visit each other, and PHILCAG would sometimes host sporting events and invite their 229th friends.

One day just before Christmas 1969, Jerry joined a group of 229th Soldiers for a volleyball competition and beer bust. The Philippine government had flown in copious amounts of their national treasure, San Miguel Pale Pilsen (beer). San Miguel came in short, squatty amber-colored bottles. Unlike the English who preferred their beer cool and the Americans who liked it cold, the Filipinos liked their beer really cold. They had a knack for refrigerating beer to just the point of freezing so that when the cap was popped, half an inch of icy slush would form at the neck. The first sip of San Miguel was like drinking a Beer Slurpee.

The Americans loved San Miguel and enjoyed the volleyball and comradery. It gave Jerry a chance to meet and socialize not only with the Filipinos but also with some of the officers from headquarters and the other 229th companies.

The competition was intense but one sided. The

Filipinos were volleyball naturals, but perhaps they had an unfair advantage. The Americans were drinking San Miguel without the knowledge that its alcohol content was seven percent. With each San Miguel the Americans consumed, swatting the volleyball became more problematic and awkward.

One of Jerry's volleyball teammates was the Battalion Surgeon Captain Craig Thomas. Thomas knew most of the PHILCAG doctors—he had scrubbed with them a few times and considered them excellent surgeons—so the event gave him the opportunity to socialize with old friends. Captains Thomas and Swayze found themselves in friendly competition with the Filipinos, and in the process, made an immediate connection that both men thought would be an enduring friendship.

Breaks from the daily grind of combat were rare, and most days were like all others. Although most of the Soldiers, particularly the short-timers, could recite the number of days they had left in-country, few could remember the day of the week.

It was Wednesday, 30 December 1969.

Captain Jerry Swayze was scheduled to fly peter-pilot with CWO David Hogan* on a mission extracting troops from the field. The LZ that morning was in an area of enemy activity in War Zone C, north of Firebase Grant.

Hogan was a seasoned aviator and a relatively short timer with just a couple of months left in-country. Hogan would be Yellow Two backing up Captain Roger Baker in Yellow One, and he'd be getting artillery clearances to ensure that the flight didn't become victim to friendly fire. Hogan had intended to let Swayze fly left seat—the AC's seat—since he would be evaluating Swayze's competence on this mission and recommending Swayze for the position of AC. It wasn't according to Hoyle— whoever that guy Hoyle was—but it was standard practice when a peter-pilot was nearing the end of his training to let him fly left seat so that he could become adjusted to controlling the bird from the AC's seat.

Before the mission was scheduled for liftoff, Hogan, Swayze and the crew of 772 had scrambled on an emergency one-ship medivac mission for a unit under fire. They would deliver the casualty to the 45th Surgical Hospital at Tay Ninh West. The pilots and crew of 772 rushed to the flight line. Hogan entered the port door and took the AC's seat. Swayze, a little surprised, took his familiar co-pilot's seat. They strapped themselves in with the Huey's four-point harness. Swayze donned his Army-issue Bausch + Lomb© aviator sunglasses. It was all business until they reached altitude. David then told his co-pilot that he would switch seats with him when they returned to Tay Ninh West. Jerry was relieved; he would fly left seat today after all.

The medivac mission was routine, if it can be considered routine to place a bloodied, wounded Soldier clinging to life into the cargo bay of a Huey.

Back at Tay Ninh West, Hogan and Swayze made the short hop from the hospital helipad to the flight line, where Captain Baker was waiting with the Yellow One flight for their return. There was just enough time to take their position between Yellow One and Yellow Three piloted by WO1 Bob "Jake" Jacobs. There wasn't enough time to switch seats. There was a moment of disappointment before Hogan said that he would swap positions at the first refueling. Swayze would fly left seat after all, with Hogan getting artillery clearances.

Captain Baker (Yellow One) led the flight from Tay Ninh West, with Hogan (Yellow Two) and Swayze in the number two ship.

After the short twenty minutes to the LZ, Captain Baker began his descent. On short final, it looked like it would be a cold extraction, but at 150 feet above ground level, Baker's crew chief, David Holt, keyed his intercom, "Taking fire!"

M60 machine guns began spewing lead from both sides of Cherry Buster. Door gunners and crew chiefs in the other Hueys followed suit; they were saturating the ground with hot lead.

High in a tree along the LZ's tree line, an NVA sniper adjusted his well-concealed body among the branches. He had his choice of targets. He selected the second Huey because it was at his eye level, about 170 feet above the ground; that would make for a straight shot. He took a deep breath and began slowly releasing the air from his lungs. When his lungs reached normal capacity, he stopped and held his breath. He adjusted his aim and started slowly squeezing the trigger. He knew the instant the 7.62mm bullet left the muzzle that it was a good shot. It was his last conscious thought before a Cobra's Minigun ventilated his body.

In Huey 772, aircraft commander Hogan and Peter-Pilot Swayze were taking care of business. Swayze was at the controls and Hogan was on the radio, when suddenly the Plexiglas® windshield shattered, sending shards of plastic flying inside the cockpit. Hogan caught bits of the plastic in his face. Thinking that he was hit, he reached for his face, but he suddenly realized that his bird was in a nose-down attitude—not a good attitude at 170 feet. Hogan looked to his peter-pilot and saw that Swayze was slumped over his cyclic stick with blood covering his face. Hogan grabbed his cyclic and tried to pull it back, but he was pulling against Swayze's weight. Quickly switching his right hand for his left on his cyclic, Hogan reached over with his right hand and grabbed Swayze by the back of his collar. He simultaneously pulled Swayze off his cyclic while he pulled back on his own. Huey 772 regained normal attitude.

Hogan immediately broke formation. He keyed his mic, and in a calm and professional "Houston, we have a problem" tone, transmitted to the flight:

"Yellow Two breaking left. Fire received from one o'clock...One-half click. My peter-pilot's been shot, and I think he's dead. Heading to Tay Ninh hospital."

Every pilot in the flight was on high alert. Roger Baker in Yellow One responded immediately:

"Roger that Yellow Two, got your co-pilot wounded, you're clear to break off for Tay Ninh."

Baker knew that a lone Huey returning to base

158

would be a tempting target for the enemy. A gunship escort should keep them safe. Without un-keying his mic, Baker continued:

"Yellow One to Tiger Two-Six, break off to flight and chase them back to Tay Ninh."

Then, it was on with the mission.

Back at Tay Ninh West, the men who were manning the Tactical Operations Center had been following the mission. All seemed routine until Hogan's radio call "...fire received" got their attention, but that was almost expected. "...peter-pilot's been shot" shocked everyone into a moment of suspended animation. "...and I think he's dead" sent a wave of disbelief throughout the room. Captain Fred Zacher was Operations Officer, and that radio call hit him especially hard. He knew that Hogan's peter-pilot was his hootch mate and friend. "...I *think* he's dead" meant there was some hope. Zacher continued with his duties following the action, and kept up the hope that his friend would arrive at Tay Ninh's hospital in time.

After breaking left, Hogan flew low level over the jungle canopy; it was best to stay just above the treetops so that any enemy lurking below the canopy would not see them coming until it was too late. Hogan glanced over at his co-pilot. It looked bad; blood was flowing from his mouth. Concerned about Swayze's ability to breathe, Hogan directed his crew chief and door gunner to pull the seat pins, tilt Swayze's seat back and try to clear his airway. Hogan radioed Tay Ninh Tower and asked that they notify the hospital of his pending arrival. He then concentrated on milking every last knot of forward air speed out of 772. The trip took about twenty of the longest minutes Hogan and his crew had ever experienced.

Word of Hogan's "co-pilot shot" radio call had made its way around the Charlie Company area. A group of concerned North Flaggers began congregating outside the hospital, awaiting the arrival of 772. Swayze was a new arrival at Charlie Company, and some had never met the new captain—the man who was to be their new XO. That didn't matter though, as he was a North Flagger.

Once inside the Tay Ninh perimeter, Hogan set the skids of 772 down on the 45th Surgical Hospital's helipad. Hospital medics were waiting, and they quickly extracted Swayze from the blood-soaked co-pilot's seat.

It looked bad.

Inside the hospital, the doctors assessed their patient; they could do nothing for Vietnam's latest casualty.

The doctor came out a few minutes later to inform Hogan and the concerned North Flaggers that Swayze hadn't made it. He told them that Swayze had been hit just above his left eye and that the massive head wound would have resulted in his immediate death.

Death in civilian life is a tragic and emotional event. Loved ones take the time to mourn their loss. They then eventually resume their lives. In combat, the men fighting side-by-side consider each other as brothers. To lose a brother in battle is also a tragic and emotional event, but there is little time to mourn. Life—and the war—must go on.

Hogan had to get 772 off the hospital helipad; more casualties could come in at any time. After the short hop to the maintenance area, Hogan and his crew examined their bird. The Plexiglas® windshield on the co-pilot's side had been shattered, but they found no bullet holes in the skin of 772. Just one bullet had penetrated 772.

In Vietnam, aviators feared the "Golden BB." A Golden BB was a single lucky shot that, against all odds, could hit its mark and kill a pilot or bring down a ship. The crew examining 772 couldn't help but think that Captain Swayze was the victim of a Golden BB.

Huey 772 required inspection and cleaning before being placed back in service. In the maintenance area, a crew led by SP-5 John Pecha set about their work. A group of Soldiers who were not assigned any missions that day gathered around 772. As the crew began their task, the onlookers stood in eerie silence. Pecha and his crew started to clean the bits of broken Plexiglas® scattered around the cockpit floor. They suddenly stopped as if they were having a moment of reverence. There, on the floor, was a pair of Army-issue Bausch + Lomb© aviator sunglasses. They were in perfect condition, except that the left lens was missing. Scattered among the bits of Plexiglas® were slivers of gray glass, remnants of the shattered lens.

David Hogan took possession of Swayze's sunglasses; he refused to allow them to be thrown away with the trash. He didn't know then, but those sunglasses with the left lens missing would become a memorial of sorts.

Captain Craig Thomas, the Battalion Surgeon, was not a North Flagger, but a part of Headquarters Company. His clinic and hootch were next to Charlie Company's area on the Tay Ninh Base, so it was natural that he got to know and socialized more with North Flaggers than with men of the battalion's other companies. The doctor was hurt and emotionally wounded when any of the battalion's men were killed. He had seen his share of death in Vietnam; it never got easier.

On the eve of 1970, Doctor Thomas made his way to the 45th Surgical Hospital's makeshift morgue to write his report on the death of Captain Gerald Clifford Swayze. His report was technical and did not include how much he had liked Jerry Swayze when they had met at the PHILCAG volleyball beer bust just a few weeks before. He didn't write about how painful it was to see such a promising life cut short. The doctor signed his report; the man then bid a final farewell to his friend and left the morgue. Sadly, it would not be the last time that Doctor Thomas would have to visit friends at the Tay Ninh morgue.

A missing-man fly-by was arranged in honor of Captain Gerald Swayze, and a formal memorial service was conducted by the Battalion Chaplin in Charlie Company's mess hall. A less formal memorial was organized by Jerry's fellow North Flaggers.

As flights and individual Hueys returned to base on 30 December, the crews learned of Captain Swayze's death. The story of the Golden BB striking 772's co-pilot spread quickly. Days later, when the officers of Charlie Company entered their O-Club, they saw a pair of Bausch + Lomb© aviator sunglasses with the left lens missing, sitting reverently on a shelf behind the bar. Those sunglasses would remain there as a symbol of all the North Flaggers lost in Vietnam. Many a beer—and a few soft drinks—were hoisted in salute to the memory of Jerry Swayze and the other North Flaggers whose lives were cut short.

Charlie Company's XO, Captain Bill Lorimer, became CO in February of 1970. Captain Roger Baker became the XO, the position that would have gone to Jerry Swayze had he not died from a Golden BB while sitting in the co-pilot's seat of Huey 772.

Exactly seventy days after Swayze's death, Captain Lorimer was killed by a Golden BB while piloting Huey 772 from the co-pilot's seat[12].

The irony was not lost on the North Flaggers.

---

[12] The death of William Lorimer IV is covered in detail in the book *Fixin' to Die Rag* by Roy Mark. *Fixin' to Die Rag* is available on amazon.com and other online bookstores in print and eBook format. ISBN-13: 978-1484135105

13

First Team

Republic of Vietnam
March 1970

Newly minted Warrant Officers Ozzie Daniels and Phil Seefeld left the United States for Vietnam on 2 March 1970, and they were followed two weeks later by Warrant Officer (WO1) Sterling Cody.

Daniels and Seefeld's chartered flight landed at Bien Hoa Air Force Base just northeast of Saigon on 3 March.

The troops, a mixture of all branches—enlisted and officers, privates to lieutenant colonels—filed off the jet onto the tarmac. March and April are the hottest months in South Vietnam, and the heat radiating off the tarmac hit the troops immediately. Planes taking off and landing; helicopters flying overhead; buses, trucks, and jeeps scurrying about—all presented a confused visual image to most of the troops.

Daniels and Seefeld, along with the other new arrivals, were directed onto waiting buses. The buses were standard Army buses, except for the chicken wire that had been stretched across all of the windows. The purpose of the chicken wire was apparent to Daniels and most others, but one clueless individual seated near Daniels had to ask. When told that the chicken wire was to prevent a VC or a VC sympathizer from riding alongside the bus on a motorcycle and flipping a hand grenade into the bus, the inquisitive trooper's face showed signs of a man coming to grips with his mortality. The new arrivals realized that they were not necessarily being welcomed to Vietnam as conquering heroes or liberators.

The buses drove the new arrivals southeast out of Bien Hoa for about five miles to Long Binh, where Daniels and Seefeld reported in at the Army's 90th Replacement Battalion. At Long Binh, all of the new arrivals endured the seemingly never-ending processing and were issued new jungle fatigues, canvas-topped jungle boots and olive drab skivvies.

After a couple of days at Long Binh, Daniels and Seefeld were given orders to report to the First Cavalry Division's First Team Academy at Bien Hoa Army Base. Again, they boarded a bus; again, the bus had chicken wire stretched across the open windows. Their bus pulled into the Bien Hoa Army Base after a short 15-minute trip.

Bien Hoa Army Base was the First Cav's rear headquarters and home to the "First Team Academy." All new guys were required to attend the First Team Academy's in-country orientation. The course repeated much of what the men had learned in previous courses, but the Army felt that a refresher could save lives, and it also allowed new troopers to become acclimated to the tropical heat.

With their new jungle fatigues, the new arrivals now wore the same uniform as in-country vets, but the shine on their non-faded fatigues advertised their new guy status like a neon sign. And the old guys didn't seem to miss an opportunity to have a little fun at the new guys' expense.

"Hey Smitty, give your .38 to the FNG. He might as well just shoot himself now and get it over with."

There was no respect for rank; time in-country—as every new guy soon learned—was the only rank in "the Nam."

A sergeant might taunt a warrant officer with, "Hey new guy, I'm short. Forty-three days and a wake-up."

Daniels and Seefeld soon learned to ignore the snickers, sneers, and taunts, and to their detriment, they would soon regret taking everything said by anyone in faded dungarees with a grain of salt.

After a couple of days of First Team Academy, Daniels noticed that the instructors weren't taking a roll call, and since he'd been through the same course twice before, he decided to bug out. Daniels decided to check out the Air Force base on the opposite side of Bien Hoa. He'd heard that Air Force pilots would sometimes take Huey pilots on bombing runs and that Huey pilots would occasionally take jet jockeys on low-level flights. Daniels had dreamed of attending the Air Force Academy and of flying Air Force jets. Now, he had a chance to make a bombing run in an Air Force Jet, albeit only as a passenger.

Daniels knew that if there was anyone who could talk his way into an Air Force cockpit, it was he. At the

Air Force base, armed with brass balls and a silver tongue, Daniels approached a captain who looked like he was prepping for a mission.

Daniels greeted his senior officer with a casual "Good morning Captain; how's it going?"

The captain seemed friendly enough, so Daniels put his gift of the gab to work and soon had a seat reserved in the captain's A-37 Dragonfly.

The captain summoned an old, gray-haired Master Sergeant and instructed him to run the Army WO1 through the ejection seat procedure. The Captain then ran some of the Dragonfly's capabilities past Daniels.

The Dragonfly cruises at 489 miles per hour and has a top speed of 507, enough to jumpstart the adrenaline of any Huey pilot. Daniels asked about the plane's service ceiling and rate of climb and felt like a kid waiting on a roller coaster ride, when the captain said, "She'll climb at 6,990 feet per minute to 41,765 feet. But we won't get that high this morning."

That'll do, Daniels thought, as he and the captain climbed into the cockpit.

Front view of a Cessna A-37B "Dragonfly"
Lackland Air Force Base, San Antonio, Texas (March 2007)
Photo by Peter Rimar

In a pre-flight briefing, the pilot said, "Put your oxygen mask on Mister Daniels, it's S.O.P. (standard operating procedure) to wear it from start up to shut down."

As another A-37 joined them on the taxiway, the captain said, "That's my wingman, we'll be a two-ship mission this morning."

It was hot in the cockpit as they taxied to the active runway. The A-37's cockpit was not air conditioned, but Daniels knew that it would cool off at altitude[13].

After he was cleared for takeoff, the pilot gave the Dragonfly full power; Daniels grinned in anticipation. He was not disappointed; the climb out was like nothing he had ever felt. In a few minutes, they were cruising at eighteen thousand feet. A short time later, they were over the central highlands north of Bien Hoa and near their target. Daniels looked down and scanned the countryside. He saw nothing out of the ordinary other

---

[13] Temperature decreases by 5.38°F every 1,000 feet of altitude.

than a Forward Air Control Cessna O-2 Skymaster that was circling below. He looked for a bunker complex, but he could see nothing below the thick canopy. Suddenly, the FAC fired a 2.75-inch Willie Pete (White Phosphorus) rocket, and a plume of white smoke began rising from the trees.

A U.S. Air Force Cessna O-2A-CE Super Skymaster (s/n 67-21407) in flight
USAF - U.S. Air Force 315th Airlift Wing photo
060511-F-7779T-007

The captain pointed to the smoke and said, "There's our target Mister Daniels, here we go."

With nothing more than "here we go" as a warning, the pilot put the A-37 into a sixty-degree dive. The excitement that Ozzie Daniels felt was indescribable. He had dreamed of being an Air Force pilot since he was a freshman in high school. Now, he was actually in an Air Force jet, in a war zone, diving on an enemy bunker complex and seconds away from dropping five hundred pounds of high explosives on the bad guys. The dive was more thrilling than any amusement ride—anywhere!

After the bomb was released, Daniels suddenly felt a thousand pounds pushing down on his body as the A-37 pulled out of the dive and forced six Gs on its occupants.

Darkness began to invade his peripheral vision and threatened to turn his lights completely out. He held his breath and strained with all his might just to maintain a tunnel of vision and to remain conscious.

When the A-37 leveled off at altitude and the G-force returned to normal, Daniels took his first breath since pulling out of the dive. He had just experienced the power of gravity multiplied by about six times. Daniels was young and robust, but six times his 160 pounds meant that he'd just felt like a 960 pound man. It was excruciating.

"You OK Mister Daniels?"

"I'm fine sir," Daniels lied.

"Good, cause here we go again."

The second bomb run reminded Daniels of the rollercoaster rides he'd enjoyed as a kid, but the thrill was beginning to fade as he strained to overcome the G-force pushing the blood away from his brain. It's hard to have fun when your primary concern is remaining conscious.

By the third bomb run, Daniels began to fight against another sensation—nausea.

The feeling of nausea began slowly and then intensified rapidly. By the fourth dive, Daniels was struggling to keep his breakfast down and weighing his options should nausea win the battle. There was no airsick bag in the seatback pocket, and besides, he was wearing an oxygen mask. The only options were to puke into his mask, onto the kind captain's cockpit floor, or somehow keep it down. He would soon be faced with a fourth option.

"That was our last bomb, Mister Daniels."

"Oh, OK, sir," was all Daniels could stammer.

Just when the green WO1—"green" as in green around the gills—thought that the worst was over, the captain said, "What say we make a strafing run with the 7.62mm Minigun?"

The A-37 pilot made it clear that he wasn't asking for Daniels' permission to make the run when he nosed down into another dive. By then, Daniels was in sensory overload and oblivious to the outside world. During the strafing run, Daniels' focus was to stay conscious and not to upchuck his breakfast throughout the cockpit; the minigun action was of secondary importance.

After the climb out from the strafing run, the pilot pointed the A-37 toward Bien Hoa Air Base. The cold air from the jet's ventilation system bathing his face seemed to soothe Daniels' stomach somewhat; he might just get through this mission after all.

On the short hop back to Bien Hoa, the wingman came alongside, almost wing tip to wing tip. He then dropped down and began a 360° slow-roll inspection of the warbird. The captain explained to Daniels that jettisoning the bombs at low level made the aircraft vulnerable not only to small-arms fire but also to shrapnel from their bombs. Their wingman was looking closely for any bullet holes or shrapnel damage. When the wingman reported no damage, the captain took Daniels on a close tour of the wingman's fuselage. With no damage observed on either bird, they continued to Bien Hoa Air Force Base.

As they approached Bien Hoa, the pilot reduced

power and began his descent. The reduction in altitude resulted in an elevation of the temperature within the cockpit. Beads of sweat began forming on Daniels' brow, and the urge to void his stomach intensified.

When the A-37 touched down at Bien Hoa, Daniels was more anxious to exit the Dragonfly than he had been to begin his adventure an hour earlier. His heart sank and his stomach churned when the captain said that he would taxi to the re-arm point first.

The captain's "It won't take long" was of little comfort.

As they taxied to the re-arm point, the pilot opened the canopy and explained that it would be a "hot" re-arm and that the guys loading the ordnance would need to see their hands at all times.

"They need to see our hands on the windscreen; there's no way we can accidently set one off with our hands on the windshield. If you take your hands down, you'll see those guys diving for cover. Place both your hands on the top of the windshield and don't take them off until I say so. "

Daniels complied, but his nausea threatened to override the captain's order. Uncontrollable retching engulfed his body, and his instinct was to remove his oxygen mask so that he could expel his stomach's contents.

"Don't you throw up in that oxygen mask!"

It was a forceful command and unmistakably not one to be taken lightly.

Daniels' retching continued, and the captain continued with his mandate, "Don't you dare throw up in my oxygen mask!"

The retching intensified, and Daniels knew that there was no keeping it down; oxygen mask or not, he was about to puke.

The captain sensed Daniels' need to remove his mask and yelled, "Don't you take your hands down. Don't you throw up in that oxygen mask. Don't you take your hands down."

When the inevitable vomiting began, Daniels had no choice but to firmly lock his jaws to keep from filling his mask. His cheeks puffed as his mouth filled with vomit. With no other alternative, he then swallowed his vomit, only to have it come up again. The cycle of vomiting and swallowing was repeated several times while the crew finished reloading the Dragonfly.

Daniels had boldly climbed into the A-37 earlier that morning as a confident, cocksure Huey pilot. An hour later, he meekly climbed out of the cockpit timid and weak, unsure of what to say to the Air Force captain who had been so kind.

WO1 Ozzie Daniels thanked the captain and apologized for his weak stomach.

"Don't worry about it Mister Daniels. I know some great pilots that reacted the same way on their first flight."

With a salute that wasn't quite as snappy as when they first met, Daniels bid his leave.

As he walked away from the A-37 Dragonfly, Daniels realized that he was physically weak and totally exhausted. He felt as if he'd strained every muscle of his being to overcome the G-force. The nausea and retching had weakened him further.

What a way to begin my tour, Daniels thought, as he walked back to the First Team Academy.

Warrant Officers Ozzie Daniels and Phil Seefeld finished the First Team Academy's in-country orientation course on 11 March 1970. They had learned—again—about local traditions and customs, about the pitfalls of walking down a trail and driving over a patch of fresh asphalt, and where to look for boobie traps and tripwires. Daniels had also learned a valuable lesson in the cockpit of an A-37 Dragonfly, where he had learned to endure the unendurable.

Daniels and Seefeld were ordered to report to the 11th Combat Aviation Group (11th CAG) at Phuoc Vinh, about fifteen minutes flying time to the north of Bien Hoa.

The 11th CAG was the largest aviation organization within the 1st Cavalry Division. It was made up of an assault support helicopter battalion of twin-rotor Chinooks, and two assault helicopter battalions.

Both of the assault helicopter battalions—the 227th and the 229th—were made up of three lift companies and one attack helicopter company. The attack helicopter companies flew Cobra attack helicopters, and the lift companies flew H-model Hueys.

Huey pilots Daniels and Seefeld arrived at Phuoc Vinh mid-afternoon and were quickly processed and assigned to the 229th Assault Helicopter Battalion at Tay Ninh West, the Army's camp a few miles west of Tay Ninh City.

The Army Base at Tay Ninh was in War Zone C, the hottest part of Vietnam and the Area of Operation for the 1st Brigade of the 1st Cavalry Division. The 1st Brigade was making daily contact with the enemy along the Cambodian border and deep in Tay Ninh Province. Daniels and Seefeld would join the 229th Assault Helicopter Battalion flying support missions for a very busy infantry brigade.

Daniels and Seefeld, along with three other new Huey pilots, were directed to the Phuoc Vinh Airfield to catch a ride on a Huey to Tay Ninh. As they waited, the boom of outgoing artillery rounds made it clear that they were much closer to the enemy than they had been at Bien Hoa. Waiting for their ride, the new Huey pilots talked among themselves, speculating about what it would be like flying in this war zone. They were confident to their core in their flying skills and projected outward confidence in their bravery and tenacity.

Finally, a Huey touched down, and a crew chief motioned the five newbies aboard. They threw their stuffed duffle bags aboard and climbed into the Huey. The seats had been folded up and the seatbelts stored, so that they wouldn't entangle troopers getting in or out in a hurry. The new Huey pilots, having spent many hours in the pilot's seat, now sat cross-legged and unsecured on the floor. The passengers' shiny new jungle fatigues branded them unmistakably as FNGs. They had yet to see any action, and not having received incoming fire, they were considered "cherries" by the veteran crew.

The Huey lifted off and left the perimeter of the

Phuoc Vinh Airfield, and headed west into the sun. The new guys sat uncomfortably on the floor, trying unsuccessfully to appear confident and experienced. Daniels noticed the pilots and crew talking back and forth on the Huey's intercom. One would look at a newbie with a mischievous grin and speak into his mic, and the crew would then laugh in unison. He tried ignoring the taunts; he'd been the butt of derisive comments since arriving in-country and didn't want to give them the satisfaction. Daniels was sitting casually in the doorway with his feet resting on the skid, but his facade of experience was not fooling the Huey crew. He was taking in the scenery and enjoying the wind on his face when he noticed the pilot glance at him with a devious grin.

Suddenly, the pilot banked sharply to the right; Daniels panicked and thrust himself safely back into the Huey. He'd never been scared in an aircraft before; he'd been sick in the Dragonfly, but never scared. The fear of falling out of a Huey at three thousand feet was a first. The crew broke out into uncontrollable laughter. The FNGs couldn't hear the laughter over the engine noise, but the crew was plainly howling at Daniels' expense. Seefeld and the other new pilots smiled in sympathy. It may have been a "better you than me" smile, but regardless, it made Daniels feel a little better.

Daniels began watching a mountain that dominated the skyline in the distance. The mountain was South Vietnam's famous *Nui Ba Den.*

There were many myths among the local people about *Nui Ba Den.* According to one, a lovely young virgin and her handsome lover had been separated when the young man left to fight in a war. While her suitor was away, the maiden was forced to marry a powerful older man in her village. Desperate to maintain her virginity for her lover, she committed suicide by jumping from the mountain's edge. Out of respect for the girl's virtue, the people had built a temple at the top of that mountain. That mountain—*Nui Ba Den*—is therefore known as Black Virgin Mountain by the Vietnamese.

As the Huey got closer to the mountain, Daniels surveyed the almost perfectly shaped extinct volcano that appeared to be as high as the altitude at which they were flying. In fact, the extinct volcano was 3,268 feet high and stood taller than the passing Huey. An array of communication antenna adorned the summit, as a testament to the military significance of Black Virgin Mountain.

Nui Ba Den, Black Virgin Mountain, aerial view, 1971
Photo by and courtesy of Dwight Burdette

As the Huey flew past *Nui Ba Den*, the door gunner suddenly opened fire with his M60 machine gun into the rocky, jungle-covered slopes of the mountain. The new guys couldn't tell if they were taking fire over the engine noise, and the crew—on their intercom—weren't keeping their passengers in the loop. Daniels thought he saw an ever so slight grin on the door gunner's face.

When will these guys stop pulling our chain? Daniels thought that their little jokes were getting old.

Hueys often did take ground-to-air fire from the

slopes of *Nui Ba Den*.

Before the Americans entered the war, *Nui Ba Den* was occupied by the French during the colonial period, the Japanese during World War II, the Viet Minh during the first Indochina War, and then the Viet Cong. Then, in May of 1964, U.S. Special Forces captured the summit in a helicopter assault. They immediately began setting up radio-relay equipment on the peak, and by May of 1968, the camp included twenty defensive bunkers that circled the summit. Within the perimeter of the Army's two-acre site were officers and enlisted hootches. A helipad was built to supply the camp, along with a mess hall, latrines, and showers. They even had a club for the officers and enlisted men. Most importantly, however, among the array of bunkers and buildings was the pagoda. The pagoda was not what it seemed. Within the pagoda's sturdy stone walls, high-level and top-secret communications and intelligence gatherings took place. Not all of the men working on *Nui Ba Den* were Soldiers; a few were civilians and were presumed to be CIA operatives. The camp on the summit of Black Virgin Mountain was a vital and sensitive operation that was to be protected at all cost.

As the Huey was passing *Nui Ba Den* and descending toward Tay Ninh, the mountain's history was not known to the new Huey pilots. They would eventually learn that the U.S. owned the camp at the summit, but that the VC and NVA controlled the slopes and foothills. In fact, just a couple of years earlier, the enemy almost owned the entire mountain.

* * *

On the night of 13 May 1968, radio operators at Tay Ninh received an urgent request from *Nui Ba Den* for artillery fire. Before Tay Ninh could respond, the radio went silent. The camp on *Nui Ba Den* was being attacked by enemy forces. RPGs and 82mm mortars began pounding the compound. The radio antenna at *Nui Ba Den* had been destroyed by RPGs or satchel charges. Fires on the summit of *Nui Ba Den* could be seen, and explosions could be heard from Tay Ninh.

On *Nui Ba Den*, Soldiers manning the bunkers opened fire on VC soldiers who had already infiltrated the bunker perimeter. One element of the enemy force destroyed one bunker almost immediately and moved to the heliport, where they set up a command post with radios and a mortar team. A smaller element captured the bunkers around the helipad. After numerous firefights, the enemy began moving uphill toward the pagoda. Along the way, they destroyed the camp's generator and placed satchel charges in the operations building and in the officer's quarters.

The personnel manning the inside of the pagoda went on lockdown to protect the top-secret equipment and information in their charge. The enemy was unable to penetrate the sturdy pagoda, but they destroyed the extensive array of antennas on the roof.

American reinforcements arrived at about midnight. A Light Fire Team and gunship arrived under heavy anti-aircraft fire from the slopes and foothills. The fighting was over by 0230 hours.

Before withdrawing, the VC had roamed the camp, shooting wounded Americans and setting boobie traps on dead Americans and on their own dead.

Fog and rain engulfed the summit in the early morning hours of 14 May, hampering the medivac of the wounded.

When the fighting was over, American forces held the summit. The cost that they paid for those two acres was high. Of the 140 Americans, 24 were dead, 35 were wounded and 2 were missing in action. The casualty rate of over 42 percent was horrific. By comparison, Marine losses at Iwo Jima during WW-II amounted to 36 percent.

* * *

The sun was almost on the horizon when the new Huey pilots landed at Tay Ninh West Airfield. The base was not only the home of a U.S. Air Force Squadron, but it was also home to elements of the 1st Cavalry Division, the 25th Infantry Division, the 45th Surgical Hospital, an Army of the Republic of Vietnam Airborn Division, and the 1st Philippines Civic Action Group. Tay Ninh West was vast, busy, and important to the U.S. military's efforts in South Vietnam. The base at Tay Ninh was about three miles west of Tay Ninh City and just seven and a half miles from the border that protected NVA sanctuaries inside Cambodia.

The new Huey pilots were welcomed to the battalion and the 1st Cavalry Division by the Battalion Command Sergeant Major (CSM). After a clerk had finished typing from Daniels and Seefeld's written orders, the CSM told them that they were assigned to 229th Assault Helicopter Battalion's Charlie Company, located across the runway. The CSM then told the guys that it was too late for transportation to the other side of the base, so they would have to spend the night at headquarters and that he'd arrange for transportation the next morning. The CSM directed a corporal to escort the warrant officers to the visiting officers' hootch.

The visiting officers' hootch was not fancy. It was a rectangular wooden structure with half weatherboard walls. The upper part of the wall was enclosed with a wire screen. The only air conditioning was what nature provided. The structure itself offered no protection from rockets, mortars or even small-arms fire, so a blast shield had been built around the exterior. The blast shield consisted of old fifty-five gallon drums filled with sand. The drums, which stood about three-feet high, had wooden crates—also filled with sand—stacked on top and then sandbags stacked on the crates so that the shield stood about five feet tall.

At the visiting officers' hootch, the corporal said that they could take any bunk. As the corporal turned to leave, he said, "Oh, there'll probably be a rocket or mortar attack tonight to welcome you guys."

Yea, right! And give me a .38 so I can shoot myself and get it over with. When will they stop pulling our chains?

The new guys didn't bother acknowledging the corporal's warning; they'd been the butt of FNG jokes and hazing since their arrival in-country.

Better to not encourage that kind of shit, Daniels thought.

A captain emerged from a connecting room and introduced himself as Captain Hoskinson. Charles Hoskinson was on his second tour in Vietnam and was the battalion personnel officer. He told the guys that he'd cut the floor boards away and built a bunker next to his bunk, and he said that they were welcome to use it if needed.

It had been a long day, and the guys were whipped. When they hit the rack, rocket attacks and concealed bunkers were far from their minds.

The shock wave from the first mortar that struck just outside the hootch's blast shield knocked Daniels out of a sound sleep and onto the floor. Consciousness, comprehension, and reaction came quickly; he was on his feet and in a footrace with four comrades to Captain Hoskinson's bunker.

Five warrant officers, clad only in their skivvies, dove into Captain Hoskinson's bunker, landing atop their host. The captain and the young warrant officers wiggled and squirmed to fit six bodies into a space where rightfully only four should fit. When it seemed that the attack was over, they untangled their bodies and climbed out of the bunker.

Captain Hoskinson explained to the new guys how to distinguish between the sound of mortars and rockets. The captain said that the attack had been concentrated in the area of the officer's hootches. He then explained that VC sympathizers had probably alerted the NVA of the arrival of new pilots.

The realization that the midnight mortars were in their honor personalized the war for Daniels and Seefeld; they would not forget.

14

Dinky Dau

Republic of Vietnam
March 1970

Two weeks after Ozzie Daniels and Phil Seefeld landed in Vietnam, Warrant Officer (WO1) Sterling Cody boarded a chartered Pan Am jet at McGuire Air Force Base in New Jersey.

Pan Am's Boeing 707, with its four engines and distinctive Blue Globe Logo—the Blue Meat Ball—on the tail, was waiting on the tarmac when Cody arrived at McGuire. After checking in, Cody and a couple of hundred other Soldiers boarded the jet for the beginning of their odyssey. Their destination was Saigon, Republic of Vietnam. For some, it would be a one-way flight.

In 1964, when Vietnam first entered the public consciousness, many people had to consult a map to get a fix on just where that country with the strange-sounding name was. There was no consensus among politicians and news broadcasters on how to pronounce "Vietnam." By 1970, however, with the war dominating print and broadcast news for six years, it was easy to assume that everyone knew at least the basic history and geography of the country.

On the cross-country flight to Travis Air Force Base, WO1 Cody sat next to a clueless private.

After exchanging a few pleasantries, the private asked, "Sir, what part of Korea is Saigon in?"

With a deadpan expression, Cody replied, "South Central."

After refueling at Travis, the 707 flew across the Pacific, with fueling stops at Hawaii and Guam. Finally, the 707 touched down at Tan Son Nhut Air Base just outside of Saigon.

Cody endured the routine of thousands of other Soldiers before him during the endless in-country processing and the First Team Academy. Unlike many others, however, he took it all in his stride. Cody was ready for anything this war could dish out. He was the boy, after all, who had strapped wings onto his arms and "flown" off the roof of a chicken coop. He was the boy who had once fondled the boney feet of an old dead guy inside of a dark tomb. There was no way a little war was going to throw Sterling Cody off his game.

WO1 Cody arrived at Tay Ninh on 17 March 1970 and was assigned to Charlie Company, 229th Assault Helicopter Battalion. At Tay Ninh, he met his old friends Ozzie Daniels, Phil Seefeld, and several others who he had trained with at Fort Polk and were in his flight class at Fort Wolters. Those guys had gone on to Fort Rucker, while Cody had been sent to Hunter Army Airfield in Savannah, Georgia. He hadn't seen them for several months; it was a class reunion of sorts.

Charlie Company had been desperate for more pilots

when Daniels, Seefeld, Cody and a handful of other new WO pilots arrived in March 1970. It was standard practice that they fly an in-country check ride with the company instructor pilots before being cut loose on the enemy. So desperate was the company that many of the new pilots' "check ride" was as a peter-pilot on a combat mission.

Cody went about his business of flying as co-pilot in the war zone; he was a fast learner and was all business in the cockpit. The ACs—the pilots in command—who Cody flew with took notice of his proficiency and his calm demeanor under fire.

Around the base, Cody kept a low profile. Even so, his dry wit, endearing personality, and his humorous disdain of the hippy, flower power movement back home, made him well liked by his peers. Cody's attitude of kill'em-all-and-let-God-sort'em-out was the polar opposite of the peacenik hippy philosophy, so the other pilots would sometimes playfully refer to him as "the Flower Child."

Cody and the other new pilots settled into a very busy routine. Reveille was before daylight, and it was followed by long days of flying. When all of the ships returned to base, the company commander usually held a meeting to debrief his pilots. The pilots would gather at the O-Club, and Captain Baker would review each mission, looking for ways to improve operations and safety. After the meetings, the pilots would usually order a few rounds of beer to unwind from the stresses of the day.

Charlie Company was supporting the 1st Battalion of

the 7th Cavalry Regiment (1/7). The 7th Cav was made famous in 1876 by General George Armstrong Custer's defeat in Montana at the Little Big Horn. In 1970, the 7th Cav was operating in the Dog's Head area of III Corps and along the Cambodian Border (see map on page 201). It was a hard, physical, sometimes frustrating, and emotionally draining job for the pilots of Charlie Company, 229th Assault Aviation Battalion. The days were long and hot. When the enemy wanted to be seen, it seemed that they were everywhere; when they wanted to be unseen, it seemed that they were nowhere to be seen.

It was demoralizing for the pilots to know that the VC and NVA could cross into Cambodia and enjoy the immunity that Washington's rules of engagement provided. Most, if not all, of Charlie Company's pilots felt that their leaders in Washington had no clue; this was no way to fight a war.

On 30 April 1970, Sterling Cody was in his hootch shooting the shit with other pilots when their hootch maid announced, "Tomollow, you go Cambodia."

"No, No," Cody and the others protested.

Using the Vietnamese term for "crazy," the pilots admonished their maid with, "You're *dinky dau*. You know it's forbidden for us to cross into Cambodia."

It was not just Cody's hootch maid, but other pilots too who were hearing, "You go Cambodia tomollow!"

The United States' "secret" plan to invade Cambodia was not as secret as the Army thought it to be.

Dinky Dau!

It was music to the ears of many when word came

down that they would be flying into Cambodia. About 52,000 Americans had already died in South Vietnam, and in many cases, the enemy had fled to the safety of Cambodia after attacking U.S. firebases. Inside Cambodia, the enemy could relax and plan their next raid into South Vietnam, protected by the rules laid down by Washington. Inside Cambodia, the NVA would then replenish their supply of ammo, rifles, grenades, and medical supplies from vast stores of war matériel brought down from the north.

U.S. Intelligence was aware that the North Vietnamese were transporting large quantities of supplies south down the Ho Chi Minh Trail. The trail was actually a network that was comprised of the quintessential jungle trail and modern, paved roads. The roads stretched from North Vietnam into Laos and south through Cambodia. South of the DMZ separating the two warring countries, the Ho Chi Minh Trail had many offshoots that went east into South Vietnam. The Air Force had been bombing the trail since hostilities began, but the quantity of matériel flowing south seemed to increase in proportion to the number of bombs that were dropped. With an estimated forty thousand NVA and VC ensconced in the border region of Cambodia, President Nixon decided that it was time to take action. Most U.S. troops and their commanders thought that it was past time.

Charlie Company supported the Cambodian Incursion with troop insertions, extractions, and "log" or resupply missions. Most of their missions were in support of the 1st and the 5th Battalions of the 7th

Cavalry Regiment (1/7 and 5/7).

The VC and NVA fought back as if their lives depended on it, which it did. Charlie Company pilots also flew command and control (C&C) missions, which involved ferrying commanding officers of the infantry and engineer units around the battlefield. The Soldiers of Charlie Company had been working long, hard hours before entering Cambodia, and the invasion began taxing the men to their limits. Nevertheless, there were no complaints; it was payback time, and it was long overdue.

When Cody arrived at Charlie Company, he was given the option of a .38 caliber revolver or a .45-caliber semi-automatic pistol as his sidearm. Cody chose the .45; he felt that the Colt-45 had more stopping power than the .38 and that it was more of a "man's weapon."

Many pilots felt that they needed a little something extra in case they were forced down and had to abandon their bird in hostile territory. Cody got his hands on a sawed-off M1 Carbine. The .30 caliber M1 Garand that won WW-II was a hell of a weapon, but it was too heavy and too long, and unwieldy in the cockpit. The M1 Carbine, which was six-and-a-half pounds lighter and eight inches shorter than its longer cousin, was a little better, but it was still too long for the cockpit. Cody's Carbine was modified so that it was ideal for the confines of the cockpit by sawing off the barrel and part of the stock. The result was a rather long, semi-automatic pistol with rifle characteristics. Cody taped two thirty-round magazines back-to-back for a little extra oomph.

On the fourth day of the Cambodian Incursion, Cody spent most of the day in the Dog's Head supporting ARVN troops. He got back to base at Tay Ninh early and decided to test fire his new M1 Carbine. As Cody was walking to the firing range, he came upon his CO, Captain Roger Baker.

Baker asked if he'd heard the news.

"No," replied Cody, "The war's over?"

With a smile, Baker replied, "No, you're an Aircraft Commander now, so be ready tomorrow morning." Cody had noticed that some of the more experienced ACs had finished their tours and returned to the world, but he wasn't expecting this. Like always, he took the news in his stride.

To say that Cody was elevated to AC prematurely because of the company's shortage of ACs would be misleading. A co-pilot became an AC only with the consent of the other ACs. They worked as a team and their mission—indeed, their lives—depended on each other. It was only after a vote by the ACs that Captain Baker became confident that Cody was up to the challenge.

Just as at Fort Wolters, where WOC Cody became the first to solo, here again, WO1 Cody was the first among the new arrivals at C/229th to be elevated to the position of Aircraft Commander.

As a new AC, Cody needed a personal radio call sign. It was the custom within Charlie Company for a new AC to be given his call sign by other Aircraft Commanders. With little debate, Cody's radio call sign became "Flower Child." It was soon shortened to "Flower."

The torrid pace of combat assaults and resupply missions (log missions) seemed never ending during the first days of the Cambodian Incursion. On the morning of 4 May, the fourth day of their foray into Cambodia, a corporal woke up Sterling Cody at 0500 hours. The "after-meeting meeting" of the night before had adjourned in the O-Club only four hours earlier, so it was difficult for the teenaged pilot to clear away the cobwebs.

Cody spent much of the day "logging"—flying log missions—for 1/7 units in the Dog's Head and inside Cambodia. Late in the afternoon—early evening actually—with darkness approaching, Cody returned to 1/7's base at Fire Support Base (FSB), Illingworth (see map on page 201). A sergeant came up to Cody and said that the battalion commander's helicopter—an OH-6A—was down for maintenance, and asked if Cody could fly a C&C mission for the colonel.

"Sure," Cody said.

He didn't have much fuel at the time, but with not more than an hour of daylight remaining, he figured that it would not be a problem. After a short wait, Lieutenant Colonel (LTC) Everett "Moose" Yon[14] and a major—the battalion operations officer—climbed aboard Cody's Huey. Yon took the jump seat that was in between and just behind the pilots; the major sat on the floor in the back. Colonel Yon plugged his headset into the Huey's comm system and explained to Cody that he needed to do a "Last Light" check on three of his companies that

[14] Everett Marion Yon Jr. (6 July 1934–20 May 1993) graduated from the United States Military Academy at West Point in 1956.

were setting in for nighttime defense. Yon and his operations officer—the battalion S-3—needed to know exactly where the units would be during the night so that they could set artillery and gun target lines.

Cody—call sign "Flower"—lifted off and within five minutes, was back inside Cambodia. Two Cobra Gunships, flown by CWO James Ware—call sign "Top Cat"—and his wingman provided cover from above. Cody approached the first company's position and dialed their frequency into his FM radio. By watching the glide path indicator needle, he homed in on their position. With a reliable fix on their position, Yon and his S-3 looked for landmarks that could be used as checkpoints for artillery. If their infantry company were attacked after dark, Yon's artillery would have a target line and be able to shift their fire from that known point to the attacking enemy.

Satisfied that the first company was secure for the night, Yon directed Cody west toward the second 1/7 company. Cody dialed the company's frequency into his FM radio, and LTC Yon established radio contact. Cody began homing in on the signal. As Yon and his S-3 were marking the company's location on their map, the company commander radioed Colonel Yon.

"Sir, we can hear gasoline engines a couple hundred meters south of our current position. We're in an abandoned motor pool; there isn't much left here."

Yon "rogered" the transmission and said that he'd take a look. Cody could see the motor pool, so he adjusted his heading to intersect where the company commander was hearing the noise. Cody and his peter-pilot had the best seats in the house for observation. Yon could see quite far straight ahead, but from his position in the jump seat, he couldn't see down.

The terrain was rocky with some tall trees, especially along a gravel, east-west road. Movement on the road below caught Cody's eye. It was a tank...no...two tanks. Wait, it was a convoy of tanks and troop-carrying trucks. They were heading east and rapidly approaching the position of the dismounted infantry company.

Cody keyed the intercom, "Sir, do we have any armor up here?"

Yon replied with an incredulous "No."

"Well Sir, there're tanks coming down that road."

Apparently surprised, Yon leaned forward—almost standing—so that he could see from Cody's perspective.

Clearly excited, Yon said, "Hell, those are Russian tanks; those are T-34s. Those aren't ours! Let's go down and take a look."

Yeah right, that's just what I wanna do, Cody thought but answered "Yes Sir," as he nosed down to have a look. Cody banked left and began a descent so that he could fly parallel with the road and give his door gunner a good shot at the troops on the trucks. The enemy immediately opened fire with .51 caliber anti-aircraft fire and 7.62mm small-arms fire. The lone Huey must have been a tempting target for the NVA gunners, and they were intent on taking it out.

With things getting interesting, Cody switched his radio to the emergency guard frequency[15]. He figured

[15] Guard frequencies are 243.0 MHz UHF and 121.5 MHz VHF and are reserved for aircraft in distress. All aircraft and ground stations monitored guard 24/7.

that if he was shot down, he wanted to be quick to call for help on guard.

Might as well let everyone in the area know about this, Cody thought, so he keyed his mic and said, "We've got enemy armor in the open. They're moving west to east on the road," and he gave the coordinates (see map on Page 201). Cody knew that such a tempting target would get immediate attention. The convoy was on an east-west gravel road lined with one hundred foot tall trees. The trees and the rocky terrain restricted the convoy to the gravel road.

LTC Yon and the Major moved to the right side of the Huey to observe the convoy. Cody descended so that he would pass the convoy head on and to the left; that would give the 1/7 Commander the best view.

When Cody leveled off at one hundred feet above the treetops, the enemy fire from the convoy intensified. AK-47 tracer rounds glowed green as they went by the Huey, and the .51 caliber tracers glowed orange. The .51 caliber projectiles were roughly the size of standard AA flashlight batteries, but the light from the magnesium burning off the bullets that were coming at them looked to be the size of basketballs. It was chilling to see hundreds of orange tracers whizzing past the Huey, and they all knew that there were four non-tracers between each of the basketballs.

Cody's door gunner returned fire with his M60 machine gun. The red tracers from the M60 and the green AK-47 tracers lit the late afternoon sky. The orange basketballs kept coming. When LTC Yon saw what he was dealing with, he immediately called FSB

Illingworth for artillery. He directed the artillery to the front and the rear of the convoy. The tanks and trucks became trapped between the artillery and the trees and boulders lining the road.

CWO Ware and his wingman heard the commotion on their radios and descended to strafe the convoy. The Cobra's Miniguns played havoc with the NVA troops jumping from their trucks and taking refuge behind trees and boulders.

An Air Force FAC in an OV-10 Bronco showed up and said that he had fighters on the way; he said he'd go down and have a look. As the FAC made his pass firing his four M60 machine guns, the enemy's green and red tracers flew skyward.

The NVA commander must have realized that he was boxed in between the artillery falling to his front and rear and the tall trees and boulders on each side. He must have also known what the presence of that FAC in his Bronco meant for his chances of a long lifespan and a comfortable retirement. Retribution's a bitch!

*An air-to-air right side view of an OV-10 Bronco aircraft firing a white phosphorus smoke rocket to mark a ground target
The OV-10 is used by forward air controllers in support of ground troops.
Photo from November '84 Airman Magazine
Service Depicted: Air Force
Camera Operator: TSGT Bill Thompson (ID: DFST8505744)*

As much as Cody wanted to stay and watch the mayhem, and to let his crew join the fun with their M60s, his fuel gauge indicated that it would be a bad idea. As Cody departed the area, the FAC thanked him and said that he had two F-100 fighters circling at 3,500 feet and another pair circling at five thousand feet. He then fired Willie Pete rockets to mark the target for the F-100s. With the plumes of white phosphorus clearly marking their target, the jets began attacking the convoy, first with 20mm suppressive fire and then with their five hundred pound bombs. The four F-100s made mincemeat of the armor and trucks, not to mention the more fragile enemy soldiers.

Burning T-34 tank, Russia 1941
Bundesarchiv, B 145 Bild-F016221-0016/CC-BY-SA 3.0
https://creativecommons.org/licenses/by-sa/3.0/de/deed.en

It was after dark when Cody dropped LTC Yon and his S-3 off at the firebase. On the flight back to Tay Ninh, Cody and his crew were still excited about what had happened; none of them had heard of anyone encountering NVA armor anywhere in Vietnam or Cambodia. Cody couldn't help but wonder if the entire NVA wasn't on the move to the south.

Wow...Soviet Union T-34 Tanks! Cody couldn't wait to spread the news.

They were the last ship to return to base. Cody left his peter-pilot to do the shutdown—a welcome novelty for the new AC—and headed for the O-Club.

The bar was full, and a few officers were standing around chatting. Most had been on missions inside Cambodia all day and were unwinding and telling war stories. Cody spotted his flight platoon commander Captain Dave "Pebbles" Stone, so he approached to tell Captain Stone the news. It wasn't just a couple of trucks or one armored vehicle, but FIVE Russian T-34 tanks and four trucks. This was big!

Captain Stone, clearly not on his first beer of the evening, said, "Aw, just have a beer."

It *was* a big deal. Reports came in the next day that 1/7 had counted forty-nine dead NVA soldiers among the four destroyed trucks and five Russian tanks.

Dinky Dau indeed!

The grunts of Bravo Company, 5th Battalion, 7th Regiment (B/5/7), entered Cambodia on 6 May 1970. They set about carrying out their orders to locate and destroy NVA command centers, supply depots, and weapons caches. They stayed off the roads and trails to avoid NVA ambushes. Hoofing it through the boonies and sloshing through mud and up the sides of mountains was tough going. Leeches, red ants, and snakes were a constant curse.

Bravo Company was actually looking for a firefight, but on their terms. They knew that the NVA would have defenses set up around their assets and that the harder the enemy fought, the nearer the Americans were to their goal. When Bravo Company did make contact, the fighting was fierce. Over the course of three or four days, they lost about fifteen men, including their company commander and a second commander who was flown in as his replacement. Based on the enemy defenses, they knew that they were getting close.

One of the troopers was Corporal Chris Keffalos[16]. When Keffalos first joined the company, he stood out for

---

[16] Chris Albert Keffalos, 11 October 1951 to 21 May 1970

several reasons. He was young, and although he may not have been the youngest in his company, he looked much younger than his eighteen years. In fact, he could have passed as a high school freshman. Chris was a little nervous and was prone to stutter at times. The men of Bravo Company took to the new kid and promptly nicknamed him "Shakey." Shakey became a favorite within the company, and he eventually became a legend.

By 20 May, Bravo Company had encountered the enemy on twenty occasions and had fought their way to the base of Hill-423. A large NVA force held the high ground, which gave them the advantage. After the battalion commander had consulted with regimental and division commanders, a full-on frontal attack was ordered. Bravo Company would lead the charge with the objective of seizing, controlling and occupying Hill-423.

The morning of 21 May began with an artillery barrage on the hill. Cobra gunships and Air Force jets joined in the assault. The North Vietnamese hunkered in their caves and bunkers, and like the Japanese on the island of Iwo Jima twenty-five years before, they were annoyed by, but were little affected by the assault. Like the Marines on Iwo, the 7th Cav would have to root the enemy out the hard way. Over the course of the day, Bravo Company fought their way up the hill. They encountered many bunkers and stiff resistance, but the arms caches remained elusive, until one Soldier who was out in front of the others, Corporal Chris "Shakey" Keffalos, turned to the Soldiers following him and yelled "Cache!"

Just then, a gook at the top of the hill appeared and opened fire with his AK-47. Shakey was hit five times. He fell and rolled down the hill several meters. A medic got to Shakey immediately, but it was too late.

In the minds of Bravo Company, the outcome of the fight for Hill-432 was settled at that moment. Hill-432 was now Shakey's Hill, and no gook would be allowed on Shakey's Hill.

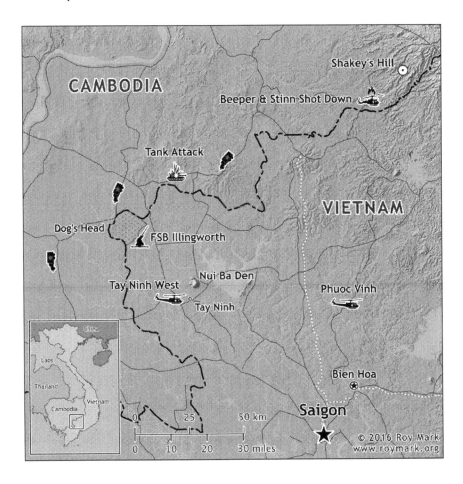

When the killing was done, the Soldiers of Bravo Company found dozens of bunkers. The bunkers were humongous; each one was a virtual weapons warehouse. Soldiers carried out AK-47s, ChiCom pistols and grenades, anti-aircraft guns, sniper rifles, and Soviet-made SKS semi-automatic carbine rifles and two hundred-tons of ammunition. It was big, and everyone knew that their sacrifice would have a major effect on the enemy's ability to kill Americans in the months or even years to come.

After a week of offloading matériel out of bunkers, Bravo Company was airlifted five miles away to Fire Support Base Neil for a three-day rest. They were removed from Shakey's Hill, but Shakey and his hill would live with them into old age.

15

Rock and Roll

Cambodia
May 1970

The grunts of the 7th Cavalry were kicking ass and taking names in Cambodia. The pilots of 229th Assault Helicopter Battalion inserted the infantry into the battle and extracted them when the fight was over or when things went sour. The Cobra pilots of 229's Delta Company—The Smiling Tigers—flew cover for insertions and extractions and enjoyed reaching out and touching the enemy with their Miniguns and rockets whenever possible.

Two weeks into the invasion of Cambodia, the pilots of Charlie Company were on a high. They were extracting revenge on the enemy, which had eluded them in their previous sanctuaries. Thousands of North Vietnamese Regulars were killed; Charlie Company's loss was zero. On 15 May, the score changed.

CWO Neil "Beeper" Blume flew to the headquarters of 8th Engineer Battalion at Phuoc Vinh, where he picked up 8th Engineer's CO, LTC Scott Smith. Smith and two 8th Engineer Sergeants wanted to evaluate potential firebase sites inside Cambodia.

Smith's engineer battalion was one of several units that were placing heavy demands on the overworked Charley Company. In addition to having engineer elements with almost every infantry unit on the ground, the engineers had a hand in the siting and construction of the many firebases required by the First Team. Infantry units always wanted to be within the range of at least one ground artillery firing unit, but preferred having two artillery units available for supporting fire.

With the NVA on the run, infantry units were moving swiftly to maintain contact with, or to re-engage, the enemy. The constantly changing positions of the infantry required 8th Engineers to site and build new firebases for the supporting field artillery units. During the Cambodian Incursion, there were eight or nine firebases in full use and being improved, and several more were under construction. It was like a massive game of chess.

Many of the firebases were carved out of the dense jungle, so the needed dozers, graders, and small trucks required by the engineers were airlifted to the sites by twin-engine, tandem-rotor heavy-lift CH-47 Chinook helicopters. The Chinooks of the 228th Assault Support Helicopter Battalion did the heavy lifting, and the Hueys of the 229th Assault Helicopter Battalion ferried demolition men and their explosives, equipment operators, repair and maintenance personnel, concertina wire, replacement and spare parts, and a host of other essential matériel to the engineer work sites.

Charlie Company also helped the engineers with

evacuating and sometimes destroying the vast quantities of enemy documents and matériel that were captured at Shakey's Hill and several other locations. Charlie Company pilots were called upon to fly Colonel Smith and his staffers on reconnaissance missions and regular visitation and supervision flights.

On one such mission, CWO Beeper Blume approached a site that Colonel Smith wanted to survey. As he circled the site, he, his crew, and LTC Smith scanned the area for threats. Satisfied that there were none, Blume brought his Huey in for landing. As he was hovering a few feet above the ground, a lone NVA soldier stepped out from behind a tree and pointed a rocket-propelled grenade at the hovering Huey.

Door gunner John Stinn saw the man in the black pajamas and opened fire with his M60 machine gun just as the enemy launched the rocket, sending it into the fuel cell of the Huey. The Huey burst into flames and settled to the ground (see map on page 201).

John Stinn and the two 8th Engineer Sergeants, Staff Sergeant Arnold Robbins and Sergeant Melvin Thomas, were killed in the attack. Blume, his co-pilot, and crew chief, along with LTC Smith, suffered minor injuries, but survived the attack and were evacuated.

It was a sobering wake-up call for everyone in Charlie Company. John Stinn was very popular around the base; he had worked in an admin position for eight months and had been the company's mail clerk. The loss of any comrade is heartbreaking, but none more so than a close buddy. Stinn, the guy who delivered mail from wives, girlfriends, moms, and siblings, was a friend to everyone, from the CO to the cook. Some of Stinn's friends were stunned. Not realizing that he'd volunteered to be a door gunner, many thought that he was still their mail clerk. It was John Stinn's first combat mission[17].

War is hell and waits for no man. The men of Charlie Company grieved their loss but continued with missions into Cambodia. Hueys took hits, but brought their pilots home safely, until 11 June.

AC WO1 James Bulloch was returning from Cambodia after dark. He was without a co-pilot, so his crew chief, Specialist 4th Class (SP4) Raymond Uhl, was riding up front. Bulloch's door gunner SP4 Alonzo Taylor and three passengers were in the back.

Near Tay Ninh, Bulloch flew into the worst thunderstorm anyone in Charlie Company had yet experienced. He did not to fly out of it. A search and rescue mission found the crash site later that night when the storm subsided. There were no survivors. The passengers killed in the accident were SP4 Franklin Meyer of Charlie Company, and from Alpha Company, SP4 John Dossett and SP4 Vernon Bergquist.[18]

While plans for a memorial service were being made, Charlie Company lost a pilot to combat inside Cambodia. AC WO1 Leslie Tatarski and his peter-pilot WO1 Larry Wall flew into Cambodia to resupply an ARVN unit that was being overrun by the enemy. When they reached

---

[17] The story of the RPG attack that killed John Stinn is told in depth in the book *Fixin' to Die Rag* by Roy Mark.

[18] The story of the accident is told in depth in the book *Fixin' to Die Rag* by Roy Mark.

the besieged unit, they saw that the jungle canopy was too thick to land. Under intense small-arms fire, Tatarski hovered down into a small opening in the canopy, and his crew began kicking out much-needed ammo and medical supplies. Suddenly, Tatarski slumped over the controls, and the Huey began to flounder. Peter-Pilot Wall grabbed the stick and, quite remarkably, was able to fly the crippled Huey to an aid station back in Vietnam. Unfortunately, WO1 Leslie Tatarski did not survive[19].

During the second month of the Cambodian operation, Ozzie Daniels and Phil Seefeld were elevated to ACs.

The invasion of Cambodia—the leaders in Washington insisted on calling it an "incursion"—ended for Charlie Company on 30 June 1970.

Charlie Company had inflicted death and destruction upon the enemy, but they had lost five of their own. It was little consolation, but they had lost only two to the enemy, and the others to that awful crash in the nighttime thunderstorm.

In addition to leaving Cambodia, the battalion received orders to pack up and move south to Bien Hoa, near Saigon. Most, if not all, of Charlie Company's men were glad to be leaving Tay Ninh to the South Vietnamese ARVN units. The fate of the country was being handed to the South Vietnamese through President Nixon's "Vietnamization" policy.

Most of the men had spent at least a few days in

[19] The story of how Leslie Tatarski was killed is told in depth in the book *Fixin' to Die Rag* by Roy Mark.

Bien Hoa on their way to Tay Ninh; they were anxious to return. The facilities at the larger Bien Hoa base were more civilized than those at Tay Ninh. Although conditions were better within the confines of the base at Bien Hoa, conditions outside the wire did not change. Pilots were still flying into hot landing zones; their Hueys were still taking hits; grunts were still climbing aboard with bodies bloodied from the battle.

In August, Warrant Officer Ozzie Daniels was given a direct commission as a second lieutenant. As an AC, and now a commissioned officer, Daniels began taking on more responsibilities. On 26 September, Second Lieutenant Ozzie Daniels was assigned a five-ship mission to pick up grunts of the 1st Brigade, 7th Rifle Company, at a firebase for insertion at landing zones in the field. Daniels flew ahead to survey the landing zones and left instructions for the other four ships to follow in thirty minutes. When the four-ship gaggle left Bien Hoa, they encountered a solid cloud cover to 3,500 feet. Flying above the clouds in clear skies, two of the Hueys meshed rotor blades, causing catastrophic loss of control. The two Hueys fell through the cloud cover.

Search and rescue missions were launched, only to find the charred remains of the two Hueys; all eight aboard were killed.

Ozzie Daniels and the two ACs were close. He had been hootch mates with Bob "Little Ogre" Bauer and Mark "Hokus Pokus" Holtum. Their death affected him profoundly. The two peter-pilots, Francis Sullivan and Warren Lawson, were newer arrivals. Even so, they had become part of the team, and their loss was a shock to everyone.

The loss of the four enlisted men of the two doomed ships was felt profoundly around the base. Hootch mates and friends of Crew Chiefs Donald Hall and Douglas Woodland along with door gunners Robert Painter and Ernest Laidler grieved their loss.

In October of 1970, Sterling Cody and Ozzie Daniels were granted seven days of R&R. It seemed that the brass couldn't agree if "R&R" stood for "Rest and Recuperation" or "Rest and Relaxation." To the troops, however, R&R was seven days of "Rock and Roll."

Cody opted to spend his week in Taipei, Taiwan, and Daniels chose to go to Sydney, Australia. In Sydney, he met a lovely girl named Vicki, and the couple fell in love. They vowed to be married one day.

When Sterling Cody returned to Bien Hoa, he was assigned as the battalion commander's personal pilot. He would no longer fly whatever ship was assigned to him each day. Flying the colonel's Huey meant that he always flew with the same crew. SP5 Greg Weber, a crew chief who Cody had flown with several times, and whom Cody liked and respected, was now his permanent crew chief.

Weber was interested in aviation, so his position on the colonel's ship gave him a unique opportunity. Each day as Cody flew to pick up the colonel, he did so without a co-pilot, so he began allowing Weber to ride in the left seat to get a feel for the controls. Soon, Weber was hovering and taking off better than most student pilots. After dropping the colonel off, Weber would again take the co-pilot's seat for more practice.

Hovering, takeoffs, and landings were challenging skills to master, and Weber got plenty of practice. Soon, he was flying as well as some FNG pilots. Still, he had lots to learn, and Cody encouraged his crew chief to apply for flight school after his tour.

One day in November, Cody picked up his mail at the orderly room and sorted through the small stack. As he walked to the Tactical Operations Center, he noticed an official-looking letter. As he walked, he opened the letter and began to read.

"Greetings, You are hereby ordered for induction into the Armed Forces of the United States, and to report..."

You're shitting me!

He couldn't believe it. It was actually funny. He'd been in the Army for more than a year; gooks had been shooting at him in Vietnam for eight months and now he was being drafted?

A few other pilots stopped to chat, and Cody announced, "I'VE BEEN DRAFTED!"

They all got a kick out of the government's ineptness and howled with laughter when Cody read on.

"Willful failure to appear at the place and hour of the day named in this Order subjects the violator to fine and imprisonment."

"Well," Cody told his friends, "if hippies can burn their draft *cards*, I sure as hell can burn my draft *notice*."

With that, he whipped out his Zippo Lighter®, held the notice high, and set it alight. His audience cheered as the government document burned down to Cody's fingertips. As the ashes floated to the ground, his audience went about their business, and that was that.

The remainder of Sterling Cody's tour in Vietnam was relatively uneventful. He was promoted to Chief Warrant Officer in February 1971 just as he was counting the days to his March DEROS. During his 12-month tour, he had lost friends to enemy fire and accidents. It was a long year spent in harrowing conditions. He was happy—no ecstatic—to be returning to the world, but a little sad to be leaving his brothers-in-arms.

Cody made the rounds, shaking hands, exchanging "good lucks" and promising to keep in touch. One gesture touched Cody, and it came not from a fellow pilot.

When CWO Sterling Cody bid his farewell to his enlisted crew chief, SP5 Greg Weber gave Cody his Zippo Lighter®. He talked about how he enjoyed flying with Cody and how much he appreciated the flying lessons. Cody tried to refuse such a personal gift, but Weber insisted, saying that it was the point of the gift.

On one side of the Zippo Lighter® was engraved the name "Greg." On the other side was engraved:

LIVE BY CHANCE
LOVE BY CHOICE
KILL BY PROFESSION

The Zippo Lighter® presented to CWO Sterling Cody by SP5 Greg Weber in 1971

16

Jittery Prop

Pacific Ocean
May 1985

Jittery Prop was an ongoing operation in 1985 conducted from the U.S. Navy's Destroyer *USS Deyo* (DD-989). U.S. Army Captain Sterling Cody would launch his mission with two helicopters: one UH-1 Huey was chained to the helideck of the *Deyo*, and the other Huey was secure inside the ship's hangar. Each Huey was ferrying Special Forces Soldiers to the objective, and each was carrying a highly skilled and specialized Warrant Officer pilot. Their objective was to snatch a Soviet-made Hind helicopter gunship from a heavily defended airport.

In the weeks leading up to this moment, Cody had ensured that the pilots were qualified to use night vision goggles and to conduct deck landings at sea. Now, it was almost time to launch. The *Deyo* was cutting its way through moderate seas as Cody gathered his mission members in the *Deyo*'s Officers' Mess. With maps spread out on tables, Cody reviewed the mission with his men a final time. He pointed out the coastal air defense radars on a map and reminded his pilots that Surface-to-Air Missiles (SA-6) and radar-controlled anti-aircraft guns would likely light up their screens.

CWO Sterling Cody had caught his freedom bird out of Vietnam in March of 1971. The war was winding down, and many Nam Huey pilots were offered an early release from active duty. Most of the pilots were eager to see the Army in their rear-view mirrors, but not Sterling Cody. He had been accepted into the Army's "Boot Strap" program; the Army would pay CWO Cody's full salary while he attended college at the University of Nebraska. Twenty-year-old Cody saw the Army as his future.

After hitting the West Coast, Cody was granted thirty days leave. He headed east, and after a connection at Reagan National Airport, flew to Weyers Cave Airport in the Shenandoah Valley.

Buck Cody met his son at the airport and drove him home to Waynesboro, Virginia.

Later that day at the family home, Buck said, "Well, son, you made it back. What can I get you?"

Cody said, "I'd really like to have a nine-shot Colt .22 pistol for target practice and to shoot snakes."

"Yeah, I thought that's what you'd want," Buck told his son, "I've shopped around and found one in the Waynesboro Gun Shop."

Buck handed his son a crisp new fifty dollar bill and said, "Here son, welcome home."

The next day, Sterling drove to the gun shop in Waynesboro and found the .22 pistol in the display case.

When the salesman handed it to Cody, he looked it over, looked down the sights, looked down the barrel and said, "I'll take it."

The salesman said, "Fine," and pulled out a form that he handed to Cody saying, "Just fill out this form."

After Cody had filled in the form, the salesman looked it over and suddenly placed it on the counter.

"Sir, I can't sell you this gun," the clerk said, "you're not twenty-one."

"A few days ago, I was flying Army helicopters," Cody told the man. "I was firing machine guns and rockets at enemies of the United States, and you're telling me I can't buy this peashooter?"

"Sorry son; it's the law in the Commonwealth of Virginia," the man explained.

Combat Veteran CWO Sterling Cody would have to wait seven months before he could legally buy the pistol.

Dinky Dau!

Cody couldn't even legally cry in his beer; he wasn't of legal drinking age. Neither could he voice his displeasure at the ballot box; the Twenty-sixth Amendment to the Constitution wouldn't grant him permission to vote until later that year.

Double Dinky Dau!

Sterling called his dad, and Buck Cody immediately drove to the gun shop and bought the pistol for his son. The Commonwealth be damned.

CWO Phil Seefeld accepted the Army's offer of an early out and returned to Nebraska, where he joined the Army National Guard so that he could continue to fly. He would fly Hueys out of Lincoln Municipal Airport with the 24th Medical Company Air Ambulance.

Second Lieutenant Ozzie Daniels returned to the U.S. in March of 1971. Vicki, Ozzie's girlfriend, arrived from Australia about a week later. After a short engagement, Ozzie and Vicki were married that summer.

Because Daniels had accepted the direct commission, his obligation to the Army was extended. Ozzie and Vicki lived at Fort Benning, Georgia, until he left active duty in May of 1972. The couple then moved back to Nebraska, where they lived with Ozzie's parents while they made plans to immigrate to Australia. Ozzie worked on the family farm, and Vicki helped her mother-in-law around the house.

In 1971, CWO Sterling Cody registered at the University of Nebraska under the Army's Operation Boot Strap program. Cody was responsible for the tuition, but with the Army paying his full salary and with money from the G.I. Bill[20], he was able to make ends meet. Cody had taken the College Level Examination Program test at boot camp and was awarded college credits. The academic standards at VFMA had prepared him well. In Vietnam, Cody had taken advantage of the correspondence courses offered at the education center at Tay Ninh. When he enrolled at the University of Nebraska, he was awarded credits based on his military

---

[20] According to The Servicemen's Readjustment Act of 1944, the G.I. Bill was created to help veterans of World War II. Among the benefits offered under the bill was assistance tuition and expenses for veterans attending college or trade schools. The Readjustment Benefits Act of 1966 extended these benefits to all veterans of the armed forces.

training; with his credits for meteorology, navigation, and military science added to his other credits, he was able to enter the University of Nebraska as a junior majoring in criminal justice.

During Cody's one-year tour in Vietnam, female companionship was virtually non-existent. Now, on campus with coeds everywhere, hormones flowed, and Cody came alive. He met a beautiful blue-eyed brunette in his Elements of Criminal Justice class and fell madly in love. Catherine Clark and Sterling were soon engaged. Alluding to the Criminal Justice class where they had met, they told their families and friends that they had sentenced each other to life, without parole. The couple was married on 25 March 1972.

Cody was able to maintain his flight currency by occasionally flying with Phil Seefeld's National Guard unit at the Lincoln Municipal Airport.

One fine day at the Daniels' Farm, Ozzie and his family were gathered at the kitchen table enjoying a home-cooked meal. Ozzie—now a civilian—thought he may have been having a flashback to Vietnam when the familiar "WHOP WHOP WHOP" entered his consciousness. No one else seemed to notice; was it real or was he hearing things? The "WHOP WHOP WHOP" got louder, and everyone paused to look around. It *was* real.

"That's got to be Phil," Ozzie said as he jumped from the table and ran outside.

Ozzie looked up and saw a Huey circling the house. He ran to an opening behind the barn, where he gave the Huey hand signals and directed it to land. Daniels approached the Huey and greeted Phil while the co-pilot was shutting down the bird. When the co-pilot emerged and removed his helmet, Daniels was stunned to see Sterling Cody standing on his farm. Daniels had no idea that Cody was even in the State of Nebraska, much less flying with the National Guard. The surprise was mutual; Cody had thought that Ozzie was still at Fort Benning.

The three brothers-in-arms had a mini-reunion as they walked to the house. Inside, Phil invited Ozzie and his new wife, and Ozzie's father for a ride in the Huey. Ozzie took the co-pilot's seat; his wife Vicki sat on the bench seat in the back with her father-in-law Wayne Daniels. It was the old WW-II bomber pilot's first ride in a helicopter.

Sterling Cody—always the chowhound—accepted an invitation from Mary Daniels to join her in the kitchen for a piece of homemade apple pie.

Cody was more than a little apprehensive about taking civilians on an unauthorized flight. He was planning a long career in the Army, and this could not only get him kicked out of the Army but out of college as well. Cody formulated his defense as he scarfed down his second piece of apple pie: *I was the co-pilot. The Pilot-in-Command ordered me out.*

It was a great reunion, and nothing became of the unauthorized flight. What the Army doesn't know...

Sterling Cody made the best of a good situation and graduated in just two years with a Bachelor of Science degree in Criminal Justice. After graduation, Cody served in aviation assignments around the world before going to Officer Candidate School and receiving a commission as a second lieutenant. He was subsequently based in Virginia, the Western Pacific, Pensacola, Fort Benning, Georgia, and Fort Rucker, Alabama. Along the way, Sterling and Catherine Cody were blessed with a daughter and, later, a son. Shannon was born in 1973 and Paul Cody in 1978.

By the time Cody arrived at Fort Rucker in 1980, he had been promoted to captain (O-3). Most of the Army's Huey pilots had trained at Rucker, but it was Cody's first tour at Mother Rucker. He'd heard Ozzie Daniels tell the story in Vietnam many times of his failed attempt at stealing Enterprise's famous boll weevil. Ten years later, he finally cast his eyes upon the little critter.

Cody's initial assignment at Fort Rucker was as an instructor pilot. He later became Head of Standardization.

One day, Cody's CO called him into his office and told him that he was being transferred to 210th Combat Aviation Battalion, 114th Combat Support Aviation Company, at Fort Clayton in the Panama Canal Zone. He would take command of a platoon, but the company commander was due to be relieved soon, so Cody would take over as company commander when the current CO was relieved.

The 114th—The Black Knights—had been in Vietnam, but eight years after the war, it was unlikely that any current Black Knights were Vietnam Vets.

Captain Cody arrived in Panama with Catherine, ten-year-old Shannon and five-year-old Paul in August of 1983. His first order of business was to report in. Cody located the battalion headquarters, but he saw that the building was closed for renovation. A sign directed him to a fire station a short distance away. Inside the firehouse, Cody saw a small, unimposing man—a lieutenant colonel—sitting at a desk next to a fire engine.

Cody walked up, saluted, and said, "Sir, Captain Cody reporting for duty as ordered."

The man stood and said, "Hi, I'm Colonel Duck."

Cody burst out laughing and said, "Come on Colonel, what's your real name?"

"Donald," replied Colonel Duck.

Both men had a good laugh.

It was an exchange with a superior that could have resulted in an uncomfortable situation, but Cody's fun-loving personality meshed well with LTC Duck's sense of humor. After controlling his laughter, Duck explained that his real name was Theodore. It was the beginning of a pleasant and professional relationship.

LTC Duck went on to explain that the battalion had recently suffered a string of nighttime accidents and that since Cody had headed up the Night Vision Goggle Instructor Pilot Course at Fort Rucker, he felt that Cody would be a big help.

When Sterling Cody arrived in Panama, Central America was the latest hotbed of the Cold War between the United States and the Soviet Union. The Cold War began in 1945 at the end of WW-II, as tensions escalated and ebbed at flashpoints around the world. The cold war turned hot in 1950 when the Soviet Union's client state in North Korea invaded the U.S.-sponsored South Korea. The Korean Peninsula continued to flash hot from time to time, even after an armistice was signed three years later. The two superpowers came close to nuclear war in 1962, when the Soviet Union attempted to place nuclear missiles in Fidel Castro's Marxist Cuba. The U.S. effort to prop up South Vietnam from 1954 to 1974 failed in part because of North Vietnam support from the U.S.S.R. When the Soviet Union invaded Afghanistan in 1979, the United States immediately began supplying Afghan rebels in a proxy war that was still hot when Captain Cody arrived in Panama in June of 1983.

In nearby Nicaragua, the Marxist Daniel Ortega was the leader of a military junta that was supported by the Soviet Union. Ortega and his Sandinista National Liberation Front were orchestrating a Marxist-Leninist program of land reform, nationalization of private industries, and wealth redistribution. The Soviet Union, keen to spread their ideology in South and Central America, immediately began to support the Communist Junta with cash and military equipment. The U.S., just as eager to blunt Soviet influence in the region, began to support the counter-revolutionary "Contras" in an attempt to overthrow Ortega's Communist Junta.

Tensions between the two superpowers were running high. Neither country was willing to allow the other any gain of influence. A slight miscalculation or misunderstanding could lead to outright war between the two nuclear behemoths.

In late 1983, soon after Cody arrived in Panama, the United States invaded the small Caribbean island nation of Grenada and defeated a Cuban force there. The Cold War could turn hot at any moment, at many spots around the globe. The threat of nuclear annihilation seemed to be the only thing preventing nuclear annihilation. Thus, when Captain Sterling Cody arrived in Panama, the country was at peace, but all of Central America and Nicaragua, in particular, was one incident away from a hot war.

In May of 1985, Captain Cody was summoned to Colonel Duck's office. When he entered the room, the Colonel directed Cody to have a seat. Based on the Colonel's demeanor, this was not to be a social visit.

The Soviet Union, the Colonel explained, had presented Daniel Ortega in Nicaragua a gift of twelve Hind helicopter gunships. They were the latest model of those Russian birds, and the United States Government wanted to have one to assess their capabilities.

"We," the Colonel said, "are going to go into Nicaragua and snatch one of those Hinds from under Daniel Ortega's nose."

What do you mean WE? Cody thought, knowing that the Colonel would lead from the rear.

"You, Captain Cody," the Colonel continued, "will be the air mission commander."

It was a long and detailed meeting. The Colonel explained that the *USS Deyo* had been conducting Operation Jittery Prop for some time and that the *Deyo* would ferry them to within twelve miles of the Nicaraguan coast. That in itself was risky, since Daniel Ortega's government was claiming territorial waters out to a two hundred mile limit. Based on the United Nations Convention on the Law of the Sea, the U.S. recognized territorial waters extending only out to twelve miles. U.S. Navy ships regularly tested Nicaraguan resolve by sailing within their two hundred mile limit, and the Nicaraguan Navy never failed to monitor and occasionally harass U.S. Navy ships within that limit.

Cody would launch two Hueys in the dark of night from the *Deyo* as it skirted the twelve-mile limit. That would surely get the attention of Nicaragua's military.

The Army had flown in two Army Warrant Officer Pilots to fly the Hind out of Nicaragua. They were specially trained to fly the Russian gunship. A team of Special Forces (SF) Soldiers was on base and standing by for the mission.

It would be a nighttime mission launched from the helideck of the *USS Deyo*, so Cody would have to train his pilots to use night vision goggles and conduct deck landings at sea. The *Deyo*, the Colonel said, would arrive the next day to begin crossing the Canal from the Atlantic side. Cody suggested that he fly his team across Panama and board the *Deyo* before she began the crossing, as it would give everyone the opportunity to become oriented to the ship before their training began. LTC Duck agreed, but cautioned his captain to keep the details of the mission under his hat.

A port bow view of the destroyer USS DEYO (DD-989) underway south of Italy on 10 Dec 1991
Camera Operator: PH2 PAUL A. VISE

Cody would be Mission Commander and Pilot-in-Command of one Huey and would carry one Warrant Officer Pilot and four SF Soldiers. The second Huey would bring the other Warrant Officer Pilot and four other SF Soldiers. The SF Soldiers would immediately set up a perimeter around the Hueys and the Hind.

As Platoon Commander, Cody knew his men and the ships they flew well. He chose his best pilots and crew. He also chose his two best UH-1 Hueys and had them modified to carry an extra internal fuel tank. The addition would increase the Hueys' two-and-a-half-hour range by two additional hours; it was a critical addition for the mission.

Cody gathered his men, and the two Hueys flew the length of the Panama Canal to the Atlantic side. There, they boarded the *Deyo* for what Cody told them was routine deck training and night vision goggle qualification. The extra fuel tanks were a new innovation, so Cody informed his men that they'd practice deck landings to become accustomed to the extra weight.

The Soldiers felt a little out of place on the Destroyer; it was easy to get lost navigating the gray hallways—passageways in Navy speak—and multi decks of the ship. Learning Navy jargon was the least of their concerns; they were more interested in the flight deck and hangar.

The helideck was at the tail end of the ship; a Sailor corrected one of the pilots and said that it was called the "fantail," and not the rear end. The pilots were more concerned with the size of the helideck than naval terminology. The helideck was small...very small! And to become deck qualified, they would have to make ten landings on this thing—three at night, at sea, with the ship underway.

They didn't have to measure the flight deck; a Naval officer gave Cody a diagram with the dimensions. The pilots looked at the diagram, at each other, and then at Captain Cody.

"No sweat," Cody said, "We'll have two feet to play with before the rotor hits the hangar door."

The eight-hour trip through the Canal was time well spent. The Army Officers got to know their Naval host, and at least where the important parts of the ship were. The enlisted crew could find the mess deck and the officers could find the Officers' Mess. They knew where they could take a leak and even learned to call it the "head" and not the latrine.

Once on the Pacific side of Panama, their training began in earnest. The *Deyo* sailed out into the Pacific beyond Taboga Island for deck training. Each pilot had to make ten deck landings to be qualified. Landing on a rolling deck with two feet of clearance between the main rotor and the hangar door—"Hatch" in Sailor speak—was tricky. Before the pilots were completely comfortable with that, they had to do it again at night.

They practiced moving a Huey out of the hangar and onto the helideck. Cody pushed his crews; they had to get the Huey out of the hangar and into the air inside of ten minutes.

Over the course of one week of deck training, a Navy Lieutenant Commander (O-4) Huey Instructor Pilot certified Captain Cody and his pilots for deck landings. In turn, Cody qualified the Lieutenant Commander on the latest night vision goggles. Captain Cody was so impressed with the Lieutenant Commander's piloting skills, not to mention his expertise in deck landings, that he decided to make him the pilot-in-command of the second Huey. It would be unusual for an Army Captain to be in command of a mission that included a higher-ranking naval officer, but the two men worked so well together that Cody was comfortable with the arrangement.

The deck training was paramount, but Cody made time for night flights away from the ship to allow his door gunners time to get in some time firing their M60 machine guns in a low-light environment.

It was a busy seven days of what everyone in the company, except for Cody and his CO, thought was regular training.

Once back at base, a meeting was held to brief key personnel of the command structure. The "command structure" began with the brigade commander—a two-star general—and included his chief of staff, aides, and Cody's battalion and company commanders. The pilots and crewmembers who would fly the mission were also present. Battalion and company personnel gathered in a small conference room, awaiting the general and his entourage. They spread maps and diagrams out on a large conference table. A detailed drawing of the Managua Airport was centered on the table. The General entered with the flair of...well, the flair of a general who was ready to cut to the chase.

Colonel Duck spoke, and the company commander spoke. Known Nicaraguan air defenses, including missiles and 23mm and 37mm anti-aircraft guns around the airport, were pointed out on the map. Possible routes to the target were drawn on the map. The plan and contingencies were discussed in detail.

The General then spoke, pointing out the importance of the mission. He also emphasized to Cody the importance of arriving at the objective at exactly 00:45 (12:45 a.m.) on the target date. He didn't explain why that was important and no one asked. Cody thought that the Army might have some sort of diversion planned and figured that it must be above his pay grade.

With the briefing winding down, the General stood and leaned over the table to study the map.

"I'd take this track," the General said with authority.

"Sir," Captain Cody retorted with an equal amount of authority in his voice, "If you'd like to come and sit in the jump seat, we'll take that track; otherwise, we'll take the route I choose."

The General gave Cody a hard look. The expression on Colonel Duck's face was that of a man who was about to be drummed out of the Army.

Cody continued, "I don't know where all the anti-aircraft guns are, sir, but as we go in, I'll determine that, and run my own zigzag courses. I have an idea about how I'm going to get in there from the satellite photos, but I'm not sure. If I take fire, I'm obviously going to vary the route."

The briefing ended without the General accepting Cody's offer to come along in the jump seat. After the meeting, one of the pilots marveled at Cody's remarks to the General.

"Aww," Cody said, "You can say anything to a general as long as you say 'Sir' at the end."

The fact that Cody was one of the few combat veterans still around in 1985 didn't hurt.

Cody had one of his pilots fly the second Huey to the *Deyo* that afternoon and secure it in the hangar. He would follow the next morning after the *Deyo* shoved off.

Pilots and crew stored their gear in their quarters, which were designed for quick access to the hangar and helideck. They had time to kill; the Deyo was scheduled to sail the next morning on what most of the Sailors and Soldiers thought was another routine training exercise.

Late that night, eight SF Soldiers walked up the Deyo's gangplank, saluted the Officer of the Deck, and requested permission to come aboard. No questions were asked, and no explanations were given.

The next morning, the ship's boatswain's mate of

the watch blew a long blast on his whistle and passed the word, "Underway—shift colors." The ensign (U.S. Flag) on the fantail was hauled down, and another ensign raised to the gaff, which is the diagonal spar projecting aft from the mast. The Destroyer *USS Deyo* (DD-989) was underway once again, conducting Operation Jittery Prop.

One hour later, with the *Deyo* cutting its way through the Pacific, Captain Sterling Cody gathered his pilots, his crews, and the SF Soldiers in the ship's wardroom. Maps, diagrams, and satellite photos were again laid out on a table. Cody was all business as he went over every detail of the operation. They would fly in low level, snatch the Hind gunship, and make their escape to Honduras. Cody pointed out on a drawing of the airport exactly where the Russian-made Hind gunships were sitting on the tarmac. Intelligence knew from satellite images, which one of the twelve were flown that day. They'd target that one, expecting it to be airworthy. Nicaraguan coastal defenses were anticipated to be stiff; anti-aircraft fire was expected when they approached the airport. Cody didn't mix any punches about how dangerous the mission would be.

After fielding a few questions, Cody dismissed the men.

As they steamed north past Costa Rica, Cody took the opportunity to take his Hueys and crews on flights away from the ship. More target practice for the door gunners wouldn't hurt; it would be better to keep everyone busy. On night flights, they threw out floating debris with chemical light sticks attached as targets for the door gunners.

During the day, from the ship and from the air, they saw hammerhead sharks and occasional batches of sea snakes. The snakes moved in flocks that looked like bowls of spaghetti. The snakes and sharks were a powerful motivating force; don't be shot down in these waters.

On the second night, the *Deyo* entered the two hundred mile limit claimed by Nicaragua and began slowly moving toward the twelve-mile limit.

When the Deyo's Captain gave the word, Cody and his crew went topside and began unchaining their Huey from the helideck. The Lieutenant Commander and his crew entered the hangar to ready their ship for a quick exit to the helideck. Cody blasted off from the deck at exactly 23:15 hours (11:15 p.m.), gained altitude, and set a course southwest, away from Nicaragua. He maintained that course for sixty seconds and then descended to two hundred feet above the sea before turning back toward the *Deyo*. When he reached the ship, he went into a holding pattern to await the launch of the second Huey. After a mad scramble to get the second Huey out of the Deyo's hangar and airborne, it left the ship, and picked up the same course as Cody before returning to the vicinity of the ship. Then, the two-ship gaggle set a course for the Nicaraguan coast twelve miles away.

It was a dark moonless night. At sea, without the benefit of lights from towns, scattered villages, and car headlights, their night vision goggles couldn't pick up enough ambient light to be useful. It was like flying in a can of chocolate syrup, while visualizing sharks and sea snakes in the ocean below. Flying only by their instruments at two hundred feet above the Pacific Ocean was dangerous stuff, but it was necessary to avoid enemy detection.

About six miles from the coast, Cody's AN/APR-39 radar warning receiver lit up as he'd never seen before. They were picking up radar from all angles as mobile anti-aircraft units turned on their sensors. The enemy had them on radar; it was a sign that they were locking on for the kill. It was a tense few moments; waiting to be shot out of the sky does tend to make a person anxious. The minutes passed. Were the Nicaraguans asleep at the control? Perhaps the Nicaraguan response—or lack thereof—was the result of the Deyo's jamming radar, or maybe it was the product of an Air Force high-flying Electronic Jamming Aircraft preventing the Nicaraguan and Russian gunners from locking onto their targets.

Cody considered the Nicaraguan Army to be bush league at best, but thanked his lucky stars for whatever kept him in the sky rather than shot out of the same.

Once the two Hueys were inland, lights from villages and vehicles generated enough light, so the pilots were comfortable donning their night vision goggles.

To avoid detection, the two Hueys flew "NOE" (Nap-of-the-Earth); they flew so low that they went under power lines, in river gullies, and around hills. It wasn't treetop flying; at times, they had to look up to see the tops of trees.

Captain Cody navigated toward Managua Airport, checking his watch from time to time and doing mental calculations so that he would arrive at 00:45 hours, just as the General had directed. The airport lights came into view; they were right on course and right on time.

Cody spotted twelve Hind gunships sitting on the tarmac well away from the terminal area. As he was making his approach, a gigantic explosion erupted on the opposite side of the airport.

Wow, looks like their fuel storage tanks, Cody thought. *Thanks, General.*

Cody figured that the General had arranged the diversion to increase their chances of a successful mission. He wondered if the SF guys knew anything about the diversion, because he sure didn't. If they did, they kept it to themselves.

Those SF guys are a secretive bunch; they wouldn't say shit if they had a mouthful.

The two Hueys set down near the Hinds, and the SF Soldiers jumped out and formed a perimeter. The two Warrant Officer pilots raced to the Hind and began a quick pre-flight inspection.

A Russian Hind Mil Mi-35M (51 yellow)
By Yevgeny Volkov (http://russianplanes.net/id99985) [CC BY 3.0
(http://creativecommons.org/licenses/by/3.0) or CC BY 3.0
(http://creativecommons.org/licenses/by/3.0)], via Wikimedia Commons

Things were happening fast, but for Cody, sitting at the controls, waiting to get the flock out of there, things seemed to be moving in slow motion.

Cody's mind was racing.

My favorite thing in life: sitting stationary with my engine running on an enemy airfield waiting to get the shit shot out of me.

The Warrant Officers got the Hind up to operating speed. The Special Forces scurried back to the Hueys and the now three-ship gaggle lifted off, silhouetted by light from the raging fuel tank fire. Cody didn't expect to be pursued. Nicaraguan pilots weren't that good, especially at night, and they didn't have night vision goggle capabilities.

Adios Amigos!

The gaggle departed to the northeast toward Honduras. Everything had come off like clockwork. Now, all they had to do was to get out of the country before Nicaraguan pilots began flying again at dawn.

The flight of two Hueys and one Soviet gunship made its way across the border into Honduras. As dawn broke, they landed at a dirt airstrip; they were expected. A fuel tanker was waiting to refuel the Hueys, and a large tent had been erected to conceal the Hind from Russian satellites during the day. They'd fly it out the next night.

After refueling, the two Hueys were on their way to Sosa Soto, the principal American Air Base in Honduras.

It was a successful mission. The United States had managed to acquire the latest version of the Russian gunship. Captain Sterling Cody had brought everyone home safely. The two UH-1 Hueys had completed the mission to perfection—as usual—and Daniel Ortega had got the message loud and clear.

We can be in your pocket anytime!

17

Fish House

Colombia
16 February 2001

After Captain Sterling Cody's adventure in Panama, he was appointed as Company Commander of the 114th Combat Support Aviation Company. In August of 1985, he was assigned as 210th Combat Aviation Battalion's Operations Officer (S-3) and was promoted to Major.

The battalion had begun transitioning from UH-1 Hueys to the more modern and advanced UH-60 Black Hawks the same year. The new four-blade, twin-engine medium-lift utility helicopters were manufactured by the Sikorsky Aircraft Corporation and had been introduced into the Army in 1979. Cody and the battalion's pilots were impressed with the Black Hawks. They were great helicopters, but they were replacing a legend. General Maxwell Thurman would later say that when the last of the new Black Hawk helicopters was flown to the aircraft bone yard, the crew would get into their Hueys and fly home.

As part of their training, the battalion's pilots

conducted high-altitude flights into the Andes Mountains of nearby Colombia. Cody once landed on one of the rocky and barren peaks at 17,680 feet. The new Black Hawks were equipped with oxygen and were up to the challenge of high altitudes.

In September of 1986, Cody was transferred back to the United States. Major Cody's new assignment in the U.S. was at Fort Monroe, Virginia, working for the Deputy Chief of Staff of the Training and Doctrine Command. Then, in 1989, Major Cody was sent to the United States Army Command and General Staff College (CGSC) at Fort Leavenworth, Kansas. The ten-month CGSC course offered instruction in military history, military planning, decision making, leadership, and leadership philosophy.

Fort Leavenworth is also the home of the maximum-security U.S. Disciplinary Barracks for personnel of all branches. Inmates of the prison reside at Leavenworth considerably longer than do the students of CGSC. Cody often told his friends that he had been shipped off to Leavenworth for the "short course."

Sterling Cody lived on base with Catherine and their two children, Shannon, who was now sixteen, and eleven-year-old Paul.

After graduating from CGSC in June of 1990, Major Cody was assigned to the Defense Nuclear Agency in Washington, D.C. When Cody arrived in Washington, D.C. to begin his new job, work was underway to implement the Intermediate-Range Nuclear Forces (INF)

Treaty. The 1987 INF Treaty between the United States and the Soviet Union stipulated the elimination of intermediate-range and short-range nuclear missiles.

Cody worked side-by-side with Russian counterparts on the safe and secure dismantlement of nuclear weapons. One of Cody's responsibilities was the manufacture of the soft armor blankets used to protect nuclear weapons during their transportation to the deactivation site. To that end, he coordinated with the manufacturing contractor in Florida as they constructed the ballistic blankets. The thick blankets were about ten feet long by six feet wide and made of layered para-aramid synthetic fibers. The blankets were wrapped around nuclear weapons to protect them from inadvertent penetration in the event of rail or airplane accidents or small-arms fire.

The Russians didn't have the technological expertise to manufacture soft armor blankets, so Cody traveled to Russia with the American-made blankets and assisted with the safe transportation of Soviet nuclear weapons to their deactivation site at Tomsk, Russia. He was promoted to lieutenant colonel shortly afterward.

The end of the Cold War in 1991 brought with it years of downsizing for the U.S. Army and a period of reflection for Sterling Cody. He'd come a long way since joining the Army as a Private in 1969. In December of 1993, with twenty-three years of service, forty-three-year-old Lieutenant Colonel Sterling Cody retired from the Army.

Civilian Sterling Cody thought that the tranquil life of

a restaurant owner would be a nice change of pace. He found land for sale in Prince Edward County, Virginia, that he thought would be ideal for a restaurant. Cody worked with an architect, and they came up with a perfect design that included living quarters above the restaurant for him and his family. He worked with the contractor daily to ensure that every detail was just right. As the building neared completion, he hired a professional restaurant manager with an impressive résumé. It was all interesting and exciting leading up to the grand opening.

When the restaurant opened in 1994 and things settled into a routine, Cody came to realize that his life was going nowhere and that he missed the occasional adrenaline fixes that came with flying helicopters in dangerous situations. So when a civilian contractor talked with him about flying Black Hawks for the U.S. Government in South America, Cody embraced the offer with open arms.

The contractor offered him a good deal. The government would fly him to Colombia for a month or so, and fly him back home for time off. He'd have some control over his schedule, and he could keep the restaurant. His manager could run the business while he was gone, and Catherine could look after things.

Where do I sign?

Civilian Sterling Cody's restaurant had been an immediate success, and with his manager running the day-to-day operations, Cody felt comfortable with his frequent trips to South America. When not flying for the government, he relaxed at his home above the restaurant and often socialized downstairs with friends and customers.

On a cold and rainy winter day in 1997, Catherine told her husband that she would go to Fort Bragg, a three-hour drive to the south, to attend a Bible Study and visit with friends.

"Why not wait until tomorrow?" Sterling asked his wife. "I'll drive you down first thing tomorrow morning."

Catherine insisted, however, and left the same day. A few hours later, a policeman entered the restaurant and broke the news. Catherine had been killed in a horrific traffic accident.

Sterling's daughter was married and his son Paul was off at college when their mother died. With his kids grown and on their own, Cody continued his frequent trips to South America.

The U.S. Government had begun an active anti-drug campaign in Colombia in 1989, when President George H. W. Bush allocated over three hundred million dollars of military and intelligence assistance to fighting drug cartels in South America. The focus of those operations was in Colombia. By 1991, the budget for the anti-drug campaign had grown to over seven hundred million dollars, and an undisclosed amount was earmarked for secret military and spy units. Those units were referred to as "black ops." Cody's work as a contractor fell under the black ops umbrella.

The Colombian government was not only fighting a hot war with the drug barons, but was also fighting for its survival against a Communist insurgency.

The Revolutionary Armed Forces of Colombia (Fuerzas Armadas Revolucionarias de Colombia, or FARC in Spanish) was formed in 1964 as a Marxist-Leninist peasant force. The FARC army and the drug lords were fighting the same enemy in the Colombian government. After the drug cartels had formed their own armies, it was often difficult for the Colombian Army to distinguish between FARC and drug forces. By the time the U.S. joined with the Colombian government in the fight against the drug cartels, they were actually fighting on two fronts.

The company that was paying Sterling Cody's salary had a contract with the State Department, so in effect, Cody was working for the Department of State. The government supplied Cody with the tools of his trade, namely, a UH-60M Black Hawk helicopter.

Life was good for the retired Army pilot; he looked after his restaurant in Virginia on his days off and was paid well to pursue his passion of flying helicopters on special operations missions in South America.

The restaurant business fit well with Cody's lifestyle. He could walk away for weeks at a time, confident that his manager would keep close tabs on operations. When he wasn't flying, he enjoyed the comradery of customers and friends at the restaurant. On one such evening, Melissa Clark, an old family friend, stopped by for a visit.

Sterling and Melissa enjoyed each other's company, and were soon seen as a couple by their other friends. As their friendship grew, Melissa began taking an active part in overseeing the business when Sterling was in South America.

In early February of 2001, Cody caught an Air Force C-130 at Pope Air Force Base in North Carolina for what was anticipated to be another regular tour in Colombia. After arriving and spending a few days at a hotel in Colombia's capital city of Bogota, Cody went seventy miles south to the quaint little town of Apia.

Sitting 5,350 feet above sea level in a lush river valley, Apia was a ripe town for tourism. Cody, however, saw little of the town. He spent his time, when not flying, at the airfield holed up day and night, at the flight operations center. Living conditions were basic but adequate. Bunks were set up, so that contract flight crews were close to their ships. Some missions needed urgent attention.

Just after midnight on 16 February 2001, the call came in for another emergency mission. Cody would lead a gaggle of two UH-60M Black Hawks across the Andes Mountains to a Colombian naval base at Buena Ventura. The base was on the Pacific coast and was under heavy attack. The Colombians were on the verge of being overrun, and the commander had asked for immediate help. Cody wasn't told who was assaulting the base. Colombian Naval Marines were running counter drug operations from the base, so the attack could have been a retaliatory strike by drug cartel forces or FARC's continued war on the government. It didn't matter to Cody who the bad guys were—FARC Communist or drug cartel armies—he'd kill 'em all and let God sort 'em out.

Cody, his co-pilot Terry Brock*, his two door gunners and the crew of the other Black Hawk pulled on their boots, grabbed their survival vests, and rushed to the flight line to fire up their ships.

Their survival vest had pockets for a personal firearm, ammunition, a strobe light, survival knife, a snakebite kit, fishhooks and line, Meals Ready to Eat and a handheld waterproof survival radio. Knowing that there are a thousand uses for duct tape, pilots also included a small roll in their survival vest

Their UH-60 "M" model was a specialized variant of the Black Hawk and featured advanced avionics, FLIR (Forward Looking Infrared Radar), and more powerful YT706-GE-700 engines. They were equipped with an additional self-sealing fuel tank, an air-to-air refueling boom, and oxygen that allowed for operations at high altitudes. They'd need that oxygen as they crossed over the Andes.

Their aircraft were always pre-flighted and fueled, so the crews strapped in, put on their oxygen mask, and within ten minutes, were climbing rapidly to 18,000 feet. It was a dark night, and the oxygen improved their night vision. Even so, they could barely see the summit as they crossed over to the Pacific side of the Andes. Cody had landed a Black Hawk on the summit in 1985 during high altitude training, so he knew that it was like a barren moonscape.

The descent to the Pacific Coast was steep and calculated at 140 knots indicated airspeed. As they passed through ten thousand feet, the gunners test fired their weapons, and Cody contacted the Colombian Naval Commander on his FM radio. The Colombian said that they were taking mortar and small-arms fire and that the heaviest part of the assault was focused on the main entrance to the base.

Cody radioed back, "We'll attack in a racetrack pattern. Have your men cease fire and take cover when our attack begins."

Palms became moist and muscles tensed as they approached the Colombian Naval Base. Green and red tracer rounds were crisscrossing and occasionally ricocheted skyward. Cody led the way as the two Black Hawks set up their approach so that they would parallel with the main gate of the base. That would put them in a position to lay down suppressive fire on the bad guys. It also put them in a position to receive fire from the same bad guys.

On cue, the defenders ceased fire. The Black Hawks were then free to fire upon the source of any tracers.

Cody slowed to forty knots as the two Black Hawks entered the fray. When the enemy spotted the threat, they redirected their fire skyward. The Black Hawk's door gunners opened fire, and the fight was on. The Miniguns saturated the ground; green AK-47 tracers and the familiar .51 caliber orange basketballs began whizzing past the Black Hawks.

The Black Hawks leveled off at two hundred feet as they passed along the front wall of the base. It was not Cody's first rodeo, and he didn't let the sound of hot lead hitting his ship distract him from job one—flying the mission.

The Black Hawks were heavily armored; it took a lot of lead from small-arms fire or a very lucky shot to bring one down. The two Black Hawks flew into red and green tracers as the door gunners opened up with their six-barreled Miniguns. The Gatling-style rotating barrels of the Miniguns could spit out 7.62mm bullets at two thousand to six thousand rounds per minute and strike absolute terror into any bad guy who hadn't yet been ventilated.

As Cody turned to the north to set up the racetrack pattern, he heard more rounds hitting his aircraft. The sky was filled with green and red tracers, and he knew that there were many nontracers between each fireball. Bullets continued to impact Cody's Black Hawk as he rounded the racetrack and began his second approach. His second pass was almost identical to the first, but at the end, he turned to the left and set up for a hover in front of the main entrance to the base. The second Black Hawk was well behind Cody as he slowly turned to allow both of his door gunners to open up on the enemy.

"Damn," Cody said over the intercom, "the controls are getting sloppy!"

Cody was having to make exaggerated moves of his cyclic to get a response and then had to compensate in the opposite direction.

"I think we're gonna lose it," Cody told Ernie.

Cody forced his Black Hawk to make a final turn and headed out to sea.

A thousand thoughts fought for dominance as Cody assessed the situation.

Don't wanna crash on land, bad guys all around.
Damn, my ankle hurts.
Better to ditch in the water.
My boot feels like it's full of blood!
Have to take our chances with the sharks.

About three hundred yards from the coast, Cody descended to about ten feet above the water, keyed his intercom, and told his crew to get out.

Ernie jettisoned his door and was gone. Cody didn't see the crew leave, but a quick glance assured him that they had jumped.

Cody continued out to sea for another twenty or thirty yards to make sure the rotor blades didn't strike the bobbing crew when the Black Hawk hit the water. When he was sure that it was safe, Cody executed the maneuver to set the helicopter gently—relatively speaking—into the water. When the rotor blades hit the water, the Black Hawk juddered violently. Cody held tight as seawater began rushing in around his feet. He was waiting for the main rotor blades to stop turning; he didn't want to risk decapitation with a hasty exit. The helicopter began listing to the left and sinking fast. Cody jettisoned his door.

Oh crap, I should have already done that.

He unbuckled, pulled off his oxygen mask, inflated his water wings, entered the water, and swam away from his sinking Black Hawk. He loved that ship; it was the latest model and had all the bells and whistles. And, with just two hundred hours of flight time, it was the helicopter equivalent of an automobile which still had that new car smell.

"AMF my friend" Cody mumbled to himself, as he watched his Black Hawk sink to the depths, "You're a fish house now."

Cody looked around and saw the beach about three hundred yards away. Then, he heard the sharp survival whistle of one of his crew. He looked toward the sound but couldn't see anyone, so he swam in the direction of the sound. After a few yards, he saw heads bobbing in the sea. A few more yards and he was reunited with his crew. After checking that everyone was all right, pilots and crew began a slow swim to the beach.

Cody was sure that his right ankle was bleeding. During the swim, the movie *JAWS* played in his mind's eye. In Cody's version of *JAWS*, it wasn't a Hollywood animatronic shark that was stalking him, but rather, the real hammerhead he'd seen from the *USS Deyo*.

When they reached the surf, Ernie suggested that they take refuge in the jungle beyond the sandy beach. They didn't know who the enemy was, much less where they were, but they did know the likely outcome if they were captured. The FARC were notorious for holding prisoners for ransom—sometimes for decades—and drug cartels generally killed their enemies without a second thought.

Cody directed his men to set up a defensive perimeter. They only had their side arms, Cody's .45 and the crew's 9-mm pistols to protect themselves against the unacceptable.

Cody reached down and rubbed his ankle in a vain attempt to relieve the pain. The leather was wet and sticky; he knew that it wasn't seawater. As he rubbed his ankle, he felt two holes in his boot's leather; a piece of metal was sticking out from the largest hole.

Ernie said, "Let's take a look at your foot."

He shined a flashlight on the foot, reached down and pulled the protruding metal from Cody's ankle. A mixture of blood and seawater drained out. Ernie removed the boot from Cody's right foot, tore open a combat bandage from his first aid kit, placed the bandage on the wound, and then wrapped the ankle with duct tape. With his ankle wrapped tightly, the pain was relieved, and Cody was good to go, albeit with a painful limp.

They sat quietly listening to the sounds of the jungle. They couldn't risk calling for rescue on their emergency survival radios because the bad guys might hear the call and home in on their position. They weren't despondent. In fact, they were optimistic; they knew that no man would be left behind and that it was just a matter of time before a rescue party arrived.

The long hours of darkness finally gave way to dawn. The stranded crew continued their vigil until, finally, around mid-morning, they heard a helicopter.

Ernie and the crew chief ran to the open beach and looked skyward. A gray-colored Black Hawk was coming in their direction parallel to the beach. Ernie pulled out his survival radio and made the call. Within minutes, the friendly Black Hawk was landing on the beach. Ernie returned to the jungle and helped Cody to the rescue helicopter. After the rescued crew had boarded the Black Hawk, the helicopter crew informed them that they had come from Bogota and that they would take the guys back to Bogota for medical evaluation and debriefing. When Cody asked about his wingman, he was told that they had made it back to Apia safely.

After the trip over the mountains to Bogota, Cody received care at a clinic on the flight line. A doctor from the U.S. Embassy tended to Cody's ankle. He explained that a 7.62mm bullet had apparently split apart when it came through the helicopter, and then penetrated the boot leather before the two pieces lodged in Cody's foot. The wound wasn't serious; no bones were broken. As the doctor was explaining the injury to Cody and preparing a packet of painkillers, a nurse was cleaning the examination room. She picked up Cody's dirty, filthy sock and his right boot and unceremoniously tossed them into a waste bin.

Damn! Now I'll have to break in a new pair of boots.

By nightfall, Sterling Cody was on an Air Force C-130 heading north. He had been awake for thirty-six hours and was stacking Z's before the cargo plane got clearance to taxi to the active runway.

As Cody slept in the cargo bay of the C-130, the tropical heat of Colombia gave way to the February cold of North America. It was cold when they landed at Pope Air Force Base in North Carolina, and even colder by the time he finally arrived home in Virginia.

Later that month, inside his restaurant, Sterling Cody sat with Melissa by the fireplace. As he sipped bourbon and she enjoyed some red wine, they reflected on their future—a future that was about to take a sudden and drastic change of direction. Sterling also reflected on the recent past.

"That Black Hawk was the best helicopter I ever flew," Sterling told Melissa. "Oh well, it's a fish house now."

18

Objective Yogi

Iraq
19 March 2003

Every generation has a seminal moment or two seared into their memory. For Sterling Cody's grandparents, it was the moment that they learned of the sinking of the RMS Titanic in 1912 and the RMS Lusitania three years later. The traumatic moment for Sterling's father, the Greatest Generation, came on a Sunday in 1941 when the Japanese attacked Pearl Harbor, Hawaii. Baby Boomers and Generation X'ers will forever remember the exact moment they learned of President Kennedy's assignation and the attacks of 9/11.

Sterling and Melissa were in their restaurant when news flashes hit the wires and airways informing the shocked nation of the 9/11 attacks. As with all Americans, the images on their TV screen were painful to watch. That morning, as the scenes of devastation played on every television channel, Sterling and Melissa vowed their love for each other and decided to get married as soon as possible.

They spent the days following 9/11 running the

restaurant and making wedding plans. Their future together was bright and assured. Then, on 17 September, the phone rang. That phone call— another of those seminal moments for Cody—put all wedding plans on hold.

Melissa had answered the phone, and she told Sterling, "It's a colonel; he wants to talk to you."

Cody was busy getting things ready for another day at the restaurant.

"Ahh, it's probably just one of my old pals...tell him I'm busy."

A few hours later, the phone rang again. This time, Sterling answered. A polite but firm voice informed LTC Sterling Cody that he had been recalled to active duty, and was to report to the Chief of Staff of the Army at the Pentagon within forty-eight hours.

Sterling rented a room in a large house in Springfield, Virginia, a few miles south of the Pentagon, and began working five to seven days a week. Five-day work weeks were rare and seven-day weeks commonplace. The flurry of activity within the Pentagon left no doubt that a response to the 9/11 attacks was imminent.

The Pentagon's obvious target was Afghanistan. The Taliban government was hosting and protecting Osama bin Laden and his al-Qaeda terrorist organization, and when they refused President George W. Bush's demand that they hand over bin Laden and expel al-Qaeda, the die was cast. The United States would dismantle al-Qaeda, remove the Taliban from power and deny terrorism a safe haven in Afghanistan.

On 7 October 2001, just twenty-six days after 9/11, the U.S., the United Kingdom, and other allies launched Operation Enduring Freedom. At the Pentagon, the pace of activity increased from hectic to fever pitch. Cody stayed busy locating equipment from around the country, and even in South America, to fill requests from commanders in Afghanistan.

Cody finally managed to take a few days of leave, and got married on 14 December 2001. It was a simple ceremony at the Mecklenburg, Virginia County courthouse, followed by a quick honeymoon at Nags Head on North Carolina's Outer Banks. On the return trip, the newlyweds had to wait for the ferry back to the mainland. Sterling and Melissa were standing beside their car admiring the coastal scenery when a flock of seagulls flew overhead. It was a peaceful moment for the newlyweds as they enjoyed the crisp sea breeze and the gulls squawking overhead. They talked about their future. Sterling had two weeks remaining on his recall before they could return to their civilian life running the restaurant.

Then, one of the seagulls made a deposit...on Sterling's head.

"Damn," Cody said as he instinctively ducked, after the fact. Melissa handed Sterling a tissue to clean his hair as best he could.

"Well, it's not the first time I've have been shit on..." Sterling told his wife.

Before he could continue with, "and it won't be the last," his cell phone rang, as if on cue. It was one of Cody's buddies at the Pentagon.

"You've just been extended until July 2004."

When Sterling told Melissa the news, she took it like a trooper. It might have been the first time that a seagull had shit on them, but life...well, you live your life and take your chances.

LTC Cody fulfilled his duty without complaint, but as Christmas 2002 approached, he felt that he had not contributed directly to the war effort. Then, on Christmas Eve, Santa presented him with an opportunity.

Cody was called to the G-3's office and was given an important assignment by the Chief of Staff directly. A Ranger Battalion in Afghanistan was in desperate need of drinking water. It was not a minor inconvenience for the Rangers; without drinking water in those arid mountains, their fighting capability, not to mention their lives, were on the line. Drinking water would be the best Christmas gift they could receive.

Cody returned to his office and began a search of Army bases around the country for a "water buffalo." He wasn't searching for livestock; he was searching for a four hundred gallon water tank mounted on a trailer.

It was Christmas Eve; by 1800 hours (6 p.m.), most military facilities around the country were on skeleton staffing. Cody was having little success until one of his counterparts from the Air Force drifted in to shoot the breeze. He was in the middle of a divorce and figured that Christmas Eve at the Pentagon was preferable to what awaited him at home.

"Whatcha doin here so late Cody?" the Air Force officer asked.

Cody explained the frustration he was having trying to locate a water buffalo.

"No sweat," Cody's friend said, "I know where one is at Andrews Air Force Base."

The Air Force officer got on the phone, and a few calls later, Cody's problem was solved. He got verbal authorization to release the water buffalo to the Army—paperwork to follow—and, like a Christmas gift from the heavens, a C-117 Cargo jet was sitting one hundred yards away and scheduled to depart for Afghanistan. The water buffalo was manifested on the flight, and the Rangers had their water by Christmas Day. The Air Force officer got an after-hours drink compliments of Sterling Cody.

While the U.S. was driving the Taliban from power and building military bases across Afghanistan, LTC Cody was bored to tears with staff work. It was important work that someone had to do, but he was a pilot and not a desk jockey.

By the end of 2002, planning was well underway to invade Iraq and topple dictator Saddam Hussain from power. The United States had begun pre-positioning war matériel in Kuwait during the summer, and the airlifting of arms and equipment intensified in the fall.

On 28 December, Cody was directed to attend a meeting by a colonel with the Joint Staff. The meeting was to be held in one of the many secret meeting rooms in the lower levels of the Pentagon that belonged to the Joint Staff. With seventeen miles of hallways and one hundred and thirty-one stairways, navigating the Pentagon wasn't easy, but by now, Cody was familiar with his part of the massive building. Meetings and conferences were a daily fare around the Pentagon, so Cody figured that it was just another planning session to locate equipment for a unit preparing to deploy to the Persian Gulf.

The meeting began with the colonel stating that the group was tasked with forming a lean force to seize bridges crossing the Euphrates and Tigris Rivers in advance of the Counterattack Corps (countering the 9/11 attacks) that would enter Baghdad and topple Saddam and his Ba'ath Party from power. The force that would seize the bridges was designated "Task Force Martha."

The primary objective of Task Force Martha was to seize and control a bridge crossing the Euphrates River—designated Objective Yogi—and if possible, a second bridge—code-named Juba—that crossed the Tigris River. The two bridges, if captured intact, would greatly facilitate the Counterattack Corps' taking of Baghdad. If the mission failed, the Iraqis could blow the bridges, forcing Counterattack Corps engineers to build temporary bridges across the rivers. The delay would then allow Saddam time to strengthen his defenses or to mount a counterattack. It was a critical mission behind enemy lines. The group was given seven days to develop a course of action and identify the structure of the task force.

Perhaps no one was more surprised than Cody when the colonel said, "Task Force Martha will be commanded by Lieutenant Colonel Cody."

The colonel knew Cody well; when he introduced

Colonel Cody as the task force's commander, he expressed confidence in his ability to get everything done in the limited time available.

"Lieutenant Colonel Cody," the Colonel said, "is a cross between Colombo, MacGyver, and the Red Barron. We'll need those skills on this mission."

Mission Commander LTC Cody quickly put together his Operations Order.

OPERATIONS ORDER
Task Force Martha
17 March 2003

SITUATION:

Enemy: Enemy forces control Objectives Yogi and Juba which must be secured to facilitate the Counterattack Corps advance into Baghdad.

Friendly: Counterattack Corps commander will take control of Yogi and Juba after seized by Task Force (TF) Martha.

MISSION:

On order during the hours of darkness TF Martha will seize and hold the bridge (Objective Yogi) crossing the Euphrates River until relieved by the Counterattack Corps commander.

If practicable TF Martha commander will split his force and seize bridge crossing Tigris River (Objective Juba). Priority is to secure Objective Yogi.

EXECUTION:

TF Martha will proceed to LZ Dog during the hours of darkness and await attack order.

On order of the Counterattack Corps commander, TF Martha will seize Objective Yogi and if possible Objective Juba and hold until relieved.

TF Martha will depart LZ Dog on a heading of 085° at an altitude of 100 feet Above Ground Level (AGL) at 120 knots Indicated Air Speed (IAS). Strict Radio Silence will be observed.

Yellow Flight will cross on the south side of Objective Yogi applying suppressive fire and will return on the north side and land on the west approach to Objective Yogi.

White Flight will land on the west side of Objective Yogi and secure the west end of the bridge.

Engineers will immediately clear the bridge of demolition charges.

Divers will check the water for demolitions.

All prisoners will be thoroughly searched, disarmed, and moved to the command post on the west side of the river.

ADMIN AND LOGISTICS:

Aircraft will refuel on the west side of Objective Yogi from CH-47 Milk Cows.

Assault Force will cross-level ammunition after securing Objective Yogi.

COMMAND AND SIGNAL:

Aircraft will be provided by Central Command (CENTCOM). Primary targeting method will be laser designation.

Engineers will mark Objectives, Yogi and Juba.

Air cover will be continuous until the artillery from the Covering Force is in range. Artillery fire will be adjusted using technique (Shift from a Known Point).

On order, White Flight with designated assault group will seize and hold Objective Juba.

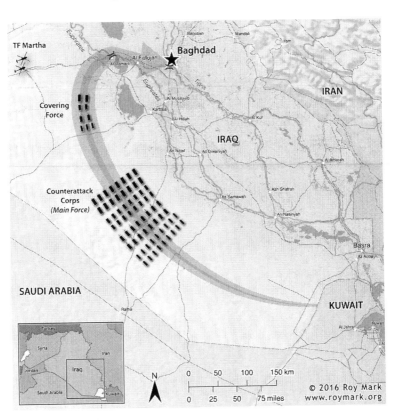

Over the next week, Cody and the group worked together to develop a force structure of 392 Soldiers, forty UH-60 Black Hawks, engineers, explosive experts, and scuba divers.

During subsequent meetings, LTC Cody insisted that the forty Black Hawks for Task Force Martha had to be intact units; crew integrity was vital. He was also firm that the helicopters be equipped with FLIR and that the pilots have night vision goggle experience.

Cody's insistence on crew integrity was the result of having studied the failed rescue mission of the fifty-two American Embassy staff who had been held hostage by the Iranians in 1980. The string of events that had led to the failed effort and the death of eight military rescuers in the Iranian desert had begun with the operational loss of three helicopters, one of which was lost when pilots who were unfamiliar with the particular helicopter that they were flying incorrectly interpreted a sensor indication as a cracked rotor blade. Those losses, Cody believed, could have been prevented by ensuring crew and equipment integrity. Crews should know their pilots; pilots should know their crews; and they all should know *their* ships intimately.

Cody then went to work finding all the parts—the Soldiers, the helicopters, the equipment, and the ammunition. Time was short. Everyone knew—or at least sensed—that the buildup for the Iraqi counterattack was reaching a crescendo. Locating the men and equipment in such a short time wasn't easy. Most of the U.S. Black Hawk fleet was already in the

Middle-East, and Cody's stiff pilot criteria made the search more difficult. Within two weeks, however, he had located forty Black Hawks and crews from active Army units, Reserve, and National Guard units. Cody knew from experience that the Reserve and National Guard pilots were nothing to sneeze at; their abilities were equal to and often exceeded those of their active Army counterparts.

Soon, Black Hawks were flying in from around the country. Special Forces, Rangers, and support personnel met the Black Hawks at Quantico for briefings. At first blush, Task Force Martha appeared to be a hodgepodge of Soldiers—some wearing green jungle fatigues and others in tan desert fatigues; some helicopters were painted green, others gray and some with camo paint schemes.

Task Force Martha may have appeared a motley crew, but they meshed well together. There wasn't time enough to fit everyone in new uniforms and paint the helicopters in desert camo, so they wore their irregular appearance as a badge of pride. Regular Army Soldiers and National Guardsmen trained alongside Special Forces and Rangers. Divers and engineers went over plans to dismantle any explosive charges that the Iraqis may have set up to blow the bridges. Their task would be formidable; Yogi and Juba were massive structures that were the size of the bridges crossing the Mississippi River in St. Louis. Within days, Task Force Martha was ready to move out.

From the base in Quantico, Task Force Martha flew offshore and landed on an Iwo Jima-class amphibious assault ship. The rotor blades were retracted, and the Black Hawks stowed below deck, out of site of surveillance satellites. After a long voyage, the ship entered the Persian Gulf, and sailed north between Saudi Arabia and Iran before entering Kuwaiti waters. Task Force Martha then flew to its staging area in what was now a massive military arsenal on the Kuwait-Iraq border.

The Counterattack Corps being assembled in Kuwait was built around George Patton's old Third Armor Division out of Germany and consisted of tanks, Bradley Fighting Vehicles, self-propelled artillery, bulldozers, 20mm Gatling guns, Stinger missiles, and supply and fuel vehicles. With all of the parts in Kuwait, they assembled along a line of departure stretching several miles along the Iraqi border.

After the buildup, on 15 March 2003, President George W. Bush gave Saddam Hussein and his sons forty-eight hours to leave Iraq or face war. Saddam had threatened the U.S. with the idiom "Mother of All Battles" shortly before his defeat in the first Gulf War of 1991. Now, twelve years later, the U.S. was justified in retorting, "You Ain't Seen Nothing Yet...Mother!"

Just after dusk on 18 March 2003, Task Force Martha crossed the Kuwaiti border into Iraq. The gaggle of forty UH-60 Black Hawks was composed of two groups of twenty each, designated Yellow and White Flights. Task Force Martha carried a contingent of 392 Rangers, Special Forces, engineers, divers, and 81mm mortar squads. They flew on night vision goggles one hundred feet above the ground and observed strict radio silence.

Their destination was a GPS point in the desert designated as LZ Dog, eighty miles west-northwest of Objective Yogi. The second bridge—Objective Juba—was five miles from Yogi and on the edge of Baghdad City.

Task Force Martha landed at LZ Dog at about 2300 hours (11 p.m.) on 18 March. The desert floor at Dog consisted of hard-packed sand topped with a dusting of loose sand, so digging in was impossible. A minute or two after the last Black Hawk landed, six Boeing CH-47 Chinook "Milk Cows" landed and shut down. The large tandem rotor heavy-lift helicopters carried fuel for the Black Hawks.

The Black Hawks hovered over to the Milk Cows in twos, setting down to the right and left just behind the CH-47s. The Black Hawks kept their engines running during the process; hot refueling saved time. The six Milk Cows were able to refuel twelve helicopters at a clip. As their fuel cells were topped off, the Black Hawks returned to their positions, and their crews draped camouflage nets over their birds and settled in for the night.

Task Force Martha listened to the silence of the desert until after midnight, when they began hearing bombing in the distance; Baghdad was under aerial attack.

Mission Commander Cody walked among Task Force Martha, reminding his men that all movement must be kept to a minimum. On his rounds, the commander talked with his men, offering words of encouragement. As he chatted with one Black Hawk crew, a young Army reservist door gunner voiced concern that his ship was not painted with the desert tan camo paint scheme he'd seen at the staging area.

"Aw, that's no problem Soldier," Cody offered to the entire crew, "Helicopters are like cats...they're all gray in the dark."

A covering force of about 1,800 Soldiers—a microcosm of the 15,000-man Counterattack Corps—left the line of departure, led by tanks and Bradley Fighting Vehicles. The Covering Force was operating independently and in advance of the Counterattack Corps to intercept, engage, delay, and disorganize any Iraqi forces before the enemy could attack the main body of the Counterattack Corps. The Covering Force moved quickly and encountered nothing but empty desert. The Counterattack Corps followed, trusting that the Countering Force would clear the way and that they would find the two bridges into Baghdad in friendly hands.

Task Force Martha waited. Some within the force had combat experience, but most did not. Some young men were contemplating their mortality for the first time in their lives. This is what they had signed up for, however, and they were all prepared to do their job. They waited as they listened to the sounds of bombing in the distance.

At 0100 hours Zulu (military designation for Greenwich Mean Time) on the 19th, the commander of the Counterattack Corps transmitted the order to seize the bridges. It was 0400 hours (4 a.m.) local time when the camo nets were pulled off the Black Hawks and their turbine engines began to whine. LTC Cody took his position in the jump seat between and just behind the pilots of Yellow One.

Forty Black Hawks, their pilots on night vision goggles, flew in tandem at 80 knots on compass heading 265° directly to Objective Yogi. As planned, the mission would fail or succeed in the twilight.

A UH-60L Black Hawk helicopter flies a low-level mission over Iraq, January 2004
Photo by SSGT Suzanne M. Jenkins, USAF

As the outline of the massive bridge appeared on the horizon, Yellow One began to bleed off airspeed. He set up his flight of twenty Black Hawks to approach the Euphrates River on the downstream or west side of Objective Yogi. As the foot of the bridge appeared on the port (left) side of his Black Hawk, Mission Commander Cody ordered his door gunner to open up on the bridge. It was the signal for all the door gunners of Yellow Flight to open fire. Twenty M60 machine guns began concentrating fire on the approach end of Yogi.

Door gunners continued firing as the flight crossed the river and did a one-eighty at the east side of the bridge. Crossing back to the west bank, door gunners sprayed lead at the upstream (north side) of the bridge.

Once back on the west bank, Yellow Flight landed at the foot of the bridge, and eighty Special Forces and Rangers immediately began their assault on the bridge. Small-arms fire was intense. Special Forces set up a blocking position on the highway leading to the bridge. LTC Cody set up his command post about one hundred yards from the foot of Yogi.

The textbook method for capturing a bridge is to assault both sides simultaneously, so as Yellow Flight was landing, the twenty White Flight ships passed around Yellow Flight and descended on the east side of the Euphrates at the foot of the bridge.

Defenders opened up with small-arms fire even as White Flight was landing. Rangers and Special Forces troops jumped from their helicopters and immediately assaulted the defensive positions.

Small-arms fire raged from both sides of the bridge. Within forty-five minutes or so, fighting on both sides of Yogi had ceased. It was a one-sided fight: no Iraqis survived, while the Americans suffered no casualties. Once assured that all Iraqis had been neutralized, the Rangers and Special Forces set up defenses, and the engineers and divers went to work checking the bridge for demolition charges. While Yogi was being checked for explosives, the six CH-47 Milk Cows arrived and landed on the east side of the Euphrates, and began hot refueling White Flight.

After refueling, White One (flight leader of White Flight) reported back to Cody.

Cody issued a simple, clear order: "Go take the second bridge."

White Flight's twenty Black Hawks flew the five miles to Juba. White One was at a disadvantage on several fronts. First, unlike the assault on Yogi, he was assaulting Juba with twenty Black Hawks instead of forty, and his twenty helicopters carried half the assault troops that had assaulted Yogi. Second, and very importantly, White One had to assume that the element of surprise was compromised.

Again, it was necessary that they assault both ends of the bridge simultaneously. White Flight split with ten Black Hawks landing at the foot of the east end of Juba and ten continuing across the Tigris to the west side of the bridge. This time, Iraqi forces were waiting and ready for the Americans.

Assault troops stormed the east end of Juba, and mortar crews set up positions at about three hundred yards from the bridge.

The second group of ten Black Hawks continued across the Tigris River with their door gunners firing on the bridge as they went. The east side of the Tigris was a built-up area on the outskirts of Baghdad; office buildings, houses, telephone poles, and power lines restricted landing. With no clear place to land, the ten Black Hawks hovered forty feet above the ground. Ropes were thrown from the helicopters, and assault troops began fast-roping to the ground. Incoming fire intensified and the fight was on.

The Black Hawks immediately returned to the west side of the Tigris River; they didn't want another Somalia style "Black Hawk Down" diverting Task Force Martha to a rescue mission.

The firefights on both ends of Juba were intense, but the one on the east side was the most difficult. The defenders undoubtedly felt that they were guarding the front door to their capital city. The Americans had to utilize their hip-pocket artillery, their 81mm mortars, to finally dispatch the enemy to Allah.

When the fighting was over, engineers and divers inspected the bridge for demolition charges; none were found.

The Americans at Juba had killed fourteen defenders; none surrendered, apparently preferring martyrdom to captivity. Unlike at Yogi, taking Juba cost two American lives, and several Soldiers were wounded.

Back at Yogi, the Abrams Tanks and Bradley Fighting Vehicles of the Covering Force began arriving. Their mission would be accomplished when the Counterattack Corps arrived at Yogi.

About thirty minutes after the arrival of the Covering Force, the lead elements of the Counterattack Corps began arriving. A lieutenant colonel from the commanding general's staff sought out LTC Cody and thanked him for securing the bridges into Baghdad.

The Counterattack Corps' pause at the foot of Yogi was momentary; they had urgent business to attend to in Baghdad. Tanks and Bradleys began crossing Yogi at top speed. Once reformed on the west side of Yogi, the Counterattack Corps hauled ass and was crossing Juba into Baghdad about fifteen minutes later.

Task Force Martha had done its job by opening the door to the city of Baghdad; the Counterattack Corps' job had just begun.

Task Force Martha flew back to Kuwait and was disbanded. Their Black Hawks had served them well, but they were unceremoniously shipped back to the U.S.

LTC Sterling Cody was back at his office at the Pentagon within forty-eight hours.

Some of Cody's friends gathered at his desk, asking about how the mission went.

"Just another day at the office," Cody replied.

It took little prompting, however, before Cody opened up with the details of his mission.

Someone asked if he had put up a sign at the foot of the bridge saying, "You are now entering Baghdad compliments of Task Force Martha."

"Nah," Cody replied, "that's only in the movies."

After the laughter had died down, Cody added, "But if they ever make a movie about it, I'll insist on that sign.

ABOUT THE AUTHOR

Roy Mark grew up in New Orleans and joined the U.S. Marine Corps in 1963. He served as a radio-telegraph operator at Camp Pendleton and onboard the *USS Mount McKinley* (AGC-7). After four years of service that included a brief period in Vietnam, he attended college at Southeastern Louisiana University.

Following a career in the oil industry that included writing technical manuals in oil well blowout prevention, Mr. Mark retired from Arco Oil and Gas Company in Indonesia. He continued to live in Indonesia until he relocated to Chiang Mai, Thailand, in 2001.

Since his retirement, Mr. Mark has written *The Mark Family History* in 2005, *Fixin' to Die Rag* in 2014, and *Live by Chance, Love by Choice, Kill by Profession* in 2017.

Roy Mark continues to live in Thailand, enjoying his retirement with frequent trips to countries around Southeast Asia and occasional trips back to the U.S.

Please visit Roy Mark's social media sites:

RoyMark.Org   Facebook.com/Roy.Mark.Books

You may also enjoy this great book by Roy Mark:

FIXIN' TO DIE RAG

FIXIN' TO DIE RAG is the true story of Charlie Company of the First Cavalry Division's 229th Assault Aviation Battalion during 1970. It was a tough year for Charlie Company, as it lost men to the enemy, to accidents and to bad weather.

Available at all online and "brick & mortar" bookstores
Paperback and e-book format.

Made in the USA
San Bernardino, CA
06 May 2017